Oh, the danger and the desire...

Peter Spaulding, lawyer *extraordinaire,* is sending Jenny calla lilies. Plotting major changes in her life. And talking about feelings.

Jenny Spaulding is trying to sort hers out. Asking herself questions like, "After we solve this case, is there a future for Peter and me?"

But his kisses are still heavenly, and his touch is fire in her blood....

After a year of silence and separation, Jenny and Peter are together again—to work once more as a team of amateur sleuths.

Falling in love was the easy part.

Following through is murder.

ABOUT THE AUTHOR

When Robin Francis wrote *Button, Button,* Intrigue #147, she became so attached to the hero and heroine that she decided to write some more novels featuring the same amateur sleuths, and a series was born. Here is the second book in A SPAULDING & DARIEN MYSTERY series. Jenny and Peter will be back in October, in #171 *All Fall Down.* Robin Francis is currently at work on a fourth book.

Robin tells us that like her heroine, Jenny Spaulding, she enjoys writing. And like her hero, Peter Darien, she enjoys baseball, basketball and Brahms. Like most of us, she wishes she could afford a Maserati, like Peter has.

Books by Robin Francis

HARLEQUIN INTRIGUE
147–BUTTON, BUTTON

HARLEQUIN AMERICAN ROMANCE
253–TAKING A CHANCE
295–THE SHOCKING MS. PILGRIM
301–CHARMED CIRCLE

Double Dare

Robin Francis

Harlequin Books

TORONTO • NEW YORK • LONDON
AMSTERDAM • PARIS • SYDNEY • HAMBURG
STOCKHOLM • ATHENS • TOKYO • MILAN

First edition April 1991
Second printing May 1991

ISBN 0-373-22159-2

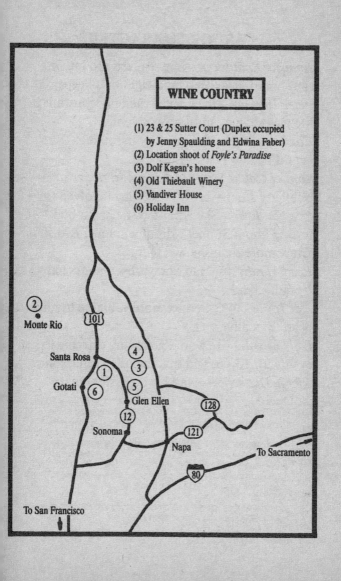

WINE COUNTRY

(1) 23 & 25 Sutter Court (Duplex occupied by Jenny Spaulding and Edwina Faber)
(2) Location shoot of *Foyle's Paradise*
(3) Dolf Kagan's house
(4) Old Thiebault Winery
(5) Vandiver House
(6) Holiday Inn

Monte Rio

101

Santa Rosa

Gotati

Glen Ellen

128

Sonoma

121

Napa

To Sacramento

80

To San Francisco

CAST OF CHARACTERS

Jennifer Spaulding—She realized too late that she should have been her neighbor's keeper.

Peter Darien—He believed the only constant in life was change, until he met Jenny.

Edwina Faber—She was the first to die. Who would be next?

Sonnet Cole—Was her disappearance a publicity stunt—or was foul play involved?

Eve Vandiver—She admitted she had a bad feeling about Sonnet's disappearance. Did she know more than she was telling?

Reed Vandiver—Had Sonnet been abducted from his bank?

Hal Joyce—Was Sonnet more valuable to him dead than alive?

Dolf Kagan—He would go to any extreme to get even with Joyce. Did that include kidnapping?

Rickie Detweiler—Had his obsession led to violence?

Prologue

Sonnet Cole was steamed. A hormone deficiency had stunted her growth. At eighteen, she had the body of an underdeveloped twelve-year-old. But the anomaly hadn't stunted her mind. She knew when she was being taken advantage of; she knew a parasite when she saw one.

She narrowed her eyes, regarding Hal Joyce's reflection in her makeup mirror. As he hovered behind her, expression solicitous, jowls shiny with sweat, Joyce had the look of a fat, bloated slug.

"You're disappointed," he observed. "Can't say I blame you. On the surface, this movie deal seems like the next logical step in your career."

Sonnet's fingers tightened around the handle of her hairbrush. "It's not just a movie, Hal. It's a Dolf Kagan film."

"So what am I, chopped liver? And what's *Foyle's Paradise?*"

"The country's top-rated sitcom."

"Right on, sweetie, and don't you forget it."

"But Kagan's offer is the break I've been waiting for. Have you any idea how many actresses would give their eyeteeth for the chance to work with a director like him?"

"Yeah, yeah," Joyce replied wearily. "I imagine Kagan made it sound as if his version of *Peter Pan*'ll be a shoo-in for the best-picture Oscar, and the title role's the juiciest plum since Selznick cast Scarlett O'Hara."

"It's a role that worked miracles for Mary Martin."

"Or she worked miracles with it," said Joyce. "But you're not doing bad yourself, kiddo. You've got top billing, your own Winnebago. You earn more money in a week than most people earn in a year—"

"I'm worth it!"

"Sure you are, babe. No one's denying that you're the reason thirty million viewers tune in to *Foyle's Paradise* every Thursday."

"If I do this movie, I'll bet our ratings would go up."

"Not for the weeks you're off the show."

"But I don't have to be off the show. Not if you shoot around me."

"Be reasonable, Sonnet. Much as I'd like to go along with your request, I can't revise my shooting schedule to satisfy your whims. As executive producer, I'm responsible for the whole ball of wax. I have obligations to the sponsors, the network, the rest of the cast and crew."

Sonnet studied him, unmoved. "You're all heart, Hal."

The bitterness in her tone was not lost on Joyce. He helped himself to a handful of facial tissues from the box on the vanity, and used them to mop his face. "Listen, sweetie, you may not believe this, but it's not just the show I'm concerned about. I have your welfare at heart, too. Take it from one who knows, Kagan's a shark—"

"He's a genius, only you're too jealous of his talent to admit it."

"He's a man-eater, Sonnet. A full-grown barracuda. He eats little girls like you for breakfast."

"I can take care of myself."

"Not with this guy, you can't."

"So you won't let me out of my contract?"

Joyce gave her shoulder a conciliatory squeeze. "Sorry, kid, no can do. Even if I were inclined to release you, the network wouldn't stand for it."

Sonnet rose, drawing herself to her full four-feet-four inches. Hal towered over her, bulky and sweating, but she was not intimidated by his girth or by the aura of power he exuded. She shook off his hand, gripping the hairbrush like a weapon.

"What's to stop me from walking off the set?"

"Nothing. Not one blasted thing—except common sense." Hal tossed the wad of tissues toward the wastebasket. "If you walk out on me, you'll never work as an actress again. I'll see to it personally. That's a promise, Sonnet, baby, and it's my final word on the subject."

With that declaration, Joyce made his exit, and Sonnet swung away from the mirror to glower at his broad, retreating back.

Rage boiled up inside her, threatening to spill over. Her fingers itched to slap the patronizing smirk off his face. She was tempted to throw the hairbrush at him; instead, she waited until he left the Winnebago, then ran to the door, slammed and locked it.

Privacy secured, she returned to the vanity, dragging the brush through her hair with punishing force. The scrape of the bristles fueled her anger.

"Parasites," she muttered, and in a fit of temper, hurled the hairbrush at the door.

She was surrounded by parasites, by blood-sucking leeches. Hal Joyce was merely the most disgusting of the lot!

She snatched up a jar of cold cream, whirled and fired.

"Parasites!" she shrieked, and with a sweep of her arm, sent the clutter of makeup on the vanity crashing to the floor. A crystal flagon of perfume shattered and the scent of jasmine filled the dressing room.

Sonnet confronted the mirror, tears of frustration glittering in her eyes.

Everyone wanted a piece of her, up to and including her parents, who'd grown accustomed to the goodies her income could provide. Darling Daddy, with his Porsche and his chorus girls; dearest Mom, with her country club and shopping sprees.

"We love you, baby," they proclaimed. "We want the very best for our daughter." But when push came to shove, whose side were they on?

"Not mine," Sonnet told her mirror. "They don't give a damn about me."

As for that cockroach Marty Riordan, he was supposed to be her agent. She paid his salary, for God's sake! When it was time to collect his ten percent, he could account for every penny, but when it came to protecting her interests, he couldn't add one and one.

Sonnet's features contorted with fury at the thought of Riordan's betrayal.

Marty must've taken a kickback, she realized. Hal must've slipped him a payoff under the table.

There was no other explanation. Riordan couldn't have believed he was doing her any favors, negotiating the latest pact, delivering her into bondage.

They thought they were clever, her parents, her agent, her ever-lovin' executive producer. Conspiring against her. Lining their pockets at her expense. Locking her into an iron-clad contract that wouldn't let her sneeze without Joyce's approval. But if they thought she'd take this lying down, they were sadly mistaken.

The rest of world might be convinced her parents were devoted to her, but she wasn't buying that phony bill of goods anymore. Marty Riordan could find himself another lamb to fleece. And Hal Joyce could take her contract and stuff it where the moon don't shine.

In the four years she had worked for Joyce, she had learned a number of unsavory truths about him. A few of his secrets would be cause for embarrassment, sordid enough to make even an executive producer blush, and one or two concerned activities that were downright illegal. Or if they weren't, they ought to be. And if ever the need arose, she would not hesitate to use Hal's secrets to her own advantage.

So let him plead. Let him bargain. Let him threaten all he wanted. But if he tried to carry out his threats, if he tried to get her blacklisted, if he ever so much as looked at her cross-eyed, he'd regret it. She would see that he regretted it if it was the last thing she did.

Sonnet straightened her spine, appraising herself in the mirror.

To hell with the makeup. She didn't need it. She might not be the fairest in the land, but she wouldn't trade places with anyone. She looked adorable, irrepressible, almost thirteen—

Except that her eyes contained a terrible wisdom.

She softened her glance, rehearsed a smile. There, that was better.

Her gaze drifted downward, her smile fading as she stared at the damp imprint Hal Joyce's hand had left on her blouse. She'd have to change before her lunch date with Kagan. That smudge was like a brand, marking her as Joyce's property. It made her feel dirty...unworthy....

Sonnet tore off the garment with reckless haste. Several buttons popped off, joining the litter on the floor, but she didn't care. Never, under any circumstances, would she wear it again.

She balled up the blouse and flung it into the darkest corner of the wardrobe, then selected a new one and put it on.

It seemed appropriate that this should be the first of July, the beginning of the long holiday weekend. This year she would celebrate the Fourth a bit early.

As far as she was concerned, today was Independence Day. *Her* independence day. From this day forward, she would be her own woman. Indebted to no one. With no commitments. Free to follow where ambition led her. Free to accept whatever parts *she* wanted.

And just now the most attractive offer on the horizon happened to be Dolf Kagan's.

Sonnet found her sunglasses, and tied a scarf around her head to disguise her trademark carrot-colored hair. She usually adored being recognized by her fans—the bigger the mob, the better. But this luncheon with Kagan was primarily a business meeting, which called for some discretion.

She checked the clasp on her Medic-Alert bracelet, and studied the effect of the stainless steel bangle amid her scarlet plumage.

The bracelet was ugly, utilitarian; she hated her dependence on it, yet she wore it always, with perverse pride. It was a way of rubbing peoples' noses in her affliction, saying "Hey, I'm not perfect. Want to make something of it?"

Besides, she wasn't an idiot.

If disaster struck, if she was in an accident, carted unconscious into the emergency room, and if, God forbid, no one recognized her, the bracelet would warn the medical staff that she required special treatment.

Sonnet grabbed her car keys and Gucci tote. On the way out of the dressing room, she paused for a last glance at her mirror.

If any of the others were still on the set, she didn't want to leave them with the impression that the run-in with Hal had shaken her confidence.

She lifted her chin and blew herself a kiss, preparing to run the gauntlet to her car.

"Let 'em think what they please," she declared. "If anyone doesn't like it, the hell with them! The hell with them all."

Chapter One

That first of July brought Jennifer Spaulding a new beginning.

The sun seemed brighter, the air sweeter, the white-and-yellow daisies that blossomed on the wallpaper in her kitchen suddenly seemed more vivid.

And all because of a phone call from a man she'd known only briefly and hadn't seen for a year.

"Hello, Jenny. It's Peter."

Peter Darien.

He of the rangy build and craggy features weathered to the color of saddle leather. He of the sun-streaked hair, crooked smile and gentle, gold-flecked gray eyes. The hot-shot lawyer whose avocations ranged from baseball and basketball to Brahms.

"A man for all seasons," she had called him once, referring to his fondness for sports. It hadn't taken her long to discover how well that description fit.

Two weeks...

That was all they'd had together. But by the time they parted, she felt as if she'd always known Peter. They had shared more experiences in those two weeks than most couples share in a lifetime. They had seen each other in every conceivable mood. They had laughed and loved and fought and despaired.

They had tracked down her father's killer.

In a time of grief, Peter Darien had given her solace. In a time of danger, he had bolstered her courage. He had seen her guilt and offered absolution. He had seen her doubts and given her trust. He had seen her loneliness and given her hope. He had seen her need and given her passion.

She remembered a warm June night, Peter's face dark with urgency, the sweetness of his touch, the taste of his kisses, the proud, hard length of his body sheltering hers—

"Hello, Jenny. It's Peter."

Was it any wonder the sound of his voice left her stunned and incoherent?

She had no clear recollection of how she replied, but she must have managed some response because they talked for almost twenty minutes. When the conversation was over, she made her way through the maze of mover's cartons from the kitchen to the living room.

"That was Peter," she announced.

Betty Holtz looked up from the books she was packing, brown eyes round and owlish behind the lenses of her glasses. "Peter Darien?"

"He's the only Peter I know."

"Hallelujah!" Betty pranced among the cartons like a pom-pom girl, waving jubilant fists in the air. A fringe of rust-colored curls bobbed about her forehead as she foraged through the books she'd been boxing and held up a copy of *Justice Denied,* the exposé coauthored by Jenny and her father. In the month since its release, the book had shot to the top of the bestseller lists and made Jenny a budding celebrity.

She sank down upon a packing crate, still half-dazed, and found herself looking at the authors' portrait on the back cover of the book. Although it wasn't particularly flattering either to her or her father, the photograph had been chosen because it showed them together.

"It was the dedication that did it, wasn't it," Betty queried.

"It certainly wasn't my picture," Jenny answered.

Betty grinned. "It was the dedication. 'For Peter, with love. J.S.' I knew that would get to him. I just *knew* it! Do you mind if I say I told you so?"

"No. I think you've earned the privilege."

"May I also say it's about time?"

"Amen." Jenny ducked her head, plucking absently at a tear in the knee of her jeans. "He's coming over for the weekend."

"From Sacramento?"

"Uh-huh. He'll be here by two o'clock."

Betty sobered. "How can you take this so calmly?"

Calmly? Jenny's hands were trembling. Her pulses raced. Her mind refused to function. She wanted to sing and shout and tell the world that Peter was coming to see her.

But her excitement was on the inside. On the outside, she supposed, she must look calm, sitting on the packing crate.

"I guess it hasn't sunk in yet," she murmured.

"Well, come on, Cinderella. Get with it. We have less than three hours to get you ready for the ball."

Jennifer might have debated the wisdom of Betty's reaction. She might have argued that Peter and she had survived some trying times last summer and he hadn't seemed to think any less of her because she didn't always look her best.

She might have said that superficial things like clothes and cosmetics weren't important and that too much emphasis on physical attractiveness would only cheapen their feelings for each other.

She might have told Betty that Peter knew she was in the midst of packing. They had talked at some length about the house she was leasing, about her need for privacy and office space. She had told him she'd reached the stage where she was living out of boxes and that the movers were scheduled to arrive bright and early the morning of July 5.

So it followed that he wouldn't expect her to look like a fashion plate. Even if he was disappointed, he wouldn't let on, not when he chose comfort over style and avoided neckties and starched collars.

Peter was Mr. Casual, the quintessential laid-back Californian, and with the other tensions of meeting again after not seeing each other for a year, he might prefer her to wear something informal. Why bother to primp and fuss when there was an excellent chance he'd approve of her jeans? If they were on the ratty side, so what? He'd probably take one look at the holes in the denim and tell her she had great knees.

Jenny smiled to herself, remembering how much Peter admired her legs....

Maybe she should wear shorts. Her new white linen shorts would be perfect—except that she had packed them on Thursday, and linen had a tendency to wrinkle.

Jenny ran shaking fingers through her sherry-brown hair, taking stock of her appearance. She needed a shampoo. Also a manicure.

She had no wish to look like Cinderella ready for the ball, nor did she want to look as if she'd turned into some sort of household drudge. She wanted to strike a happy medium. She wanted Peter to find her appealing.

"Betty," she said, heart skipping with anticipation, "where did I pack the iron?"

ACCORDING TO THE LATEST figures from the California Department of Transportation, there are twenty-five million vehicles registered in the state. On that hot July Saturday, it seemed to Peter Darien as if the lion's share of those vehicles were clogging the highways between Sacramento and Santa Rosa, creating a gridlock that kept him from Jenny.

Like most of his generation, Peter had always believed the only constant in life was change. Every day of the week, wherever he happened to be, he saw abundant evidence that nothing was permanent. New governments rose from the ashes of old. Styles of architecture and clothing and music flourished, then vanished without a trace. People came and went, and unfortunately, so did emotions.

Therefore, it seemed self-evident that the old saying about absence making the heart grow fonder was a crock. It was a nice sentiment, even a noble sentiment, but a crock nonetheless. As recently as last summer, Peter would have sworn "out of sight, out of mind" was closer to the truth.

And then, one Friday afternoon last June, Jennifer Spaulding walked into his office....

From the moment he saw her, Peter was intrigued. She was a study in contradictions: a knowing light in guileless blue eyes; a tranquil brow and an insouciant, upturned nose; a hint of defiance in the set of her jaw, a hint of vulnerability in her smile; an unforgiving hairstyle and a soft, generous mouth.

Within minutes of her arrival, idle curiosity became fascination.

Her smile made him think of moonlight strolls, of sweet music and dry champagne. He found himself wondering if her mouth was as passionate as it looked. He envisioned how she would look with her hair tumbling about her shoulders, clinging to her skin like a tawny, silken shawl, and when Jenny confided she was searching for proof that her father's death had not been a suicide, he'd volunteered to help with the investigation.

He had offered his assistance grudgingly, against his better judgment, and Jenny had accepted with reluctance.

It became obvious that she considered him more of a hindrance than a help, and he was taken aback, annoyed. But despite his annoyance, over the next two weeks, she proceeded to knock his foolish beliefs about male-female relations into a cocked hat.

Not that he'd admitted it at the time. Not even to himself. At the age of thirty-three, he was no stranger to romance, but his experiences with the opposite sex hadn't prepared him for Jennifer Spaulding.

In the year since she'd left him at the Sacramento airport, Jenny had never been far from his thoughts, but he'd never had to pursue a woman before. He wasn't sure how to go about it, and even if he'd known all the angles, he wasn't sure that Jenny would welcome his pursuit. So instead of following her to Santa Rosa, instead of phoning or writing her, he had waited for Jenny to contact him.

Months went by without word from her. He was preoccupied with work. It was October before it occurred to him that Jenny might never get in touch.

His pride was hurt. Stubbornness set in. "Forget her," he told himself. "It was fun while it lasted, but it's over."

Through autumn and winter, he kept busy with other interests. By spring he was congratulating himself, convinced the worst was over. The diversions seemed to be working. He hardly thought of Jenny at all. Only once or twice a day.

It wasn't until he saw her photograph on the dust jacket of her book that he recognized the futility of ignoring his feelings. In the quarter of an hour it took him to buy the book and rush home to his apartment, he finally acknowledged how much Jenny meant to him.

He couldn't lie to himself any longer; couldn't tell himself he didn't care. What good was pride? Being obstinate had gotten him nowhere. He missed Jenny, and he wanted to be with her. He'd give anything to see her smile—that wide, beguiling, quicksilver smile that moved him so profoundly. And he longed to hear her voice.

Before this desire had fully surfaced, he was at the phone, dialing her number. He felt a resurgence of hope when, paging through Jenny's book, he discovered the dedication, and before he could reconsider, Jenny answered the phone....

Peter had undergone his change of heart at 10:55 that morning. By eleven-thirty he had packed a bag and set off for Santa Rosa. And at one o'clock he was stranded on a secondary road thirty miles from his destination, waiting for a flagman to wave the westbound traffic through.

He fiddled with the air conditioner and adjusted the volume on the cassette player. He counted the eastbound cars as they drove past. Now and again he checked his watch.

At 1:07 he was still waiting, and his patience was wearing thin. He drummed his fingers on the steering wheel, keeping cadence to the "Toreador Song" from *Carmen,* and glanced toward the copy of *Justice Denied* on the passenger seat beside him.

Arrested by Jenny's photograph, he wondered, *What if she's changed? What if my absence hasn't made her heart grow fonder? What if she's seeing someone else?*

She'd never struck him as the fickle kind, but anything might have happened in a year.

Oh, she'd sounded the same on the phone. She'd said she was delighted to hear from him, and she hadn't objected to his spending the holiday weekend in Santa Rosa, but she might've responded that way to any friend—

"Whoa!" Peter forced his gaze away from Jenny's picture. "Idiot," he muttered, chiding himself. "Stop borrowing trouble."

If he had to worry about something, why not worry about making it to Santa Rosa? He'd been stalled for fifteen minutes, and the westbound lane hadn't moved. It was begin-

ning to look as if he'd be caught in this bottleneck all night.
And the kicker was, the engine was overheating.

He cut the engine and the tape he was playing fell silent.
The cooling blast of the air conditioner stopped. Hot dry air
gusted into the car as he cranked down the window. He
stuck his head out, scanning the cars and trucks ahead,
trying to estimate how many there were.

The line of vehicles snaked around a curve and up a hill
and vanished in the shimmering heat haze near the top.

Peter shaded his eyes and squinted into the distance, but
he saw no sign of the flagman.

He was going to be late, might as well face it. If he got the
go-ahead now, there was no way he could make it to Jenny's
place by two o'clock.

This delay was not an auspicious way to begin the weekend. Peter hoped it wasn't an omen of things to come.

JENNY HAD TO GO THROUGH several cartons before she
found the iron. The white linen shorts were easier to locate,
but they were as badly wrinkled as she had supposed they
would be.

Once she was settled at the ironing board, Betty reminded her that the cupboards were bare.

"If you'd like, I could pick up some groceries before I
make myself scarce."

This tactful suggestion helped Jenny emerge from her
trance. With Betty's collaboration, she made a list: an assortment of cheeses and sourdough bread, cold cuts and
smoked salmon, soft drinks, wine, a six-pack of beer in case
Peter preferred that, Dijon mustard, mayonnaise, lettuce
and tomatoes.

"If you see any good-looking strawberries, you might
pick up a basket of those. And we'll need a few things for
breakfast."

Pencil poised above the list, Betty waited for Jenny to go on. "What about some of those marvelous croissants from Petrini's bakery?"

"Croissants would be lovely." Jenny moistened her forefinger and tested the iron. "If you happen to think of anything else we might need—anything at all—"

"Never fear. I'll pick it up and you can reimburse me later."

Jenny nodded agreement, one eye on the clock.

"Take care," Betty cautioned on her way out the door. "Try not to burn yourself."

Jenny promised she would do her best, but her attention began to wander before her friend's car had left the driveway.

While she ironed the shorts, she remembered candles and flowers and half a dozen other items she should have asked Betty to get at the mall. While she ironed her navy-blue camisole, she tried to recall whether Peter drank his coffee black or with sugar and cream, and while she pressed her white linen wraparound skirt her thoughts leapt ahead to the moment of Peter's arrival.

What should she say to him? How should she behave?

He hadn't said he was coming to Santa Rosa exclusively to see her. He'd simply asked whether she would like some company for the weekend, and she had drawn her own conclusions.

What if her conclusions were wrong? What if she had misinterpreted the phone call?

Jennifer sighed and found a hanger for the skirt, and while she tried to come up with an opening line, she ironed a set of sheets and pillow slips.

"This is totally out of character," she said as she made up the sofa bed.

Never before had she found it necessary, or even desirable, to iron sheets. But the knowledge that she was building the reunion with Peter beyond reasonable proportions didn't stop her from ironing another set of sheets for her bed, just in case.

Four nights, she thought. Four nights and four days. A lot could happen in that length of time.

At one-fifteen, when Betty got back, Jenny was just stepping out of the shower.

"Guess who I saw on my way to the shopping center," Betty called.

"Elvis Presley."

"Someone nearly that surprising," Betty answered.

Oh, Lord! Jenny thought. Peter's here early. "Wh-who?" she stammered, fumbling into her robe.

"Your next-door neighbor."

"Mrs. Farber?"

"None other."

Jenny leaned against the washbasin while her heartbeat returned to its normal rhythm. "What's so surprising about that?"

"Nothing, I guess. But you've lived here— What? Three years? And in all that time, I've only seen her through her front window. Day or night, rain or shine, there she is, spying on your visitors."

Jenny walked into the kitchen, still toweling her hair. "It's not just my visitors Mrs. Farber spies on. She'd rather snoop than sleep. Not much happens around here that she's not aware of."

"Ever vigilant," Betty summarized. "That's not a bad motto for a savings and loan. It brings to mind rigid security, a place patroled by vicious guard dogs, with a vault protected by one of those old British battleships—"

"The word you're looking for is *dreadnought*," Jenny broke in. "A term synonymous with Edwina Farber."

"Tsk, tsk! There's no need to be so rough on her, even if she is the eyes and ears of the world."

"And the mouth! If there's one thing Edwina enjoys more than minding other people's business, it's spreading rumors about it. She's a nuisance, a menace, a one-person grapevine! She's the main reason I decided to move."

"I understand, Jenny. Honestly, I do." Betty smiled with some bemusement. "I almost didn't recognize her without those ruffled curtains in front of her face, but there she was on the corner, big as life, waiting for the bus to Crossroads Plaza, so I stopped and introduced myself and asked if she'd like a ride."

Jenny bent over at the waist, making a turban of the towel. "Naturally she took it."

"Naturally. In case you haven't noticed, it's a scorcher out today."

"I noticed," said Jenny. Less than ten minutes out of the shower, and already she was feeling the heat. Her gaze strayed to the window, to the patch of lawn hedged by wilting hydrangea bushes, and she made a mental note to unpack the table fan.

"It's got to be a hundred degrees in the shade," Betty went on, "but Edwina was wearing this ratty old sweater."

"Brown," said Jenny. "Two sizes too big for her."

"That's the one!"

"She always wears it. I think it belonged to her husband."

Betty began unloading the grocery bags, handing the perishables to Jenny. "I was glad I stopped for her, poor old thing. She was pale and sort of trembly, as if she'd been out in the sun too long. I was afraid she might be suffering from heatstroke, but when I asked if she was feeling all right, she insisted she was fine."

"I'll bet that didn't stop you from fretting about her, though."

"No. I still felt uncomfortable about leaving her, so when I dropped her at Long's Drugs, I offered her a lift home.

She wanted to know how long my errands would take, and I told her about an hour, and she said she only had to have some prescriptions filled, which shouldn't take more than half that time, but if it would ease my mind, she'd wait for me at the coffee bar in the food court.''

Jenny shut the crisper drawer with more than necessary force. "That's Edwina for you. You go out of your way to help her, and she makes it sound as if she's doing *you* a favor."

"That's true," Betty replied. "But the point is, when I got back to Long's, she wasn't there. Not at the coffee bar. Not at the prescription counter. I looked for her everywhere. No Edwina."

"She must have come home."

"That what I thought, so I tried to call her, but there was no answer. So then I thought she might've remembered something she had to take care of at one of the other stores in the mall. But after I'd waited ten minutes and she still hadn't shown, I talked to the pharmacist. He said Edwina had been in, all right, and ordered her refills. She told him she'd wait for them, but she hadn't picked them up."

Betty folded the last grocery bag and put the cash-register tape on the kitchen table. "I don't know whether I should be offended because Edwina stood me up, or alarmed because she took off without her medicine."

Jenny closed the refrigerator and turned to confront her friend. "If I were you, I wouldn't worry about Edwina Farber. She can have Long's deliver her prescription, and I imagine she's home by now."

"She's not. I tried her door when I got back. Her place is locked up tight."

"Well, I'm sure she'll be home soon."

"You're probably right, but how do you explain the way she left the mall?"

"She must've forgotten that you were giving her a ride."

Betty rejected this possibility with a dubious lift of her eyebrows. "I realize Edwina's pushing eighty and maybe her memory's not as sharp as it used to be. I can see how it might've slipped her mind that I was going to pick her up, but how on earth could she forget her prescriptions?"

"You said it yourself, Betty. Her memory's failing. She's had a number of episodes lately where she's not entirely functional. She gets confused, disoriented. Sometimes she has spells of paranoia. Last Sunday, for instance, she went running through the neighborhood, babbling about someone breaking into her apartment while she was at church."

"Had there been a break-in?"

"That's hard to say. Hank Augustine, from across the street, came over to check her story out, but he didn't find any jimmy marks or broken windows. Not long ago, she had expensive new locks installed, and they were intact. Hank did say that the place looked as if it had been searched. Pretty thoroughly, I gather. Cabinet doors were ajar and drawers had been left open—that type of thing. But Edwina might've done that herself."

"Was anything missing?"

"Hank didn't seem to think so. He said there was thirty dollars and change on the bureau."

"A burglar wouldn't have left without the money."

"Not unless he was interrupted," Jenny qualified. "But Hank played it safe and phoned the police. A patrol car got here within twenty minutes, but by then Edwina had spaced the whole thing out. She couldn't recall why the police had been summoned, and she refused to cooperate with the officers. In fact, she became downright abusive. She even accused Hank of being involved in some sort of plot to harm her."

Betty frowned. "How strange."

"And pathetic," Jenny added. "It's sad that Edwina's deteriorating this way, but there doesn't seem to be much anyone can do about it."

Betty gave her a sharp-eyed glance. "I know what you're up to, Jenny Spaulding. You're reminding me that I'm not responsible for Edwina. You're trying to reassure me."

"Is it working?"

"Not really, but I appreciate the effort."

"Would you feel better if I promise to stop by Edwina's later and make sure she got home safely?"

"It wouldn't hurt." Betty fished a package of cigarettes from the pocket of her skirt, shook one out and lighted it. "While you're at it, could you see that she gets her prescriptions?"

"Are you sure you wouldn't like me to keep an eye on her all weekend?"

"I hate to impose, but would you?"

Betty had taken her seriously! Jenny began going through the cupboards, using the pretext of hunting for an ashtray to hide her dismay.

The gypsy soul she had inherited from her father told her she wasn't her neighbor's keeper. *Don't permit this intrusion on your weekend,* urged a small inner voice. *Think of Peter. Think of yourself.*

But the stern New England conscience Jenny had inherited from her mother warned her not to be selfish. She might turn her back on Edwina Farber, but she could not turn her back on her friend.

"Don't be silly," she heard herself answering. "It's no big deal."

"But what if Peter's made other plans?"

Jenny produced the ashtray and a facsimile of a smile. "If he has, he'll change them. He won't mind." *He wouldn't, would he?*

Her uncertainty must have showed. Or perhaps the matchmaker in Betty would not let her risk spoiling their reunion.

"No," she said. "It's just not right. But if you'll keep an eye on Edwina for the rest of the day, I'll take over tomorrow."

"Fair enough," Jenny replied. "If you'd rather do it that way, it's a deal."

A few minutes later, Betty announced it was time she headed home. She was animated and cheerful, visibly relieved, when Jenny walked her to the door. But once Betty was gone, Jenny was left with a nagging sense of foreboding.

The foreboding grew stronger as she lingered in the doorway, looking across the drive toward Edwina Farber's end of the duplex.

She had seen Edwina's apartment countless times. It was identical to hers. But today, somehow, it seemed different.

The broad front window that faced the street was vast and empty. Not a breath of air disturbed the sheer lace curtains, and the ruffles hung still and lifeless. The windowpane reflected an oddly distorted image of the house on the far side of Sutter Court—and Edwina Farber's absence.

Evidently, Jenny's neighbor had not yet come home.

Jenny folded her arms about her waist and hugged her elbows close to her sides.

In spite of the heat, she was shivering.

Chapter Two

Two o'clock came and went; Peter did not arrive.

Jenny prowled from room to room, wondering if his car had broken down or if something else had come up. A family emergency or a meeting with a client. If he had changed his mind about driving over for the weekend, why didn't he call?

At two-fifteen, the telephone rang. She scooped up the receiver, said an anxious hello.

"Jenny? Eve Vandiver here. My goodness! You must've been perched on top of the phone."

Was that a car? Jenny trailed the telephone cord toward the living room so that she could see the foot of the drive-way and part of the cul-de-sac through the front window.

The street was quiet. Not a car in sight, except for her orange Toyota. Her imagination must be playing tricks on her.

"What can I do for you, Eve?" she inquired.

"You should be asking what I can do for you."

"All right," Jenny replied, only fractionally less distracted. "What can you?"

"That depends on whether you're busy tomorrow night."

"As a matter of fact, I'm expecting company." *What could have detained him?*

"The more the merrier. Bring her along."

"Him," said Jenny.

"Your company's male? That's even better. Eligible men are scarce as hen's teeth. I've been racking my brain, trying to figure out who I should invite to be your escort—"

"Why do I need an escort?"

"For my dinner party. Didn't I tell you?"

"No, Eve, you didn't."

"Then I guess I'd better start at the beginning. I'm not planning anything elaborate. It's basically an impromptu get-together in honor of Hal Joyce."

"*The* Hal Joyce?"

"Would you be amazed if I said it is?"

"No, I wouldn't. Not with all the socializing you and Reed do. But I'd be amazed to find out you know Hal Joyce and never mentioned it to me."

"Look, Jenny, don't get the wrong idea. We're not bosom buddies or anything."

"You know him well enough to give a party for him."

"Yes, but the truth is, we only just met."

"How?" Jenny asked. "Where did you meet him?"

"Right here, in Santa Rosa. You're aware, aren't you, that the cast and crew of *Foyle's Paradise* has been in the area filming location sequences?"

"Isn't everybody? There was an article about Mr. Joyce in last Sunday's paper. Something about him looking for a house to use for exterior shots of the Foyle house."

"That's old news. The latest update is, the search is over. He's found the house, and it's mine. Reed's, too, naturally." Eve acknowledged her husband's co-ownership with her infectious whinnying laugh. "To give credit where credit's due, it's actually all Reed's doing. He had a conference with Mr. Joyce at the bank last Monday and in the course of their discussion, Hal told him the sort of place he was looking for. Reed was completely flabbergasted. He said, 'You've just described my house.' He brought Hal by that afternoon—"

"And you're already on a first-name basis?"

"There's no reason not to be, Jenny. Hal has the reputation of being a tough customer, but he's really a very nice man. He's built like a sumo wrestler and he looks quite fierce, which leads you to believe he deserves his reputation, but then he opens his mouth and out comes this voice that belongs to the Pillsbury Doughboy." Eve laughed again. "At any rate, he raved about our house and by Tuesday, we'd worked out most of the details."

A car had turned onto Sutter Court. This time Jenny wasn't imagining its approach. She went onto her tiptoes to improve her view of the street, but the sound of the motor stopped before the car reached the cul-de-sac.

She rocked back on her heels, heart sinking. "I'm happy for you, Eve."

"You don't sound happy," was Eve's response. "Let's have a little enthusiasm here."

"You're enthusiastic enough for both of us," Jenny countered. "You must be thrilled."

"It is exciting, although I must confess my first thought was that we're undoubtedly letting ourselves in for some major headaches."

"Headaches?"

"Well, you know the bar on *Cheers* has become a tourist attraction. So did the house Mary Tyler Moore used for her series, and *Foyle's Paradise* is as popular as either of those shows."

"I see what you mean," Jenny said.

"But Reed assures me that Hal will provide ample security. I mean, he'd have to protect his investment, wouldn't he?"

Jenny agreed that he would.

"And then, of course, there's Momma...." Eve left the rest of this sentence dangling, but Jenny was capable of filling in the blank.

Helene Thiebault, Eve's mother, would be appalled when she learned that her family home was about to be invaded by a television crew. And Helene was not inclined to keep her suffering to herself. She would spread it around—in this case, to the Vandivers.

Never mind that the house was a sprawling relic of a bygone era, a magnificent white elephant that required endless maintenance and a nonstop flow of cash for its upkeep. And never mind that Helene hadn't lived there for the last ten years, or that it had been her pleasure to sign the deed over to her daughter and son-in-law on their wedding day.

Helene's gifts generally came with strings attached, as Jenny had cause to know.

During her tenure on the faculty at Ringer-Dent Academy, she had watched Helene Thiebault trading donations for influence, giving endowments with one hand and issuing ultimatums with the other. As Betty once put it, "Helene walks softly and carries a big checkbook."

"Yes," Jenny said. "There's your mother. Have you told her?"

"Not yet," Eve answered timorously. "For now, we're operating on the assumption that what Momma doesn't know won't hurt us. According to the agreement Reed worked out, the production company will paint the house and put on that new roof we've been needing, so it seemed wiser to wait till the place is spruced up."

"Perhaps that will soften the blow."

"That's what we're hoping. Anyway, for better or worse, whether Momma approves or not, we signed the contract today."

"So now you want to celebrate."

"And how! I think having our house on *Foyle's Paradise* will be a kick, and since I'm such a fan, this seems the perfect opportunity to meet the stars. When I started making up the guest list this morning, you were the first person I thought of, Jenny. I know that you're a fan, too."

Jenny was. Deadline pressures and her writing schedule didn't leave much time for television, but she rarely missed an episode of *Foyle's Paradise.*

"It was sweet of you to think of me, Eve. I'd love to meet Vanessa Wayne and Leo Prince—"

"How about Sonnet Cole?"

"Yes, Sonnet most of all. She's wonderful on the show. So cute and outspoken, without being the least bit offensive. And funny! I wonder if she's that hilarious in person."

"Come to dinner tomorrow night. You'll have your chance to find out."

"I'd like to," said Jenny. "Really I would." But not nearly as much as she would like spending the evening alone with Peter.

Eve must have sensed her ambivalence. "You don't have to give me your answer now," she said. "Check with your friend when he gets in. If he wants to join the party, let us know and we'll throw another steak or two on the grill. If not, who knows? The summer's still young. Maybe we can make it another time."

Maybe we can, thought Jennifer. Because of Peter's call, she was willing to believe that anything was possible.

With Peter foremost in her mind, after Eve rang off, Jenny roamed aimlessly from room to room.

She got as far as the entry hall before she thought of the way Peter drove. She recalled his habit of revving the engine at stoplights, anticipating the green, the way he whipped in and out of traffic and passed everything on the road, racing along at top speed as if there were no tomorrow.

What if he'd been in an accident? What if he'd been injured? What if—

Stop it! Jenny scolded herself. *Don't even think about that.*

A year ago, she wouldn't have been apprehensive. The thought of serious accidents, grievous injury, would never have entered her mind. But that was before her father's murder taught her that brutal events weren't limited to headlines in the morning paper and that tragedy didn't always happen to someone else.

The horrifying truth was that violence was insidious. Mayhem was all around, waiting to pounce when you were least prepared. Terrible things could happen to anyone at anytime. No one was immune.

Not her father.

Not her.

And not Peter.

Being realistic was one thing, however; giving way to panic was quite another.

Despite his daredevil reliance on hair-trigger reflexes, Peter handled his car with skill and confidence. What's more, it was only two thirty-five. It was senseless to think the worst had happened when he was less than an hour overdue.

Even so, Jenny knew she would breathe a lot easier once she was certain Peter was safe.

Consumed by worry, she stood at the screen door, staring out at the street.

AT QUARTER TO THREE, a sleek, black roadster turned onto Sutter Court. The growl of its engine preceded it, and in the split second before it came into view, Jenny guessed it would be a powerful, low-slung model; not the Taurus Peter drove.

She watched the sports car swing around the cul-de-sac and park in front of the duplex. Her eyes widened with recognition when the driver's door opened and a big, fair-haired man climbed out. As he retrieved a duffel-bag from the passenger seat and started along the front walk, she drank in each endearing move.

"Peter! You finally made it."

He spotted her in the entry and stopped to return her appraisal. "I got held up by road work. Sorry I'm late."

"Never mind. You're here now."

She wanted to run to meet him, wanted to throw herself into his arms, but uncertainty kept her rooted to the doorstep.

Until she had a better idea what he expected of her, shouldn't she let him make the first move?

To fill the awkward silence, she said, "You got a new car."

Peter hitched the duffel's strap over his shoulder. "You cut your hair."

She stirred uneasily. "When did you trade in the Ford?"

"Last fall. When did you get your hair cut?"

"A few months ago." She opened the screen door, glancing toward the roadster. "What make is it?"

"A Maserati."

"Is it as fast as it looks?"

"It's faster. Goes like a bomb. What do you think of it?"

"It suits you."

"Thank you, Jenny. I take that as a compliment."

He paused in the doorway, studying her intently as he brushed a wisp of hair away from her face. His touch was warm, his smile quizzical. The slight roughness of his fingertips made her skin tingle.

"Well?" she challenged, meeting his gaze. "What's the verdict?"

"It's stylish."

Jennifer flinched but she didn't look away. "Now I know how it feels to be damned by faint praise."

Peter rearranged another strand, tucking it behind her ear. "Don't get me wrong. You look fantastic this way. It's just that I liked your hair long."

"That's because you didn't have to take care of it. Short hair is cooler, more practical—"

Peter threw up one hand in mock surrender. "You win, Jenny. If it's a fight you want, you won't get it from me."

"That's quite a switch for a man who could never pass up an argument."

"Is that the way you remember it?"

"Yes. Don't you?"

"I remember you didn't trust me. Apparently, that hasn't changed."

"I trust you, Peter. I do!"

"But you have your doubts about my motives."

A hot wave of color flooded Jennifer's cheeks. It was she who broke the eye contact, retreating through the stacks of mover's cartons from the living room to the kitchen with Peter close on her heels. When the refrigerator blocked her path, she sought refuge in playing hostess.

"You can leave your bag anywhere," she told him. "Make yourself comfortable, while I see about refreshments."

Peter lounged against the breakfast bar, munching on corn chips, while she made sandwiches and stirred up a pitcher of lemonade.

"It's been quite a year for you, hasn't it," he said. "You've made some drastic changes. New hairdo, new apartment, new career."

"I've made some changes," she answered slowly, "but I wouldn't call them 'drastic.'"

Peter let that one pass. "Do you ever miss teaching?"

After a moment of reflection, she replied, "I miss parts of it."

"Which ones?"

"The students. My friends on the faculty. The time I used to have for reading. And some of the classroom discussions were great. The kids would come up with an analysis of a poem or short story that was fresh and original, and they'd get so excited. Sometimes they'd seem to catch fire."

Peter sampled the olives. "That must've been rewarding."

"Yes, it was. But I can do without giving tests and grading papers, and I don't care if I never go to another PTA meeting."

"Never say never, Jenny. What'll you do if you have children?"

"Their father can go to the meetings."

Peter gave her a searching look. "Any candidates in mind?"

"Not at the moment." To avoid his scrutiny, she dropped to her knees and rooted through the cabinets for a serving tray.

"So tell me," said Peter, "how does it feel to be a famous writer?"

Jenny arose, laughing. "Michener's famous. Shakespeare's famous. They've stood the test of time. I'm only a novice. *Famous* isn't a word that applies to me."

"Don't be modest. I've read the reviews on the jacket of your book."

"*Justice Denied* has been well received, for which I'm very grateful, but any fame I have is by association with my father and Judge Eaton."

Peter nodded. Revelations about Leonard Eaton had dominated the news since his death the previous June. There had been reams of headlines about his corruption. "So your publisher chose to capitalize on Eaton's notoriety—"

"And I got lucky," Jenny finished. "I had a manuscript ready to rush into print at a time when they were looking for one. At the moment, I'm considered a hot property, but that won't last, and even if it could, I'm not sure I'd want it to. Publicity work takes too much time. It offers too many distractions. Anyway, all the hype in the world won't make me a better writer. Only writing can do that."

"And you want to be good."

"I want to be more than good, Peter. I want to be the *best*." She hadn't meant to sound so impassioned. Struggling for composure, feeling painfully self-conscious, she focused on transferring the sandwiches and lemonade to the tray. "That's enough about me. Let's talk about you for a change. What've you been up to?"

"Oh, the usual."

Peter's terse reply made it evident that this was not going to be easy. Jenny gritted her teeth and tried another approach. "How are your aunt and uncle?"

"They're fine, but Felicia's not my aunt anymore. Max filed for divorce last August."

Jenny filled two glasses with ice cubes, casting about for a suitable response. She couldn't honestly say that she was surprised, not after the way Felicia had deceived Max. For the eighteen years of their marriage, she had concealed the identity of Jaime de Silva, a fugitive from justice in at least three countries.

De Silva had fancied himself a revolutionary. He'd claimed to be a crusader for socialist-humanist causes. During the Librist uprising in Santa Marta, he had kidnapped a number of diplomats and called it political protest. He had ordered the execution of his captives and called that an act of war.

But euphemisms couldn't disguise what de Silva really was. A common criminal. A murderer whose victims had included Felicia's first husband and her parents.

He had killed Bradley Darien. Max's brother. Peter's father. And he had been instrumental in the death of Gareth Spaulding. Max's friend. Jenny's father.

Yet Felicia had fobbed off this man—this assassin—as Milo Jaffre, and prevailed upon Max Darien to offer him employment as a chauffeur.

Jenny set the glasses on the tray with a sharp, indignant thump. "Divorce can be painful, but there are times when the alternative is worse. I think your uncle's better off without Felicia."

"I think you're right, but the same thing's true of Felicia."

"You've seen her?"

Peter nodded. "I ran into her a few months ago. I was out jogging, and she was, too. She's stopped drinking, and she looks like a different woman. It would appear that being on her own has been her salvation."

Felicia jogging? The mind boggled. Jenny couldn't imagine her doing anything more strenuous than lifting a whiskey bottle. She couldn't imagine Felicia standing on her own feet, walking a straight line or wearing anything other than a peignoir.

"Is this ready to go?" Peter asked, picking up the tray.

Jenny added napkins and said that it was.

She was still trying to assimilate the idea of Felicia running as she led Peter out the back door and across the yard to the grape arbor, but once they were settled in the leafy green shadows beneath the trellis, she gave up the effort as a lost cause.

"I don't understand women like Felicia," she said.

"In what respect?"

"Her involvement with de Silva. From what I've learned about him, he had no conscience. He couldn't have cared for Felicia at all. If he had, he wouldn't have used her the way he did. But she lied for him. She cheated and schemed for him. She deceived her husband—''

"And nearly destroyed herself in the process."

"Do you think that's why she did it? To punish herself?"

"I'm no mind reader, Jenny, but if I had to make a guess, I'd say she loved de Silva. God knows she did everything in her power to protect him."

Jenny exhaled on a sigh. "I suppose that's one definition of love."

"Or obsession," Peter qualified. "Why all the interest in Felicia?"

"The book I'm working on now is part of the Santa Marta trilogy."

"The series you mentioned on the phone?"

"That's right. The first is *Diary of a Journalist*—"

"The one about your father."

"Right again. And the second's about de Silva—or it will be, if I ever get it written." Jenny grimaced. Her mouth turned down at the corners. "I've done my research, read every article about de Silva I can get my hands on, and I've practically memorized his journals, but I can't seem to get a handle on the man. So I thought if I understood Felicia, that might help me understand him."

"What's to understand? De Silva was a fanatic out for revenge. Settling old scores was the only thing he cared about, even if he had to torch himself to do it."

"That accounts for the way he died, Peter. It doesn't begin to explain the way he lived."

Peter reached for another sandwich. "You know, Jenny, de Silva worked for my uncle a good many years. Max thought he knew him, but he didn't. He was taken in by the impersonation of the loyal family retainer, and frankly, so was I. De Silva seemed hardworking, trustworthy and highly intelligent. He was obviously underemployed, and sometimes I wondered why he'd settled for being a chauffeur, but I chalked it up to a lack of ambition. And once or twice, I wondered why he revealed so little of himself, but I never suspected what he was hiding."

"You weren't alone. De Silva was the consummate actor."

"Exactly," said Peter. "So when you come right down to it, do you think it's possible to figure out what drives a person like that?"

"I *hope* it's possible." Jenny poured refills of lemonade, a V-shaped furrow between her eyebrows. "My manuscript's due at the end of September, and if I don't come up with a valid theory about what made de Silva tick fairly soon, this won't be much of a book."

Peter leaned forward and took her hand. "I wish I could be more help."

Jenny turned her palm toward his. "You've helped more than you realize. Just having you here gives me confidence."

Peter laced his fingers through hers. "Have you talked to anyone who was close to de Silva?"

"I went through the motions. Part of the problem is that no one, including his brother and his kindergarten teacher, was close to him."

"Except Felicia," said Peter half joking. "Maybe you ought to interview her."

A stillness overcame Jenny. Her fingers tensed in his grasp. She had thought about contacting Felicia, but even the thought was repugnant. How could she speak to the woman whose perfidy had led to Gareth's death?

"No," she answered in a small, brittle voice. "I can't interview Felicia."

"Can't or won't?"

"Take your pick." She tried to free her hand, but Peter would not release her.

"Ah, Jenny, it's been more than a year. And Felicia was as much a victim as your father. Can't you forgive her?"

"I can forgive her, but I can't forget—" She averted her gaze, afraid of the disappointment she might see in Peter's eyes. "Please, could we talk about something else?"

He set his plate on the ground beside his glass. "We don't have to talk at all, unless you want to."

"You don't mind?"

"Nope. I can think of other things I'd rather do."

Even as he spoke, Peter gave her wrist a tug, pulling her toward him. A second tug brought her to her feet. A third, and she was in his lap, caught in a hold that barred her escape.

But escape was the furthest thing from her mind. A ripple of pleasure shot through her as his lips skimmed her forehead, her cheek, the curve of her jaw.

"Jenny," he said in a lazy drawl, "I want you to know, there's a principle at stake here."

"A principle?" she whispered.

"Actions speak louder than words." With the tip of his tongue, Peter explored the exquisitely sensitive hollow behind her ear. "Any objections?"

"None at all. I like it that you're so direct." The arms she wound about his shoulders, the eagerness with which she returned his caresses, made this clear.

"If you admire my directness, how can you doubt my motives?"

Her pulses quickened as he made a necklace of small, biting kisses about the base of her throat. "You're the one who said that, not me."

"Mmm." He kissed the pale, creamy flesh at the nape of her neck. "I noticed you didn't deny it."

"Didn't I?"

With a swiftness that made her heart leap, he trapped her earlobe between his teeth and gave it a delicate nip. "Stop stalling and answer the question."

How could she resist such sweet torment? "It's been a year since we saw each other—"

"I know," Peter groaned. "I should've called sooner."

Jenny framed his face between her palms and rested her forehead against his. "Why did you wait so long to call?"

"Because I was a fool."

Encouraged by Peter's gruff sincerity, touched by the tenderness in his eyes, Jenny kissed his chin, the corners of his mouth, his upper lip, his lower lip, and between kisses, she cried, "Why did you call today? Do you think I've been sitting by the phone all these months, waiting to hear from you? Why did you make the trip over from Sacramento? What is it you *want* from me?"

And Peter said, "I couldn't get you out of my mind, Jenny. Couldn't stop thinking about you . . . I was too stubborn to admit how much I missed you, too proud to tell you how much I need you. I was afraid you didn't feel the same way, and I was scared to death you might be seeing some other guy . . . I'm not sure what I expected when I phoned this morning. All I know is, I had to make that call. I had to see you, had to be with you, and I hoped—no, I prayed!—that it wasn't too late."

Somewhere in the midst of this interrogation, the time between questions and answers expanded, filled with silences as passionate as Peter's responses. And when their kisses grew longer and more urgent than his answers, more demanding than Jenny's questions, they retraced their path to the duplex, through the maze of mover's cartons to the bedroom.

Jenny had forgotten to unpack the table fan. The room was stuffy and airless, but they were oblivious to the heat.

And if Peter noticed the freshly ironed sheets, he neglected to mention them.

He was absorbed with Jenny. Utterly. Totally. Keenly aware that, while she seemed satisfied with all of his answers, she found his reply to her last question especially satisfying.

"What is it you *want* from me?" she'd asked.

Being a man of principle, Peter didn't simply tell her. He showed her what he wanted with kisses more persuasive than words, with caresses more devastating, with an embrace so eloquent, it left Jenny speechless.

By the time the interrogation ended, both of them were content to lie side by side, with their heads on the same pillow.

Peter was the first to catch his breath. "The defense rests," he said, "unless the lawyer for the plaintiff has more questions."

"That's all for now," Jenny replied. "But keep yourself available, Counselor. I may want to cross-examine you later."

Peter gave her a wicked grin. "I can hardly wait."

Jenny wrinkled her nose at him, undismayed by his teasing. "Just remember, you're still under oath."

SOME PEOPLE WORRY WHEN THINGS are going badly. Others worry when things are going well. Jenny tended to worry all the time, whether she had reason to or not. Through good times and bad, she expected the worst, and since the worst often materialized, she was seldom disappointed.

That Saturday was no exception.

Her reunion with Peter was the best of times. She couldn't imagine any better. Once the ice was broken, they had an idyllic afternoon. Talking and laughing. Reminiscing. Getting reacquainted. Cherishing the dear and familiar in each other and savoring new discoveries.

They had taken a precipitous plunge into intimacy, but Jenny had no regrets. She no longer questioned Peter's motives, and as the afternoon waned, she realized that she was in danger of falling in love with him all over again. But loving Peter was a danger devoutly to be wished for.

She admired him. She respected him. What was most important, she *liked* him, and she sensed that the feeling was mutual.

But even while she acknowledged all this, she was plagued by an undercurrent of anxiety.

It was eight o'clock and they were preparing to go out for dinner before she identified the source of her distress.

Mrs. Farber had not come home.

While Peter was in the shower, Jenny paid a visit next door. She rang the front doorbell, then went round to the back of the unit and knocked. She peeked in several windows, but saw no sign of Edwina.

Jenny returned to her own apartment, convinced that she ought to do something, but not sure what action to take. She was standing at the screen door, staring at Edwina's windows, when Peter came out of the bedroom.

"Something's wrong," he observed seeing her frown.

"I'm a little worried about the lady across the way. She should've been home hours ago...."

Peter's arms enfolded her, and Jenny relaxed against his chest while she went on to describe Betty's encounter with Edwina Farber at the bus top, the arrangements Betty had made to drive the elderly woman home and her subsequent disappearance from the drug store.

"I promised Betty I'd make sure Edwina was all right," Jennifer concluded, "and I did keep an eye on her place till you got here."

"But then you got sidetracked," Peter said.

Jenny tipped her head to the side and rubbed her cheek against his shoulder. "In the nicest possible way, of course, but, yes, I guess I did."

"Do you think Edwina might've come in and gone out again while we were in the bedroom?"

"Could be, except that she almost never goes out at night."

Peter drew Jenny closer. "How long has she been missing?"

"About seven hours." Jenny's gaze remained fixed on her neighbor's window. "She says she has a heart condition, but I never believed it was serious. She's always complaining about something or other, trying to play on people's sympathies. But what if she was telling the truth? What if she's had a heart attack? She could be in there right now, unconscious, too weak to call for help—"

"Why don't I have a look around?"

Peter reached past Jenny and opened the screen. He was halfway across the drive when she called, "I was just over there. Edwina didn't answer my knock."

"Did you try the door?"

"Betty did earlier this afternoon. It was locked."

"If it's been that long, it won't hurt to give it another try."

A moment later, Peter climbed the stairs to the neighbor's porch and rang the bell. A minute passed while he waited for an answer.

"Anybody home?" he shouted.

There was no response.

Jenny held her breath as he tried the knob. The door opened.

"Wait!" she cried as he stepped inside. "I'll come with you."

Although she dreaded what Peter might find, fear propelled her across the driveway. Fear and the guilty certainty that she should have been her neighbor's keeper. With very little effort, she could have been more attentive to Edwina's needs.

Peter reappeared in the doorway just as Jenny was climbing the steps. "Don't," he said grimly, motioning her to a stop. "You don't want to come in here."

"Is it . . . ?"

Peter cleared his throat. "She's in the hall, just outside the bathroom. Looks like you were right about the heart attack."

"Is she—" Jenny's mouth felt parched. She tried to swallow, licked her lips, and before she could say anything more, Peter was at her side, shepherding her back to her apartment with his hand at the small of her back.

"We'd better phone for an ambulance."

"Then she's not . . ."

Peter lengthened his stride. "The ambulance is a formality, Jenny. Edwina Farber's dead."

Chapter Three

A policeman arrived before the ambulance. Jenny waited on the porch while Peter dealt with introductions and accompanied the officer inside.

Within minutes, Peter was back. "If you feel up to it, Sergeant Beal would like you to identify the body."

The oppressive heat in Edwina's apartment struck Jenny like a blow. She clung to Peter's hand as she followed him through the murky light of the living room, with its clutter of plastic slip-covered furniture, knickknacks and doilies and dusty philodendrons.

It was hotter in the hall, and darker, but the dusk couldn't disguise the still, small form that lay crumpled on the floor, legs asprawl.

In her collapse, and in her subsequent struggle to reach the bathroom, Edwina's skirt had hiked up, exposing cotton bloomers and flaccid thighs encased in heavy support stockings. One hand was pressed to the bosom of her faded print housedress, the other gripped an empty pillbox, as if even in death, she clutched at life.

Jenny's stomach gave a sickening lurch. She wanted to straighten Edwina's skirt, to restore a semblance of dignity to the body.

"C-can't we cover her with something?"

"Not till I'm finished with the preliminary investigation," said Beal. "Is this Edwina Farber?"

Jenny peered at the ashen features that blended into the gloom, at the gaping mouth and half-open eyes, which were vacant, staring...

"Yes," she said, shuddering, "it is."

But it wasn't! The eyes were sightless and the body wax-like, an inanimate shell. Whatever spark had given it life, had rendered it human, had made it Edwina, was gone.

Beal switched on the ceiling light and bent down to examine the label on the pillbox. "Nitroglycerin," he muttered, then glancing at Peter, "you told the dispatcher she had a bad heart?"

"That's my understanding, and the circumstances seem to support it."

And I didn't believe her! Jenny thought.

She focused on Edwina's black lace-up orthopedic shoes. Like the rest of her belongings, they were serviceable and worn, badly rundown at the heels. "How long has she been—like this?"

Beal removed a handkerchief from his hip pocket and blotted trickles of sweat from his forehead, studying the body. He held his hand against Edwina's chest, testing for residual body heat and the advancement of rigor mortis. When he removed his hand, the corpse shifted slightly, then toppled to one side, exposing the telltale mottling of lividity.

Jenny gasped and Peter slid a protective arm about her shoulders.

Beal wiped his palms and put the handkerchief back in his pocket. "From the condition of the remains, I'd guess she's been dead at least seven hours."

"That would make the time of death about two o'clock," said Peter.

"Or earlier," said Beal.

"Will there have to be an autopsy?" Jenny's voice broke on the question. Edwina had suffered enough indignities.

"Well, now, that depends."

"On what?" Jenny demanded, glancing about. "Do you see any signs of foul play?"

"Easy, honey," said Peter. "Even if a death is from natural causes, the state requires a postmortem unless the deceased was under treatment for a potentially fatal illness."

The sergeant nodded agreement. The look he gave Jenny was sympathetic. "Would you happen to know who Mrs. Farber's doctor was?"

"I'm sorry, I've no idea, but if there are any prescription bottles around—"

"There aren't," said Beal. "Not in the medicine chest, not in the kitchen cupboards, not in her nightstand."

"Well, you should be able to get his name from the Long's at Crossroads Plaza. She ordered refills there today."

Beal made a note of this. "Do you know who'd be the next of kin?"

"I'm not sure she had any relatives."

"Are you sure that she didn't?"

"I'm sorry," Jenny repeated. "I didn't know Edwina very well."

"What about the other neighbors?" Peter inquired gently. "Would any of them know who to contact?"

Jenny shook her head. "Her pastor might have that information."

"What's his name?"

"All I can tell you is that she went to the Lutheran church on College Avenue." Jenny drew in a ragged breath. "I realize, it's not much to go on—"

"It's better than nothing, ma'am. It should expedite things."

Sergeant Beal's interruption kept Jenny from offering another useless apology. If she said she was sorry a hundred times, it wouldn't change a thing. It wouldn't bring Edwina back, nor would it ease her conscience. She moved closer to Peter, blinking back tears.

"I'm going to see Miss Spaulding home. If you have more questions, we'll be next door."

Peter's voice seemed to come from a great distance, and although Beal was only a few feet away, Jenny never heard his reply. He must have said they could leave, however, because moments later, Peter was ushering her through Edwina's living room and out the door.

They were crossing the drive when the ambulance arrived, followed by an official from the coroner's office.

Here and there along Sutter Court porch lights winked on as, alerted by the emergency vehicles, neighbors gathered on the sidewalk to watch the proceedings.

Jenny made it to the haven of her own apartment before her knees gave way. Peter guided her to the sofa and disappeared into the kitchen. She heard him going through the cabinets and cartons, heard his occasional muffled oath, and then he was back with a bottle of Jack Daniel's and two coffee mugs.

"I couldn't find the glasses," he said. He poured the whiskey and shoved one of the cups into her hand. "Drink it," he instructed.

Jenny took a sip. The liquor made her eyes water and stung the back of her nose. She started to put the cup down but Peter's scowl stopped her.

"Drink it all," he said sternly. "You're white as a sheet. You look like you've seen a ghost."

"Maybe I have. The ghost of summers past." She replied in a whisper, staring out the window at the ambulance. The EMT were unloading a stretcher, wheeling it onto the porch.

"If you're saying that Edwina's death brings back memories of your father, there's no comparison. Gareth died violently, before his time. Edwina was old. Her heart gave out—"

"But if I hadn't been so wrapped up in my own concerns, if I'd tried the door earlier, gotten her to the hospital, she might still be alive!"

Peter squared his shoulders. A muscle leapt at the angle of his jaw. "Maybe she would, but chances are she'd be hooked up to monitors and life-support systems, with tubes to feed her and breathe for her and get rid of wastes and keep her heart pumping. I don't know about you, Jenny, but that's not what I'd call living. That's only prolonging death."

Jenny bent over her cup. Her gaze remained fixed on the window. "At least she wouldn't have died alone."

"We all die alone, even if we're surrounded by crowds of people."

A spasm of pain clouded Jenny's features. Her throat worked as she swallowed. "That's not very comforting."

"No, but it's true."

Jenny drank her whiskey and did not respond. The instant her cup was empty, Peter poured more Jack Daniel's.

"Talk to me, Jenny. Tell me what you're feeling."

She heard the entreaty in Peter's voice; his plea struck a chord his arguments hadn't. "I feel terribly lucky that you're here," she answered softly, "and I'd give anything if this hadn't happened this weekend." As soon as the words were out, she wished them unspoken. She faltered into silence, bit her lip. "Does that sound selfish?"

"It's human," said Peter.

Jenny was not reassured. Her gaze drifted back to the window, to Edwina's apartment, ablaze with light, like a setting for a play in which the third act curtain rises on an empty stage. But even as she watched, Sergeant Beal made an entrance, stage right, along with a gray-suited man carrying a doctor's satchel. The EMT joined the procession, wheeling the body toward the door.

Jenny looked away from this sad tableau, swirling the whiskey at the bottom of her cup. "I suppose I ought to call Betty."

"Good idea. Maybe she can convince you that Edwina's death isn't your fault." Peter touched Jenny's cheek, turned her face toward his. "It's not, you know."

"Then why do I feel as if I've let everyone down?"

"Beats me. You sure as hell haven't let me down, and you kept your end of the deal with Betty. I hope, once you hear that from her, you'll be able to let yourself off the hook."

Jenny hoped so, too. She didn't like feeling guilty. She didn't like feeling that she was a failure as a friend. But worrier that she was, even as she dialed Betty's number, she was afraid it would take more than a phone call to put things right.

As it turned out, Betty was not the least bit surprised by Edwina Farber's death. "I expected to hear from you sooner," she told Jenny. "I had a hunch something like this might've happened."

"You did?" said Jenny.

"Absolutely. I've been waiting for the other shoe to drop ever since I got home. I even called the hospitals and asked if Edwina had been admitted."

Jenny sat at the breakfast bar, chin in hand, wondering why she hadn't thought of checking with the hospitals. She glanced at Peter, who was leaning against the opposite side of the counter, shamelessly eavesdropping on her end of the conversation. He grinned and gave her a thumbs-up sign.

"Betty," she said, "you're remarkable. You hardly knew Edwina. How in the world did you foresee a thing like this?"

"It's simple, really. About five years ago, my uncle died of heart failure, and he was on the same medications as Edwina. And you remember I told you how ghastly she looked? Well, my uncle used to look that way whenever he had an angina attack. So I thought about Edwina's appearance and everything else that happened this afternoon and reached the conclusion that she must have felt ill and gone straight home. That would explain why she didn't wait for me, and heaven knows it would've been a natural reaction."

"Wouldn't it have made more sense to go directly to the hospital?"

"Edwina may not have been thinking clearly. You said yourself she'd been having spells of confusion, so it's possible she didn't realize she was about to have a heart attack. At any rate, she must've got back to her apartment before I left the shopping center—"

"I thought you phoned her before you left."

"I did," said Betty. "About one o'clock, and she didn't answer. I suspect, by then, it was already too late to help her."

If this timetable was accurate, there was no way Jenny could blame herself for Edwina's death. At one o'clock, she had been in the shower, blissfully unaware of Betty's meeting with Edwina.

"That's an interesting theory," she said. And she wanted to believe it, for Peter's sake as well as her own. Unless she made peace with her conscience, this wouldn't be much of a weekend.

"It's more than a theory," Betty declared. "It's the only explanation that fits the sequence of events."

"Maybe you're right." *Please, God, let her be right!*

"I'm positive I am, but I take it you have reservations."

"As long as you mention it, there are one or two things that bother me."

"Let's hear them."

"You said Edwina's place was locked up tight, but the door wasn't locked when Peter tried it."

"Edwina must've unlocked it sometime before she died. She was probably trying to get help."

Jenny recalled the empty pillbox and the lack of medicines Sergeant Beal had reported. "What about the prescriptions? Assuming Edwina was taken ill, why did she leave the drug store without them?"

"Damned if I know," Betty said.

"And that doesn't trouble you?"

"No, but I'll tell you what does. Have you ever noticed that death has a tendency to come in threes?"

Jenny hadn't until a year ago, when her father's death was quickly followed by two others. "No," she protested, "and I can't believe you'd buy that superstition."

"It's not a superstition, Jenny. It's more of an observation. And since Edwina was the first to die, what disturbs me is, who'll be next?"

Chapter Four

Who'll be next?

Betty's question haunted Jenny far into the night. She remained wide-eyed and restless long after Peter had fallen asleep.

Sometime after midnight, she shut herself in the bathroom with the rough draft of her book. If she couldn't sleep, she might as well get some work done, and since her best ideas occurred to her when she was in the tub, she ran a bath, stocked her portable desk with pencils, legal pads and a copy of her manuscript, and fitted the tray across the tub.

She peeled off her nightgown, immersed herself in the water and lay there, staring at the ceiling, waiting for inspiration.

None came.

She began going over the manuscript. It struck her as a waste of paper. She'd written three hundred pages, but three hundred times nothing was nothing.

"Who're you kidding?" she asked herself, shoving the makeshift desk aside.

She might've been a darned good English teacher, but she hadn't been satisfied with that. She'd fancied herself a writer, and now this book—this bloodless collection of facts—would prove that she had no talent.

As soon as it was released—*if* it was released—the reading public would recognize that she had made only minor contributions to *Justice Denied,* and that she should never have been credited as coauthor. Her publisher would realize that the perceptiveness she had brought to her father's biography was a fluke. And Claude LeFevre, her editor at Aldrich & Hayes, would see her for what she was: that pitiable creature, a one-book author. Everyone would know that she was a fraud. She'd be a laughingstock, the object of ridicule—

"Stop it!" Jenny cried.

The last time she saw her father, he had accused her of losing her nerve. She, quite naturally, had denied it. But if Gareth made the same charge now, she would have to admit it was true. She was terrified of failure, and if she couldn't control her morbid thinking, failure was inevitable.

She closed her eyes and made herself relax, letting her body go limp and buoyant, allowing her mind to drift....

Who'll be next?

Her eyes flew open. She pulled the stopper, scrambled into her robe and hurriedly left the bathroom.

At 3:00 a.m., weariness drove her back to bed, to toss and turn some more. It was dawn before she finally dozed off, almost noon before she awoke, and when she followed the aroma of coffee into the kitchen, she found Peter on the phone, surrounded by sections of the Sunday paper.

He slanted a grin her way, mouthed a silent "Good morning."

"'Morning," she answered in a groggy murmur, and he returned to his conversation.

She helped herself to coffee and orange juice, buttered a croissant, then slumped into a chair at the table, rubbing the sleep from her eyes.

"I understand your concern," said Peter. "The authorities take a dim view of a hoax like this. But keep in mind, it's been less than twenty-four hours."

Jenny sipped her coffee, studying him over the rim of her cup. From his soothing, professional manner, he must be talking with a client, and judging by his jogging shorts and Nike cross-trainers, he'd been out for his morning run.

She riffled through the sections of newspaper until she found the obituaries. Edwina's was the first.

Funeral services will be held at 1:00 p.m. on Wednesday, July 5, at Calvary Lutheran Church for Edwina H. Farber, age 79, who died on Saturday, July 1, at her home. A lifelong resident of Santa Rosa, she is survived by a son, Theodore. Her husband of fifty years, Lloyd T. Farber, preceded her in death. Visitation will be held at Leicester Funeral Home on Monday, July 3, from 4:00 p.m. until 8:00 p.m. Burial will be at Sunset Gardens Cemetery, the Reverend Russell Loomis officiating. In lieu of flowers, memorials may be made to the American Heart Association or to Calvary Lutheran Church.

Jenny drank her orange juice, mulling over what she'd learned. Aside from its brevity and the implication that Edwina's death had been officially attributed to a heart attack, the obituary was remarkable for its reference to Theodore Farber.

It was odd, Jenny thought, that in the three years she'd lived on Sutter Court, Edwina had never mentioned her son. Neither had any of the neighbors. And to the best of her knowledge, Theodore Farber had never visited his mother—

"No, don't do that!"

Jenny froze, a portion of croissant halfway to her mouth.

"Two reasons," Peter declared in the same brusque tone. "You ought to stay in Sacramento in case she tries to contact you, and she's already made the front page here. If her family shows up, it'll add to the speculation."

Jenny scanned the folded newspaper in front of Peter. In banner type, at the top of page one, she spotted a headline: WHERE IS SONNET COLE? Peter's broad hand and outspread fingers prevented her seeing the rest of the article.

"It would help," he said, "if you'd tell me exactly what you hope to accomplish."

He listened intently, then pantomimed writing; Jenny handed him a pencil and memo pad. "D. Kagan," he scrawled, and beneath that "H. Joyce."

"Do you know where I can reach them?"

Although Jenny couldn't hear the caller's answer, a look at Peter's frown told her it was negative. The reply was also effusive, and his frown deepened as it continued.

"Save the flattery," he broke in at last. "We never lied to each other in the past, I suggest we don't start now."

He drew a box about Kagan's name, and Joyce's, then bracketed the boxes with question marks. "Try not to worry," he said. "I'll keep track of developments on this end and do what I can to minimize the damage. And, Sharon, you have the number here? Let me know if you hear from her."

Sharon?

An image sprang to mind of a studio portrait of a woman with fair shining hair and a provocative smile. It had been a year since Jenny saw the picture, but she could still envision the autograph. "For my darling, Peter. All my love always, Sharon."

Peter hung up the phone and propped his forearms on the table. "That was Sharon."

Jenny bit into her croissant, remembering the miniature heart that dotted the *i* in *darling,* the confident cross-stroke

that underlined *always*. She remembered every flowery cur-
licue, and the memory left a bitter taste in her mouth.

"So I gathered," she answered coolly. "What was she
doing? Checking up on you?"

"Why would Sharon want to check up on me?"

"Isn't she your girlfriend?"

Peter went from astonishment to indignation in the space
of a pulse beat. "I can't believe you asked that. One minute you say you trust me, the next you're giving me the third
degree, and I'll be damned if I can figure out why."

"Try," said Jenny. "Use your imagination."

He shook his head as if to clear it, rolled his eyes toward
the ceiling. "Are you jealous?"

"Should I be?"

"No more than I should be jealous of you."

"What does that mean?"

"It means that yesterday, while I was stuck in traffic, I got
to worrying that you might be involved with someone else."

"If you were worried, why didn't you ask me about it?"

"Because I assumed you'd play it straight with me. I
thought if I had competition, you'd tell me so up front."

Jenny lifted her chin. "I made the same assumption. The
difference is, you have no reason to doubt my honesty."

"Don't I?" Peter's voice modulated, became soft, insin-
uating. "You know what they say about a woman signaling
a change of men with a corresponding change in her
hairdo."

"That's ridiculous!"

"Yeah? Well, so's your question about Sharon. She's a
friend, nothing more. Anything else between us ended before I met you."

"But you keep her picture on your nightstand."

Peter leaned back in his chair and planted one ankle
across his knee. He appeared to be studying the toe of his

running shoe, but Jenny sensed his scrutiny. "Didn't we have this conversation a year ago?"

"Yes, and now we're having it again. Maybe this time you'll tell me the truth."

He pushed away from the table with an abruptness that made the legs of his chair chatter across the floor. "I told you then and I'm telling you now, Sharon and I dated for a while, but it never meant anything."

"Maybe it didn't to you, but it must have meant a great deal to her. Otherwise why would she call you here?"

"She didn't call me. I called her when I saw the article about her sister."

"S-sister?"

"Sonnet Cole. It seems that she may be in trouble."

Jenny's anger dissipated so swiftly, she felt hollow. "I—I don't know what to say. I had no idea—"

"Obviously," said Peter.

Her face stung with embarrassment. She should apologize, beg his forgiveness, but the words stuck in her throat. She drank the rest of her juice, pride warring with compassion for a woman who must be in an agony of suspense, worrying about her younger sister.

In the seconds it took Jenny to drain the glass, compassion won. "What kind of trouble is Sonnet in?"

"She walked off the set of her TV show yesterday after a fight with her producer, and no one's seen her since."

"But she's a baby. She can't be more than twelve or thirteen. Surely her parents—"

"Sorry to disillusion you, Jenny, but Sonnet's eighteen."

"She can't be! She's so tiny."

"And she won't get any bigger. She has a glandular condition that impairs growth."

Jenny's jaw dropped. She stared at Peter, embarrassment forgotten. "I didn't know that."

"Most people don't. It's the best-kept secret in Hollywood, but legally, Sonnet's an adult. As for her parents, Sharon said she's filed suit against them, charging them with mismanaging her money."

"Then it's not likely she'd go home."

"No, but she might turn up at Sharon's place. They've always been close."

Jenny glanced at the newspaper headline. "How did the press hear about it?"

"According to the article, Sonnet's car was abandoned at a local shopping center, so my guess is some reporter got wind of the police report. Either that, or Sonnet tipped the media herself."

"Why would she tip them?"

"For the publicity. Why else?"

"If publicity was what she wanted, wouldn't she let her family know she's all right?"

"Not necessarily."

"But that's callous, Peter. It's cruel!"

"I'm not saying she deliberately set out to hurt them, although that possibility does exist. Sonnet has quite a temper. She may have acted on the spur of the moment, and it wouldn't be the first time she's pulled a stunt like this. She's a chronic runaway—has been ever since she was in junior high. The other kids would tease her about her height. They'd call her 'shrimp' or 'short-stuff,' and she'd take off. And the more upset she'd get, the more the kids would tease. It got to be a vicious cycle, but the most insidious thing about it was, instead of learning to relate to her peers, she did everything she could to avoid them."

"She must have been terribly unhappy."

"She was," said Peter. "Still is, apparently."

"But you'd never know it from the way she seems on television."

"She's an actress, and a fine one. Sharon used to think a successful career would be Sonnet's salvation. She thought the applause and the adulation would help Sonnet cope with her problems, but in the long run, acting has become another escape, and success just another complication."

Peter filled a mug with coffee and reclaimed his place at the table, sitting astride his chair. "You see, Jenny, there's a downside to stardom, especially in a business that relies on public approval. After her first season on *Foyle's Paradise*, Sonnet was a sensation. She was deluged with fan mail. She couldn't go anywhere without being mobbed. She made the cover of *Time*. She was nominated for an Emmy. She was the critic's darling, the nation's sweetheart, the modern-day Shirley Temple. Everybody loved her— Only it wasn't really Sonnet they loved. It was Peggy Foyle, the personality kid, the cute little tomboy she plays on TV. The night she won the People's Choice Award, Sonnet told Sharon that she didn't have a friend in the world."

"Does she?" asked Jenny.

"Well, she hangs out with her stand-in, Carla Niles, but I'm not sure they're friends. It's more a case of Carla idolizing Sonnet and Sonnet admiring Carla's taste."

"And that's it?"

"Yes, except for her sister." Peter traced an idle forefinger around the lip of his cup. "Sharon may be the only person Sonnet has any faith in, the only one she doesn't think is trying to use her."

"Does she confide in Sharon?"

"Once in a blue moon, about personal matters. Never about anything that affects her career or her bank account. Basically, she's a loner."

Like my father, thought Jenny. *Like Edwina. And like me?*

Perhaps.

If she wasn't careful.

If she couldn't become more trusting.

She looked at Peter and realized, if Sharon came between them, she'd have only herself to blame. With her suspicions and accusations, it was she who had opened the door.

"Now you know as much about Sonnet as I do," he said, "so, if you'll excuse me, I'd better get to work."

Jenny met his gaze, her expression contrite. "Is there any way I can help?"

"Well, the first order of business is to get a lead on Sonnet. I want to find her before the police do."

"Of course, Peter. I understand."

He slid the memo pad her way. "It'd save me a lot of phone calls if you have any ideas where I might locate either of these men."

Jenny glanced at the names he had listed. "I don't know where Hal Joyce is staying, but I know where he'll be tonight. One of my friends is giving a party in his honor, and we're invited."

"Seriously?"

She nodded. "If you like, we can have dinner with the cast and crew of *Foyle's Paradise,* including Mr. Joyce."

"I like," said Peter.

"In that case, I'll give Eve a call and let her know we're coming."

Peter rewarded Jenny with his off-center smile. "That was relatively painless, but what can you tell me about Dolf Kagan?"

"Not much, I'm afraid. I've heard the name, but I don't recall where."

"He's Hollywood's latest boy wonder," said Peter. "He's your age, maybe a year or two younger, but he already has the reputation of being *the* rising director. He's also the CEO of an independent production company."

"Is he in Santa Rosa?"

"He was until a few days ago. Sharon said he offered Sonnet the lead in one of his films."

"That simplifies matters." Jenny reached for the phone. "Eve and her husband know practically everyone. If Kagan's in the area, I'll bet they can tell us where to find him."

"If they can't, there's always directory assistance." Jenny wrinkled her nose at Peter, and his grin widened. "While you're making your call, I'm going to grab a shower."

"Do that," she said.

On his way out of the kitchen, he gave her a kiss on the forehead.

Did that mean all was forgiven?

IF KAGAN HAD A TELEPHONE in Santa Rosa, it was unlisted. Not even the Vandivers, with all their contacts, could pry the number out of the operator, but by the time Peter was out of the shower, Eve had supplied Kagan's address.

"He has a house in the Valley of the Moon," Jenny reported as she climbed into the Maserati, "on Soledad Road, off Adobe Canyon."

Peter consulted a road map. "Out in the boonies," he remarked.

"It is fairly isolated, but it shouldn't be hard to find. It's about two miles this side of the old Thiebault winery."

"You've been there?"

"To the winery? Yes, I have."

"Then you can navigate." Peter handed her the map and pulled away from the curb. "Cross your fingers," he said. "With any luck, Kagan will be there."

"He should be," Jenny replied. "Reed Vandiver was out that way last night and he saw lights in the house."

Peter braked for the Yield sign at the corner of Sutter Court. "There are a couple of stops I want to make along the way."

"All right," Jenny said. "Where to first?"

"Plot me a course for Crossroads Plaza."

"Why do you want to stop there?"

"I checked with the police while you were getting dressed. The officer I spoke to couldn't tell me much, but he did say the Plaza is where they found Sonnet's car."

Jenny removed her sunglasses from her carryall and slipped them on, stalling while she digested this information. "Take a left, then another left, then straight ahead. The shopping center isn't far."

At the height of the rush hour, the drive from her apartment to Crossroads Plaza took less than ten minutes, and on that hot July Sunday, traffic was light. They arrived at the mall shortly after the stores opened and followed a tour bus full of senior citizens into the parking lot. When the bus halted at the main entrance to unload its passengers, Peter stopped, too.

"One of those must be it," he said, eyeing a row of empty slots across from the entrance.

"She left her car in the handicapped parking?"

"Uh-huh. That's why the manager of this place was so quick to notify the police."

"It's as if Sonnet wanted it noticed right away."

"My thoughts exactly." Peter turned his attention to the wide glass doors. There were eight of them altogether, four In, and four Out. "Tell me, Jenny, what businesses does this entrance serve?"

"Well, there's a steak house, a sporting-goods store, a B. Dalton, a branch of Citizens Bank—"

"Bingo!" said Peter. "She might have gone in there."

Jenny shook her head. "The bank's not open on Saturdays."

"Maybe Sonnet didn't know that."

And maybe, thought Jenny, she went into one of the stores.

Jenny imagined she were Sonnet, leaving her car in a tow-away zone, irate and defiant after the fight with Hal Joyce.

In that sort of mood, she wouldn't have felt like dodging autograph hounds. She would have covered her hair, worn a hat or a scarf, and she might have put on dark glasses, as well.

Jenny imagined the actress strolling through the mall, disguised and unmolested. She pictured Sonnet passing Radio Shack and the video arcade, pausing to window-shop at the jewelry store, then rounding the corner, finding herself in the main concourse. On her left she would have seen Recordland, on her right, Bon Marche, straight ahead, the food court, and beyond that, Long's Drugs—

"Reconstructing Sonnet's movements in the mall could take days," Peter grumbled.

"Right," said Jenny. "Before you could talk to all the clerks in all the stores, she'll turn up, sassy as ever."

Peter gunned the engine and swung the car into a U-turn. "That's why I think we ought to leave that part of the investigation to the police and go on to something more productive."

"Meaning Dolf Kagan?"

"Meaning the Municipal Garage on Stockton Street. I want to get a look at Sonnet's car."

"Will the police allow that?"

"I have the permission of the owner's sister."

Peter's response didn't answer Jenny's question, and she gave him directions to Stockton Street against her better judgment. As they took the freeway across town, her uneasiness increased, but she relaxed a bit when they arrived at the garage and she saw that a security guard was on duty in a booth near the entrance.

Peter saw the watchman, too. He cruised past the garage without slowing down. At the intersection with the frontage road, he made a right turn and a block later, at Exchange Street, another right. Halfway along this block, he swerved into an alley that took them back toward Stockton.

Jenny held her breath as they sped through the alleyway, between squat brick warehouses and industrial plants. Here and there, concrete loading docks jutted from the buildings, close enough that it seemed to her, if she held out her arm, she could touch them.

Just before they reached the street, Peter stopped. She looked about nervously, getting her bearings, and realized, somewhat belatedly, that he had parked near the side entrance to the garage.

"Why are we stopping here?" she demanded.

"Did you notice the red Mustang on the first tier near the booth? That's Sonnet's car."

"Great! You wanted to see it, now you have, so let's go."

"Not yet," said Peter. "Not till we plan our attack."

"Attack?"

"Teamwork, Jenny. That's what's called for in this situation."

Peter reached in front of her and opened the passenger door, then opened the door on his side and got out.

Jenny stared at him, inert and apprehensive. Her voice fell to a murmur. "You're going to sneak inside, aren't you."

"I'm going to give it my best shot, unless you can suggest another way I can get a closer look at that Mustang."

"You could make a request—go through official channels."

"All that would get me is a ton of red tape, and I don't have time for that. There may be something in that Mustang that'll tell us where Sonnet's gone."

"If there were anything, wouldn't the police have found it?"

"They can't search the car. Not legally."

Neither can you, thought Jenny. "What if you're caught?"

"I won't be. You're my secret weapon."

"Accomplice is more like it."

"Nonsense," said Peter. "I wouldn't ask you to do anything criminal. You just have to keep the watchman busy."

"How am I supposed to do that?"

"You'll think of something." After a glance at his watch, Peter circled the car and drew Jenny to her feet. When his arms went around her, he felt her resistance. He touched her mouth, shaping it into a smile. "Chin up, honey. It'll be okay. I'll give you two minutes to create a diversion, then I'll make my move."

Jenny's heart sank. Precious seconds ticked by while she remained immobile, torn by indecision.

Peter gave her a fierce, quick hug, then turned her so that she was facing the mouth of the alley.

"A minute forty-five," he said. "Better get going."

Against her will, Jenny started toward the street, keeping close to the wall of the building. Her carryall bounced against her hip, and she adjusted the strap, slinging the bag higher on her shoulder.

Without looking back, she turned the corner and continued along the sidewalk, keeping her gaze fixed on the security guard. His profile was barely visible through the window of the booth.

Create a diversion, Peter had told her, but that was easier said than done; subterfuge was not her long suit.

Why was Peter doing this? What would happen if he were caught? The police might let him off with a slap on the wrist, but would the state bar association be as lenient? He could lose his license, and for what? The dubious satisfaction of going over Sonnet's car? Would he risk his career for any friend? Was it the challenge he found compelling... or was it Sharon Cole?

A truck rumbled by, reminding Jenny of the problem at hand.

Less than a dozen yards separated her from the booth. She could see the insignia on the guard's uniform. She could see his thinning hair and beak-like nose, and she had no idea how she was going to distract him.

A few feet ahead was the open garage door. Her pace became more tentative as she approached it.

Her instincts warned her to retreat; her conscience called her a coward.

She hesitated, wondering what to do next, and from the tail of her eye, caught a glimpse of Peter, crouched low, running from car to car, working his way toward Sonnet's Mustang.

He's more likely to attract attention than I am, she thought. If she didn't act quickly, the guard would certainly see him.

Her reaction was automatic. Without thinking, without planning, she hurried toward the booth, but she had taken only two strides when the toe of her sandal lodged in a crack in the sidewalk. She staggered, arms flailing, then lost her balance and pitched forward, landing painfully on the concrete.

Her carryall sailed off her shoulder. The air left her lungs in a rush. Shards of cement gouged the tender skin of her palms and knees. She heard footsteps approaching and sucked in a breath. She dragged herself to all fours.

A pair of men's oxfords came into view: brown, highly polished. And above the shoes, pant legs: khaki, with creases sharp as knife blades. A summer uniform.

The guard was standing over her.

Her sunglasses were perched on the tip of her nose. She pushed them back into place, then lifted her head and stole a cautious look at his face.

She expected a frown, an accusation; what she got was a paternal smile and friendly hand helping her to her feet.

"Are you all right, miss?"

"I'm okay," she answered warily. "All I need is a minute to get my breath."

The guard ushered her to the booth, clucking over the abrasions on her knees. "A fall like that's enough to shake anyone up. We'll put some bandages on those cuts, and then you'd best sit a spell."

"But my things…" She motioned toward the contents of her carryall, which were scattered the width of the sidewalk.

"Never you mind, miss. I'll take care of your things as soon as I find the first-aid kit."

"Thank you," said Jenny. "You're very kind."

She felt deceitful, horribly guilty, and she was afraid her feelings showed.

Ten minutes later, her scrapes were cleaned and dressed and her belongings safe in her carryall when the toot of a car horn signaled that Peter was ready to leave.

She limped away from the booth and along the alley, vowing that never again, under any circumstances, would she let herself be roped into an assignment like this.

"What happened to you?" Peter inquired as she got into the Maserati.

Isn't it obvious? Jenny wondered. Instead of responding to Peter's question, she asked one of her own.

"Did you learn anything from Sonnet's car?"

"She's a chocolate freak. There's a gross of candy wrappers under the seats. And I found this in the glove box."

Peter dropped an envelope in Jenny's lap. Sonnet's name was printed on the front, and inside, in the same angular handwriting, was a note: "Many thanks for the tip about Vanessa Wayne. Payment is enclosed."

A newspaper clipping was attached to the note; an article praising Sonnet's work for various charities.

"It's from the *Hollywood Reporter*," said Peter. "From Lonny Pendleton's column. But the reference to Vanessa Wayne has me stumped."

"Last winter there was a rumor that Vanessa's marriage was on the rocks."

"And?"

"A month or so later, she filed for divorce."

Peter tapped the edge of the note against the steering wheel. "Wasn't she involved with another man?"

"No. Vanessa was the injured party. Her husband ran off with their daughter's nanny."

"That's right," said Peter. "Now I remember. It caused quite a ruckus, even by Hollywood standards."

Jenny stared at him, appalled. "Do you think that's the story Sonnet gave Pendleton?"

"Yes," Peter answered, tight-lipped with disgust. "I think she has an arrangement with him. I think she trades secrets for favorable publicity. And since she's gone this far, it would appear that she'll stop at nothing to further her career."

Chapter Five

Under different conditions, Peter would have enjoyed the drive to Dolf Kagan's place. The Valley of the Moon was one of the last unspoiled areas within commuting distance of the urban sprawl surrounding San Francisco Bay, a region prized for its color and quaintness.

Traffic remained light on Adobe Canyon and nonexistent on Soledad Road. They wound through hills lush with orchards and vineyards, and saw no other cars.

The countryside called for music that was lyrical and Italian—preferably something by Puccini—but instead of playing a cassette, Peter tuned the radio to a top-40 station, in case there should be news of Sonnet.

Earlier this morning he had hoped to find her quickly so that he could savor the holiday mood of the weekend. But now it seemed the mood was shattered. His preoccupation with the actress clouded his view of the scenery. It came between him and Jenny.

It was disheartening to realize that, at an age when she should have been thinking of clothes and parties and college boys, Sonnet cared only about her career. It was depressing to learn that she was ruled by ambition: ruthless enough to turn her back on her parents, calculating enough to spy on her co-workers, cynical enough to betray them.

He was beginning to wish he'd never offered to look into her disappearance. This investigation was like walking into a spider's web. He couldn't quite see the strands, but he could feel them spinning round him, and the fact that they were invisible made them seem more sinister. More repugnant. And when he'd fought his way through the tangle, some residue of the web would stick to him. He wouldn't emerge unscathed....

"This is it." Jenny pointed to a mailbox with Kagan's address stenciled on the side.

Seconds later, Peter turned onto a narrow lane that climbed a dun-colored knoll. Kagan's house was near the top.

Peter eased back on the accelerator, surveying the property. A swimming pool and tennis court were half-hidden behind the garage, and scaffolding obscured the facade of the two-story residence. Evidently the place was getting a facelift.

"Looks as if we're in luck," said Jenny. "There's a car parked around back."

"Yes, I see it."

Even as Peter replied, a man stepped out of the shadows on the porch. He was small and wiry, a bantam rooster with a ruddy coxcomb of hair that gave the illusion of height, a mustache that gave the illusion of maturity, and a paisley ascot tucked into the open collar of his shirt that gave the illusion of dignity.

"Looking for someone?" he inquired.

His clipped British accent struck Peter as phony. He introduced Jenny and himself, adding, "I'd like to speak to Dolf Kagan."

"What about?"

"Sonnet Cole. I'm an attorney, representing her sister, and I hoped Mr. Kagan would have some idea where she is."

After a brief hesitation, the man opened the screen. "I'm Kagan," he said. "You'd better come in."

Peter pocketed the keys and followed Jenny into the house, where Kagan showed them to a sitting room awash with crimson, from the fringed draperies and tassled lampshades to the wallpaper and polished tiles of the fireplace.

If there'd been a piano in the room, Liberace would have felt at home there, but Peter didn't. He paused on the threshold, while Jenny chose to sit on a plush velvet gossip bench. Kagan strutted to a sideboard that was stocked as a bar.

"May I offer you something to drink?"

Peter declined, and Jenny accepted a club soda. Glancing about the room, she said, "This is like being inside a jewel box."

Kagan laughed. "Sonnet says it reminds her of a brothel."

"Is she here?" asked Peter.

"Alas, no." Kagan rested an elbow against the mantelpiece and with a languid flap of his hand, waved Peter to a chair.

"Thanks," Peter said. "I'd rather stand."

Kagan made a gun of his thumb and forefinger, aimed it at Peter and squeezed off a shot. "If you're uncomfortable with cathouse red, old chum, we can talk somewhere else. I should warn you, however, that I cannot vouch for the structural integrity of the rest of the house. We're remodeling, you see."

"And doing a marvelous job of it, too," said Jenny. "This is the original farmhouse, isn't it?"

"Indeed, it is, my dear. And perhaps before we go any further, I should issue a disclaimer."

"A disclaimer?" Jenny echoed.

"About this room. The decor illustrates my wife's taste, not my own. The poor misguided darling is incapable of distinguishing between drama and melodrama." Kagan bowed from the waist, favoring Jenny with a smile. "And that, my dear Miss Spaulding, is the kiss of death in my line of work."

While Kagan posed and postured and exerted himself to charm Jenny, Peter watched from the sidelines, taking his host's measure, wondering if he wore lifts in his shoes, and deciding that, whether he wore them or not, he was loaded with pretenses.

Of course, it was possible that Kagan was everything his admirers claimed he was. He might be a genius, the most brilliant director since John Huston, but that didn't keep him from being a pompous ass.

Peter was familiar with the type. He'd encountered men like Kagan before. They tended to feed their own egos by putting other people down, but that didn't mean they weren't impressed with themselves. They were puffed up with self-importance, full of bombast and bonhomie, riddled with quirks and affectations. Talented, to be sure, and not averse to using their talent like a bludgeon, turning it against others. More often than not, quite effectively.

But if Kagan ran true to form, his arrogance, his seemingly impenetrable confidence, was a sham.

Scratch the surface and you'd find a mass of insecurities. Land a verbal jab, and he'd bleed neuroses all over his priceless Oriental carpet. And if an opponent scored one solid hit, Kagan would self-destruct.

Having summed up his host, Peter stepped through the doorway. He had come here for information, and the time had come to seize the offensive.

"Why don't we cut to the chase?"

Kagan whipped out his pistol again; his smile never wavered. "Are you referring to Sonnet?"

Peter nodded. "I understand you offered her a role in your next picture."

"We discussed it, yes, but I doubt that Sonnet will accept the part. She has an exclusive contract with Hal Joyce, and he's not likely to let his precious little starlet work with me."

"Did you know about the contract when you offered her the role?"

"Naturally." Kagan's smile turned wintry, became a sneer. "Joyce's penchant for luring naive young ladies into involuntary servitude is legendary. Everyone in the movie industry knows about it."

"But you went ahead and opened negotiations."

The smile cooled another degree. The gunhand came back into play. "Yes, I did."

"I assume you had a reason," Peter said.

"Well, there's always a chance, isn't there? And believe me, when Sonnet chooses to take a stand, she can be most convincing."

"Are you implying she has something on Joyce?"

"She may have. God knows, Hal's got more than his share of dirty secrets. He can't keep all of them buried indefinitely."

"So you decided to dig up a few and you handed Sonnet the shovel."

"Suppose I did. Is there a law against it?"

"No, but it may be cause for civil action if your offer to Sonnet was fraudulent."

An angry flush darkened Kagan's face. His hand formed a fist and pounded the mantel. "Listen, Darien, I'll tell you who the fraud is—Hal Joyce. That show of his, *Foyle's Paradise,* is mine. *My* concept, *my* characters, *my* creation!"

"That's funny," Peter ventured. "I never noticed your name among the credits."

"The hell with the credits! I wrote the script for the pilot my last semester in college, and the day after graduation, I headed for L.A. and started making the rounds of the producers. I had no contacts and I couldn't get past the receptionists, but I didn't give up. I knew I had a winner. And then one night I was tending bar at the Bel Air Country Club, and one of the regulars came in with this agent, Marty Riordan, who just happened to be tight with some of the studio brass. So I told Riordan my troubles and he said, 'Kid, don't sweat it. Hal Joyce has been looking for a project. If I take him your script, I guarantee he'll read it.'"

"So you gave the script to Riordan?"

"Like a shot!" Glowering at Peter, Kagan pushed away from the mantel and began pacing about the room. "A couple of days later, I got a call from Joyce himself, inviting me to lunch. After all the rejections I'd gotten, I couldn't believe my good fortune. This man was my idol. He had been since I was a kid. I'd studied his films at Northwestern. I wrote a term paper on his technique for capturing point of view. I'd heard he was down in his luck. His last two movies had bombed and he hadn't worked as a director for five years, but I didn't care squat about any of that because he'd demonstrated that he wasn't afraid to tackle major issues, and when you do that, you risk major failure."

Kagan strode to the bar, splashed Scotch into a tumbler and downed it in a gulp. "I had lunch with Joyce at his place in Malibu and I felt honored—privileged!—to be in his company. He said I was gifted. He told me my basic story idea had potential. He said the premise was a bit shallow for a theatrical movie, but he thought it might work on television, maybe even as a series. He said the script needed revisions—'punching up,' was how he put it—but he was prepared to buy the option on the condition that I agreed to collaborate."

"And what did you say?"

"That I was flattered, but I'd have to think it over. My goal, after all, was to break into movies. There were things I wanted to say about controversial subjects, and television wouldn't give me the freedom to say them."

Kagan poured more Glenlivet, scowling into his glass. "Joyce clapped me on the shoulder and said, 'Get real, boy! You're living in a dreamworld. You want to make a statement, and that's fine, just fine. I applaud your principles, but first you gotta pay your dues. Have you stopped to consider the profits you might realize from a successful television series? If the show runs two seasons, you could be financially independent. If it goes into syndication, the residuals alone can be worth millions, and with that kind of money, you can buy yourself one helluva lot of artistic freedom.'"

"Sounds like a sweetheart of a deal to me," Peter observed dryly. "How could you go wrong?"

"That's what I thought, so I signed Joyce's agreement without reading the fine print."

"It figures." Peter spoke in the same sardonic tone. "I've heard there's one born every minute."

"I don't get it," said Jenny, shaking her head. "Didn't Joyce pay anything for your script?"

"He paid for it," Kagan answered. "Quite handsomely, too, but not nearly as much as he should have. What I'd signed away was creative control of the project, although it took me a while to figure that out. At first, I tried to work with Joyce's writers. I made suggestions...argued...pleaded. But always, *always* I was overruled. By the time the network expressed an interest in running the series, I'd cut my losses and gone on to other things. So Joyce got the last word, the credit, and most of the profits. That show was my baby, and he got the *recognition*. No amount of money can compensate for that."

"So to get even with Joyce, you asked Sonnet to be in your movie," said Peter.

"No! At any rate, not entirely." Kagan fumbled with the folds in his ascot. His anger spent, he seemed diminished somehow, as if he were shrinking into himself. "I'll admit, it occurred to me that in offering the role to Sonnet, I'd be stirring up trouble for Joyce, but that was no more than the icing on an already bountiful cake. When I'm casting parts for one of my films, I consider many things, but the primary consideration is, is the actor right for the part? In Sonnet's case, the answer is yes. She'd be a tremendous asset. She has star quality, tremendous on-screen presence and tons of box-office appeal. The drawback is, she needs strong direction, and this is where Joyce made his mistake. *Foyle's Paradise* cries out for an ensemble of equals, with the cast sharing the spotlight, but instead of developing the other characters, Joyce let Sonnet steal the show. He hasn't a clue how to handle her. He couldn't get a controlled performance out of her to save his life."

"But you can," said Peter.

"Yes," said Kagan, "If I didn't believe that, I would never have approached her about the part in my film."

"And now Sonnet's missing," Jenny murmured. "What do you think she'll decide to do?"

"I wish I knew, Miss Spaulding. We'd arranged to meet for lunch yesterday at Chateau St. Jean. She was supposed to give me her decision. I waited for more than an hour, but she didn't show." Kagan sighed and guzzled his Scotch, the cock of the walk no more. "The only predictable thing about Sonnet is that she's totally *un*predictable. All I can say with any certainty is, the next move is up to her."

Peter shot Kagan an inquisitive glance. *Is it?* he mused. *I wonder...?*

THEY TOOK THE LONG WAY BACK to Santa Rosa. Peter said he wanted to see the new place she was leasing, so Jenny took him by the house on Juniper Street and gave him the grand tour.

Hand in hand, they wandered through the bright, airy living room, where everything was sunny and fresh and smelled brand-new. They explored the laundry room and kitchen, the office and two bedrooms, each with its own bath, and Peter approved of the floorplan, the ample storage space, the woodwork and track lighting. He praised the finishing touches and said he thought they gave the house character.

She showed him the attached garage and the utility shed, the fenced backyard. They sat for a while on the patio, soaking up the stillness, and he admired the landscaping.

"Those flowerbeds are like a photograph in *House Beautiful*. Not a weed in sight. And this lawn looks as if it's been manicured."

"Yes, and isn't it lovely?"

Peter agreed that it was. "The previous tenant must've put in a lot of hours taking care of this place."

Jenny looked at him sharply, wondering if his observation was intended as a compliment or as criticism. Was he implying that once she moved in, her spare time would be consumed by gardening?

During the drive to the duplex, she tested him. "That house is perfect. The moment I saw it I knew it was exactly what I was looking for."

Peter downshifted as a trio of bicycle riders pedaled into the street directly ahead of the Maserati. He swung out to pass the cyclists, concentrating on his driving, and didn't say anything.

"What I like best is its convenience," she said. "I'll be able to walk to Coddington Center to do all my shopping. There's even a post office there."

They were approaching a major thoroughfare and Peter leaned over the wheel. "Isn't this where we turn?"

Jenny told him it was, then picked up the thread of her monologue as if without interruption. "I like the neighborhood, too. All those wonderful old trees make it seem settled and peaceful."

Peter responded with a noncommittal "Umm-hmm." He made the left onto Sutter Court and parked in the driveway behind Jenny's car.

"And the rent's not much more than I'm paying here." She unlocked the front door and walked inside with Peter lagging a step or two behind. In the entry hall, she turned to look at him. "That house is an incredible find," she declared almost truculently, daring him to argue.

"It's a bargain, all right," he conceded, "and in most respects, it does seem ideal for you. But personally, I think the location stinks."

Jenny frowned. "What wrong with the location?"

"It's in Santa Rosa."

Her expression softened and so did her voice. "Santa Rosa's my home, Peter. I've made friends here. It's where I live."

"I know it is, but as long as you're moving, I wish you'd give some thought to the advantages of living in Sacramento."

She stared at him, uncertain how to reply, not sure what prompted his suggestion. "I'll consider it," she replied slowly, "and maybe next year, when my lease on the house expires—"

"There's no time like the present, Jenny. Why not make the move now? You can tell your landlord something unexpected's come up. With a property that desirable, he shouldn't have any trouble finding another tenant, so he just might let you out of the lease. And if he doesn't, I'll help you break it."

"No, Peter. I can't do that. I signed that lease in good faith. I can't go back on my word."

"Then we'll find someone to sublet." Peter opened his arms and she went into them. "You'll like Sacramento, honey. It's a great town, and it's not as if you've never been there, so you won't be a complete stranger. You know my uncle and me, and I'll introduce you to my friends, and we'll see each other often— Often, hell! I'll probably camp on your doorstep."

Wait! she thought. *Things are moving too swiftly.*

Peter was talking as if the move to Sacramento was a foregone conclusion, and she didn't have a clear idea why he was urging her to relocate.

Were her feelings so obvious? Was she that transparent? How could he take her for granted? Why was he so confident that all he had to do was crook his finger and she'd come running?

There's one born every minute, warned a shrill inner voice. *Before you make any promises, read the fine print.*

She broke away, catching Peter off guard, and managed a few wobbly steps into the living room.

"What's wrong, Jenny? Did I scare you off?"

She faltered, shaken, irresolute, sensing his dismay.

"I-it's just that I need time. This is a big decision." And whatever her choice, she didn't want either of them to regret it.

He nuzzled the back of her neck and she started. She hadn't realized that he was so near.

"Will you think about it?"

"Yes, Peter, I will." Surely there was no harm in that.

He kissed her nape again. "Seriously?"

With his arms about her waist, folding her close, her misgivings began to seem foolish. "Seriously."

"Fantastic!"

His eagerness warmed her. She felt herself blossoming. But in the next breath, he excused himself and went off to phone Sharon.

THAT EVENING, EN ROUTE TO the party, Peter asked Jenny to tell him about their hosts.

"You'll like them," she said. "They're outgoing, gracious, personable, down-to-earth."

"Go on."

Impatience roughened Peter's voice, and it dawned on Jenny that something more than idle curiosity lay behind his request. He was doing his homework, sizing up the Vandivers just as he had sized up Dolf Kagan.

"Reed's in his late thirties," she said. "Eve's a few years older, maybe forty-five or six. She raises Arabian horses and the most beautiful roses I've ever seen, and he's president of Citizens National."

"The bank at Crossroads Plaza?"

"Yes, except that's just a walk-in branch. Reed's office is in the main branch downtown."

"How'd you happen to meet them?"

"Betty Holtz introduced me to Eve when I first came to Santa Rosa, but I didn't get to know her till last year. Do you remember when that poison-pen letter was making the rounds and I was forced to give up my teaching job at Ringer-Dent?"

Peter's mouth thinned to a hard line. "I'm not likely to forget that."

"Well, Eve was the only member of the board of trustees who voted against asking for my resignation. And then last summer, when I got home from Sacramento, there was a note from her in my mail. She wrote that she believed in me, not the rumors, and she apologized for the board's action. She said she knew that it wasn't much comfort, but she hoped that someday I'd be exonerated. Till then, if I needed someone to talk to, she encouraged me to call on her.''

Jenny paused to catch her breath. "Eve sent me that note *before* the truth about Judge Eaton came out. I'll always be grateful to her for that.''

"She must be quite a woman.''

"She is,'' said Jenny, "and a bit of a rebel.''

"What does she rebel against?''

"Oh, this and that. Local issues, social pressures, her upbringing. She gets a kick out of thumbing her nose at public opinion.'' Jenny crossed her legs and smoothed the hem of her sundress over her knees as she added, "I suspect, mostly, Eve's rebelling against her mother.''

"Not openly,'' Peter said. "Otherwise she wouldn't have married a banker.''

Jenny looked at him and smiled. "You're absolutely right. It never occurred to me before, but marrying Reed must be the most conventional thing Eve's ever done. Together, they're a walking cliché. They both come from pioneer stock. Reed's father made some bad investments, so the Vandivers aren't as wealthy as they used to be, but they're terribly genteel, poor but proud—''

"Blue bloods,'' said Peter.

"The bluest,'' she replied. "If this country had royalty, the Vandivers would be it. And, of course, the Thiebaults are rich.''

"Sounds like a match made in heaven. How long have they been married?''

"About ten years.''

"Happily?''

"They seem content, and they certainly complement each other. From remarks Eve's made, I think their one disappointment is that they haven't had children. There's been a certain amount of friction with Reed's parents because he's the last of the line.''

"Tell me about it," Peter groaned. "Ever since I had my thirtieth birthday, my mom's been on my case about carrying on the family name."

"At least she treats you like an adult. Phyllis still reminds me to take my vitamins."

"Yeah? Well, that's just a phase she's going through. Give her a few years, it'll pass. And *then* she'll start nagging about grandchildren."

"Not in this lifetime. We're talking about a woman who has a pathological fear of gray hair. She's devoted to the pursuit of youth. Cosmetic surgery is the big-ticket item in her budget. In the last few years, she's had a tummy tuck, a hip tuck, liposuction and breast augmentations, and lately she's been talking about a face-lift. She lies about her age. She lies about mine. She won't even tell me how old she is."

Peter flashed a know-it-all grin. "Nevertheless, the day will come. Her attitude will change. Wait and see if it doesn't."

Jenny heard the skepticism in Peter's voice. She realized he thought she was exaggerating, but she wasn't. Not by much, at any rate. She couldn't imagine Phyllis wanting to be a grandmother, no matter how hard she tried.

"One more question," Peter said. "About the only things I watch on television are sports and the news—"

"You've never seen *Foyle's Paradise?*"

"Only bits and pieces. Before we get to this shindig, could you give me some idea what it's about?"

"Did you ever watch *The Beverly Hillbillies?*"

"When I was a kid," said Peter. "I never missed an episode."

"Well, *Foyle's Paradise* is kind of a switch on that show. This rich family loses everything and winds up working for their former servants in the mansion they used to own. But the twist is, the former servants are much more class-conscious than the Foyles, so their snobbery lands them in all sorts of hot water, and the Foyle's are free to pursue the simple pleasures. They're happy, getting back to basics.''

"Oh, brother!" Peter raised his eyebrows, expressing disbelief. "If you buy that, little lady, there's some swampland down on the delta I'd like to sell you."

Jenny laughed. "I know it's pure fantasy. That's what makes it fun. That and the relationships between the characters."

"Uh-huh. So which of the characters do you identify with?"

Jenny looked out the car window, thinking this over. "I can't say that I identify with any of them, but Peggy Foyle's my favorite."

"That's the one Sonnet plays."

"Yes. And Vanessa Wayne's quite wonderful as her mother. In a way, her character reminds me of Eve."

Peter chuckled. "Just another case of art imitating life."

Jenny smiled, unoffended. "Go ahead and laugh all you want, but there's a kernel of truth in that comment. One of the nicest things about Eve is that she honestly believes the message in *Foyle's Paradise*."

He slanted a glance her way. "Okay, I'll bite. What is it?"

"With enough love and enough laughter, a person can overcome any adversity."

Chapter Six

From Jenny's description, Eve Vandiver sounded like a real-life Pollyanna. Peter wondered what sort of hardships she'd had to endure. When they arrived at the Vandiver estate, he crossed poverty off the list of possibilities.

A private drive took them past the stables and riding paddocks. It cut through a pasture where yearling colts gamboled knee-deep in clover, and just beyond the pasture, curved through banks of azaleas. It branched to give access to a gazebo and carriage house and finally ran straight as an arrow toward the house.

Set among sloping green lawns, the stately Victorian was flanked by porches and porticos and surmounted by turrets and dormers and balconies, with lacy white gingerbread dripping from its eaves, like the frosting on a wedding cake. Fish-scale shingles decorated the attic towers. A stained-glass fanlight crowned the front door, and a pair of stone lions guarded the entry.

"It's magnificent, isn't it," said Jenny.

Peter allowed that it was, if you cared for that sort of thing. Personally, he preferred modern.

The parking apron was almost full. There was barely room for the Maserati. As he maneuvered his car in between a Rolls Corniche and a vintage teardrop Jag, from somewhere on the far side of the house, he heard the murmur of voices, music, laughter.

Nope, he thought, *no sign of hardship here.*

He and Jenny had just started along the front walk when a woman hailed them from inside the foyer.

"I hope you brought your swimsuits."

"We did," Jenny replied, holding up the beach bag she carried.

The woman stepped through the screen door, accompanied by a man, who appeared from the foyer behind her, and even as Jenny introduced the Vandivers, Peter recognized one of Eve's problems: her appearance.

Hair as black and coarse as a horse's mane framed her long bony face, and her smile of greeting bared strong square teeth that increased her resemblance to the horses she raised. But any similarity to the Arabians ended with her smile. Eve had none of their elegance, none of their grace.

Her body looked as if it had been assembled from spare parts. Everything about her was disproportionate. Her jaw was too heavy, her shoulders too broad, her arms and legs too thick for her narrow frame.

But despite her ungainliness, her lively brown eyes glowed with intelligence. She met Peter's gaze squarely, openly, and he found that he liked her candor.

By contrast with his wife, Reed Vandiver was blessed with the kind of patrician good looks most women would call handsome and a profile that would not have been out of place on an ancient Roman coin. Seen straight on, his features were finely chiseled, almost effeminate, but there was nothing soft about the handshake he gave Peter.

"Didn't I see you out jogging this morning?" Reed inquired.

"You may have," Peter answered. "Are you a jogger, too?"

"Yes, I do a bit of running."

"A bit?" Eve hooted. "Don't be so modest, sweetie." She leaned closer to Peter and spoke in a stage whisper. "He has a roomful of trophies left over from his college days, and he hasn't let himself get out of shape. He placed in the top twenty in last year's San Francisco marathon."

"I'm impressed," Peter replied, eyeing his host with new respect. "Just finishing a marathon is quite a feat."

Reed Vandiver's shrug made light of his accomplishments. With a fond look at his wife, he said, "My darling Eve, whatever would I do without you?"

"Your own boasting."

Reed chuckled at Eve's rejoinder. "I believe that's my cue to resume my duties as bartender."

Eve patted him on the fanny. "It's a tough job, sweetie, but one of us has to do it."

Still chuckling, Reed offered his arm to Jenny. "The others are around back, by the pool. Would you care to join the party?"

"Love to," said Jenny, falling into step beside him.

Peter would have followed, but Eve held on to his shirt sleeve. "I want to show Peter my roses," she called. "We'll be along in a few minutes."

Reed waved to her over his shoulder. "Take your time, love."

Her arm linked with Peter's, Eve waited till the screen door closed behind her husband and Jenny. "I heard about Edwina Farber," she said, her tone low and urgent. "My mother spotted the obituary, and when Jenny called this morning, she told me you two discovered her death."

"We did," said Peter. "So much has happened since then, though, that last night seems about a million miles away."

"Yes," said Eve. "I can see how it would. All this business about Sonnet Cole..." She heaved a sigh. "But the one who concerns me is Jenny. Is she all right?"

"That's difficult to say, Eve. Edwina's death hit her pretty hard. I know she had a rocky night, but today she seems okay." Peter hesitated. "Frankly, we've been so busy, I don't think Jenny's had time to worry about Edwina."

"Well, I guess that's the silver lining on this particular cloud." After a moment of silence, Eve seemed to shake off her pensive mood. "Now, how about those roses?"

Peter said he would like to see them, but he had the feeling that Eve had more on her mind than her garden.

As they sauntered across the lawn to a graveled path lined with tree roses, he studied her quizzically, puzzling over this woman who made no concession to her own homeliness, yet surrounded herself with beauty.

Beautiful home, beautiful husband, beautiful horses, beautiful people...beautiful flowers.

The path had widened and become a terrace, an island in a sea of roses. They sat on a wrought-iron bench beside a small fountain while Eve pointed out floribundas and hybrids, climbers and tea roses, in every conceivable shade of white and pink and red and coral. She rattled on about pruning and spraying, about fertilizer and aphids, and Peter, hearing the anxious undercurrents in her chatter, spread his arms along the back of the bench and listened to the cadence of her speech, the rise and fall of her inflections, waiting for her to get to the point.

At last, she blurted out, "Have you learned anything new about Sonnet?"

"Some personal stuff. Nothing significant."

"You don't have any leads to her whereabouts?"

"Not yet. How about you?"

"Me? What could I know? I've never met the girl."

"Then why do I get the feeling there's something you want to tell me?"

"I've no idea." Eve glanced at him nervously. Her shrill whinny of laughter didn't reach her eyes. "If you want the inside dope, you'll have to question Hal Joyce."

"That's why I'm here," Peter said flatly.

Eve hauled herself erect. "Come along, then. I'll introduce you."

"Do you think he'll cooperate?"

"I guarantee it, and you won't have to ask questions. Sonnet's the only thing Joyce and the others have talked about since they got here." Eve turned on her heel and walked away from the bench, her spine stiff as a ramrod.

Peter strode after her. "Is that why you're so jumpy?"

"Yes, if you must know, it is." She swung around and confronted him, hands fisted on her hips. "I'd like to help you, Peter. Honestly, I would. But all I can tell you for certain is, I'm beginning to get a bad feeling about her disappearance."

So am I, thought Peter. *So am I.*

He watched Eve hurry toward the house, convinced that she knew more than she was telling. She'd lied about knowing Sonnet, for instance—he'd bet his life on that—and before the evening was over, he intended to find out why.

ONCE PETER BEGAN TALKING WITH the Vandivers' guests, he had to revise his plans. After the first few interviews, he realized it would take more than one evening to uncover the truth. Everyone he approached, from the production assistants to Eve's husband, supported her contention that she and Sonnet had never met.

Reed Vandiver took a break from tending bar to confirm his wife's story. "Eve isn't acquainted with Sonnet," he told Peter, "and I've only seen her in passing once or twice on the set. In the line of duty, as it were. You're aware, aren't you, that my bank handles the finances for *Foyle's Paradise?*"

Peter said that he was. Over Reed's shoulder, he saw Jenny come out of the house with a tray of appetizers. He lounged against the bar, monitoring her progress as she wove through the crowd. When she drew near, he beckoned her over.

"Hungry?" she asked, offering the tray.

"Starving." He helped himself to some canapés. "There's nothing like sleuthing to work up an appetite."

"How about something to drink?" Reed inquired.

"Later," Peter mumbled around a mouthful of prosciutto.

Jenny offered the tray to Reed. "Try a crab puff. They're delicious."

"Which are they?"

"The ones with the pimento on top."

His hand poised above the canapés, Reed studied the selection, then chose a cheese puff garnished with chunks of Spanish olives. The instant he bit into it, he recognized his mistake. Grinning sheepishly, he said to Jenny, "Now you know my deepest secret. Pimentos and olives both look brown to me."

"Never fear. My lips are sealed."

Jenny handed Reed a crab puff, then continued on her way, and Peter returned to his inquiry.

"Did Sonnet have a personal account at your bank?"

"She may have," Reed answered. "In fact—and I say this with considerable pride—I'd be surprised if she didn't. Citizens is the largest full-service financial institution in town, and the best-known."

"But you've never actually seen her in your bank?"

"No. Not that I recall."

Peter wolfed down his last canapé and wiped his mouth with a cocktail napkin. "The reason I ask is, it might be informative to know why she stopped at Crossroads Plaza, and if she had an account with you, that could narrow things down. She may have gone into the branch at the mall to cash a check.''

"Of course. I see what you're driving at and I'd like to help you out, but there is the matter of confidentiality. Bankers, like attorneys, are bound by certain restrictions, and as president of Citizens National, I have to be above reproach. Even the appearance of wrongdoing—''

"I'm not asking you to violate your principles," Peter broke in smoothly. "All I need to know is whether Sonnet has an account at your bank.''

"Well, in that case, I'll run her name through our computer.''

"Thanks," said Peter, hoping it wouldn't come to that. But if it did, if Sonnet didn't turn up by tomorrow or the next day, it was possible one of her co-workers would know where she did her banking. Either that, or he might find a bank statement in her dressing room or at the motel where she was staying.

Eventually, he realized, he'd have to go through her things, and for that, he would need Joyce's approval.

With that thought in mind, Peter accepted a gin and tonic from Reed and set off to corner the producer.

He found Joyce at the barbecue, holding court and tending the grill, wrapped in a voluminous chef's apron that underscored his size. Rotund, balding and bullet-headed, with protuberant, lashless eyes, he was the sort of man who turned a handshake into a test of strength.

"So you're a lawyer," he remarked, when Peter had introduced himself. His voice was an astonishingly soft tenor. "Maybe you can resolve a legal issue for me.''

"I can try," said Peter.

"I've got these friends, see. For the sake of privacy, I'll call them Dick and Jane. They've been married twenty-some-odd years and in those years, they've been faithful to each other, but things are starting to get a trifle stale. The thrill is gone, if you know what I mean.''

Peter nodded. ''They're having problems in bed.''

''You've got a way with words, pal. Dr. Ruth couldn't have put it any better.'' With a sly glance at his audience, Joyce went on. ''Anyway, time goes by and both my friends are miserable. Jane starts complaining that they're not as close as they used to be. She tells Dick, 'You never *talk* to me anymore.' Dick admits she's got a point, and they arrange to see a therapist to polish up their communication skills. Pretty soon, they're talking up a storm in and out of bed, but talking's all they're doing, until one night Jane says, 'I love you, Dick, but enough is enough. If we can't put some spark back in our relationship, we might as well call it quits.'

''And Dick says, 'Janey, give me one more chance. I'll do anything to save our marriage.'

'' 'Me, too,' says Jane, 'but I've had it with living like a nun. The only way we're going to make this work is if we're free to see other people.'

'' 'You want to take a lover?' says Dick, and Jane says, 'Maybe two, and I want you to find yourself a mistress.' ''

Joyce interrupted his narrative to turn the steaks, brandishing the barbecue fork as if it were a scepter and he, the king of the hill. ''Dick thinks over Jane's ultimatum, and the more he thinks, the more he wonders how the hell he's going to keep two women satisfied when he can't even satisfy one. But then he remembers the sexy divorcée who's just moved into the apartment upstairs, and the idea of sleeping with her gets him excited, so he agrees. Within a month, he's a sexual dynamo. He's boffing the divorcée on Tuesdays and Thursdays, and Jane on Mondays, Wednesdays and Saturdays. And not only has he recaptured his lost youth, but it seems that variety's put the spice back in his marriage. Jane's happy. The divorcée's happy. And Dick can't get the silly grin off his face.''

"But it didn't last," said Peter, trying to speed Joyce's story along.

"No, it grieves me to say, it didn't. On their twenty-fifth anniversary, Dick and Jane threw a party. Everything first cabin. They hired a caterer, lined up an orchestra, and they invited all their friends, including Dick's sexy divorcée."

"Naturally," said Peter.

"The evening went swimmingly. Everyone had a blast, till the band was playing 'Three O'Clock in the Morning,' and Dick made the mistake of waltzing with the divorcée. On his way off the dance floor, he's accosted by Jane. 'That's it,' she says. 'I've had it. I'm leaving. I'm through.' 'You can't leave,' he tells her. 'I've done everything you asked of me.' 'And then some,' says Jane. 'Where did I go wrong?' he asks, and Jane says, 'I don't mind your keeping company with the slut upstairs. I don't mind you buying her gifts. I don't even mind that you were insensitive enough to ask her to our anniversary gala, but you had the gall to *dance* with her. That's one thing I cannot forgive.'"

Several of the onlookers snickered, and Joyce prodded the steaks on the barbecue grill while he waited for the laughter to die down. Smoke wreathed his face and through the cloud, he fixed Peter with his shrewd reptilian gaze.

"So tell me, counselor, in your professional opinion, is dancing with another woman grounds for divorce?"

"No," said Peter, "but it could be the last straw."

Joyce clapped him on the shoulder. "That's what I like. A plain yes or no. Most lawyers would've qualified the answer."

"I'd qualify it, too, if you were a client. You get what you pay for, Mr. Joyce, and that's especially true of legal advice."

"Call me Hal," said the producer, transferring the steaks to a platter. "You're okay, Pete. You're my kind of folks."

"And you have impeccable timing," said Peter.

Joyce acknowledged the compliment with a broad jack-o'-lantern grin and on that amicable note, they broke for dinner.

JENNY CARRIED THE LAST OF THE salads out to the buffet by the pool.

A breeze had sprung up off the Pacific. It ruffled her hair and felt refreshing and cool. The sky was clear, and the moon a pale silver crescent suspended on the horizon with Venus twinkling in its bowl—a star no less glittering than the earth-bound stars who were queueing up for dinner on the Vandivers' deck.

Smiling at this flight of fancy, Jenny went back to the kitchen for the garlic bread.

"A couple more trips ought to do it," she told Eve. "I don't know how you found time to organize all this, but everything looks lovely."

"It's easy with the help of a friend." Eve turned off the oven and advanced on Jenny, shooing her out the door. "That's enough KP for one night. Go on outside and be a guest."

"What about you?"

"I'll be along in a minute."

Eve's smile was overbright. Jenny sensed that her cheerfulness was an act and left the house with some reluctance. At the edge of the deck, she stopped to scan the scattering of tables around the pool, each brightened by a bouquet of red roses and by the amber glow of a candle in a glass-mantled hurricane lamp.

At an umbrella table on the farthest corner of the deck, she spotted Vanessa Wayne, Leo Prince and a giant Humpty Dumpty of a man who had to be Hal Joyce.

Then she saw Peter, and although he wasn't a legend like Joyce or as famous as Vanessa or as ageless and handsome as Leo Prince, it was his face that made her heart skip a beat.

He felt her watching him, looked up and grinned. "I fixed a plate for you," he called, signaling to the place setting beside his own.

She nodded to show her understanding and skirted the pool. Peter stood, and Leo Prince started to rise.

"Please don't get up." She slid into the chair Peter held for her, and for the benefit of her dinner companions, supplied her name. When Prince would have reciprocated, she said, "Introductions aren't necessary. I'm a fan of *Foyle's Paradise*."

Vanessa Wayne responded with a polite-but-distant smile, and Hal Joyce scarcely looked up from his steak. But Leo Prince more than compensated for his colleagues' indifference.

Instead of shaking her hand, the actor pressed his lips to the backs of her fingers. In a mellifluous baritone he said, "The admiration is mutual, Miss Spaulding. I can't tell you how much I enjoyed your book."

His drawl was sweet as molasses. His mustache tickled. Jenny barely suppressed a giggle. "I'm so glad you liked it."

"I *loved* it." When she tried to free her hand, Prince's grip tightened. "My only criticism is that the picture on the dust jacket doesn't begin to do you justice."

Her cheeks grew warm, her fingers numb. Prince's hold had cut off the circulation. She tried again to pull away, and Vanessa came to her rescue.

"Leo, you are such a shmuck! Why don't you let the poor girl eat before her supper gets cold?"

Prince cupped his free hand to his ear. "Hark! What's this I hear? Do I detect a trace of jealousy in the fair Vanessa's dulcet tones?"

The actress made a rude gesture. "Up yours, darling."

Hal Joyce tapped a spoon against his wineglass. "Cut it out, you two. You're upset by Sonnet's disappearance. We all are. Let's not take it out on each other."

Prince let go of Jennifer's hand. "Sorry, chief."

"It's not me you owe an apology."

Prince seemed to wilt with embarrassment at Joyce's rebuke. He stared into the open space between Vanessa and Jennifer and spoke as if he were addressing an invisible presence. "Ladies, I realize it's no excuse, but I do not deal well with anxiety."

"Leo, what the devil do you have to be anxious about?" asked Joyce.

"You know what they say, chief. There's no one so insecure as an out of work actor."

Joyce shook the crumbs out of his napkin, folded it and aligned it neatly with his plate. "I planned to make an announcement later, but if it's the job that's bugging you, I can give you a preview right now."

"Have you decided what to do with the show?" Vanessa inquired.

"Uh-huh. Me and Phil Epstein, from the network. He flew in from L.A. this morning, as soon as the story about Sonnet broke."

Prince slumped over the table, distraught, his chin sunk on his chest. "If Epstein came all the way up here, it must be worse than I thought."

Hal Joyce watched this tragic performance without blinking, without changing expression. "Leo, Leo, Leo! You've gotta take it easy. If you worry yourself into an early grave, I'll have to replace you as well as Sonnet."

The actor's head jerked up. Vanessa Wayne gasped. Peter ran his fingertips along the stem of his goblet, then lifted the glass and took a sip of water. If any of the others at the table happened to glance his way, they would think he had no more than a passing interest in the conversation. But

Jenny knew better. Beneath the tabletop his knee had pinned hers, exerting more and more pressure, communicating his tension.

Joyce leaned back, content that he was the focus of attention. His chair groaned beneath his weight, and that small sound served to break the spell. Jenny posed the question that was foremost in everyone's mind.

"Does that mean you'll go on with *Foyle's Paradise?*"

"Yes, Miss Spaulding, that's exactly what it means. We'll start taping a new episode Wednesday morning."

"How will you manage without Sonnet?" Peter asked.

"We'll begin by shooting around her. It'll take some rewrite, but fortunately we're at the beginning of a new season. We'll explain Peggy's absence by sending her off to visit relatives. That ought to get us through two or three weeks."

"And if Sonnet's not back by then?"

"That'll be a break for Carla Niles. We're going to introduce her as Peggy's look-alike cousin, Megan. We'll play up her resemblance to Sonnet and if she clicks, fine. If the audience doesn't accept her, if the ratings go down, we write Megan out. But in either case, we'll rely on the rest of the cast to pick up the slack. We have loads of talent to draw on—the finest damn ensemble in television—and it's time we took advantage of it. So from now on, we're going to look for scripts that highlight the other characters."

Vanessa's smile evoked images of a cat toying with a canary. "What an intriguing concept! I can see where it would have limitless possibilities."

"I'll bet you can," said Leo.

"And I suppose you can't?" Vanessa scoffed. "Who do you think you're kidding, Leo? It's no secret that you loathe working with Sonnet, and heaven knows you have good reason, but there you sit, pretending to be a saint, looking pious and prim, as if butter wouldn't melt in your mouth."

"Listen to the pot calling the kettle black," Leo countered, turning to Jenny. "I'm willing to admit there's no love lost between me and Sonnet. She's opinionated, egotistical and temperamental. She is without a doubt the most thoroughly aggravating actress I've ever worked with, but she's also the most talented."

Vanessa made a growling sound deep in her throat. "I've never questioned Sonnet's talent, Leo, darling, only her humanity."

"Yes, and only behind her back."

Vanessa and Leo glared at each other, and Hal Joyce intervened.

"Are you through?" he asked Prince.

"Not quite, chief. There's something I'd like to say in Sonnet's defense. She's democratic. She doesn't play favorites. It's not only me she upstages. She steals everyone's scenes, but at the same time, she puts everyone on their mettle. She brings out the best in the cast."

"Only on camera," Vanessa replied hotly. "When those cameras stop rolling, watch out!"

"Truer words were never spoken." Fingers steepled beneath his chin, Joyce contemplated the actress, his eyes hooded by his peculiar lashless eyelids. After a brief silence, his scrutiny shifted to Prince. "You scored some points, too, Leo, and I thank you for reminding me how gifted Sonnet is. She's a real trouper, and she's not afraid to take chances. But her greatest talent is for creating dissention. You and Vanessa are proof of that. And that's why I've decided to give Carla a buildup."

Leo remained unconvinced. "Carla's a nice kid, chief. I've got nothing against her personally, but she has no experience."

"Neither did Sonnet till I took her in hand." With a shrug of his burly shoulders, Joyce added, "I'll work with Carla, line up some coaching. In fact, I've already started. She's seeing a dialogue coach tonight."

"It's definite then," said Peter.

"There'll be a press release tomorrow." Joyce returned to his food, carving a bite of steak with the precision of a scientist dissecting a specimen. "No one's indispensable, counselor. Not even Sonnet Cole. Do you have a problem with that?"

"No, but you might when she turns up."

"She won't."

Peter frowned. "The press release could flush her out. She might change her mind about leaving the show. After all, she's got a good thing going with you. Why risk that for some movie deal that hasn't been finalized yet?"

Hal Joyce looked up from his plate. "You've been talking to Dolf Kagan."

"Yes. I saw him this afternoon."

"I suppose he gave you an earful."

"Our meeting was informative," Peter replied.

"Did he tell you he has a grudge against me?" Before Peter could respond to the question, Joyce sliced the air with his hand. "You don't have to answer that, counselor. I'm sure he did. And if you're half as smart as I think you are, you'll discount whatever Kagan said about Sonnet and me."

Joyce drummed a forefinger against his temple. "I know the girl. I know her moods, the way she thinks, and I'm telling you this—Sonnet and I had an argument about the movie deal. We disagreed about Kagan's motives for offering her the part, and she pitched a fit when I refused to cave in to her demands. She trashed her dressing room and took off, which was typical of her. If you won't take my word for it, ask anyone who worked with her."

"It's true," said Vanessa. "Sonnet's a volatile young lady. She often has tantrums."

"That's a fact," said Joyce, "and we'd had our differences before. She was quick to explode, but just as quick to cool down. If there's one thing she wasn't, it's a dummy. She knew which side her bread was buttered on, and she knew that I have the map to the butter churn. That's why I'm confident, if it was humanly possible, she'd have mended her fences by now."

Peter met the producer's stare with his own implacable gaze. "Assuming you're right and Sonnet wants to contact you, what do you suppose is stopping her?"

"I wish I knew, counselor."

"Do you think she's been kidnapped?"

"I'm not that optimistic. If we were dealing with a kidnapper, there'd be a chance of getting her back."

"I notice you speak of her in the past tense," Peter remarked quietly. "If you have something concrete to go on, I'd appreciate your sharing it with me."

"I've got two things," said Joyce. "The first is Sonnet's medicine. Her doctors had her on a maintenance dose of growth hormone, but her supply of pills is still in her dressing room."

"Is it possible she could have forgotten them?"

"Anything's possible, counselor, but she took that medicine faithfully, every day. It doesn't seem likely she'd leave without it."

"No," said Peter. "It doesn't."

"I also have her fan mail," said Joyce. "Only I use the word *fan* loosely. Kook'd be more like it. Flake... creep... psycho."

"Sonnet was getting letters from someone like that?"

"We all do," said Vanessa. "We're highly visible, Mr. Darien. We come into twenty million homes every week and after a while, many of our viewers begin to identify with the characters we play. They look upon us as friends or lovers, as classmates or neighbors or confidants—or, as in the case of J. R. Ewing, the villain people love to hate. So some of the viewers write to us, and most of the letters are genuinely nice. Fans give us advice or constructive criticism. They propose marriage, say how much they admire us or praise a specific performance and generally wish us well. Sometimes they send gifts. Sometimes they ask for loans, but that type of fan is relatively harmless.''

"And then there are the fans who develop fixations," said Leo. "They become proprietary, possessive. They begin to think they own you."

Vanessa shuddered. "That's when it begins to get scary."

Joyce set his knife and fork across his plate, then shoved the plate aside. "Crank mail is an occupational hazard," he told Peter. "The more charismatic the performer, the more likely it is she'll receive threats from some nut case. But the star of a TV show, like Sonnet, can't hide in a closet and wait till the threat is past. She can hire bodyguards and cancel public appearances. She can keep a low profile for a while, but if her profile gets too low, her career can go down the tubes. The bottom line is, she's at the mercy of her fans."

The candle at the center of the table flickered and almost went out, and watching the guttering flame, Jenny thought of John Lennon and Jody Foster, each the target of a deranged fan. She remembered Theresa Saldana and Rebecca Schaeffer, two young actresses just beginning their careers. They, too, had fallen victim to a fan's obsession; one badly wounded, the other killed.

A gust of wind extinguished the candle, and Jenny thought about Sonnet and shivered.

Peter's voice came from the sudden darkness. "Did you tell the police about the letters, Hal?"

"I told them, but they didn't seem interested."

"They will be," Peter said.

"Sure, when it's too late. Time's a-wasting, counselor."

"Well, if you've no objection, I'd like to see the letters."

"It's fine with me, Pete. Come by the motel tomorrow and poke around all you want, but I think you're beating a dead horse." Joyce extended his arm toward Peter, displaying the luminous dial on his Rolex. "It's been nearly thirty-six hours since Sonnet left the set. It's been more than twenty-four hours since the police found her car. If she hasn't surfaced by now, she's not going to. At any rate, not alive."

Chapter Seven

The phone was ringing when they got back to the duplex. Jenny dropped her beach bag inside the front door and raced to take the call before the answering machine could kick in. Peter sidestepped the bag and moved cautiously through the obstacle course of packing crates into the dark living room. He located a floor lamp and switched it on just as Jenny stepped out of the kitchen.

"It's for you," she said. "Eve Vandiver."

It was well past midnight, the end of a long, hectic day, and tomorrow would be just as hectic. Jenny felt punch-drunk with weariness just thinking about it.

On the drive home from the party, she had longed to crawl into bed and sleep the clock around. But the display on the answering machine indicated there were messages on the tape—probably for Peter, probably important. If she were a good hostess, she ought to play back the tape before she turned in.

She sank down on the sofa, wondering what Peter and Eve were discussing, and found that curiosity was a stimulant that temporarily revived her.

Although she kept very still, she couldn't hear much. Peter listened more than he talked, and the few things he did say were barely audible. The conversation lasted less than five minutes, but exhaustion was beginning to seep in again by the time he returned to the living room.

"That's one more lead to check out," he declared. "And it's a beauty."

"A lead?" she echoed. "What about?"

"Insurance." Peter sat on the coffee table facing her, close enough that their knees touched. He looked terribly pleased with himself. "It seems Hal Joyce took out a policy on Sonnet. If she can't fulfill the terms of her contract, he stands to gain a cool two million."

Jenny drew her fingers along the arm of the sofa, tracing circles counterclockwise against the grain of the upholstery fabric. "That's a lot of money."

"It's a lot of motive," said Peter. "With that kind of payoff, Sonnet could be worth more to Joyce out of the picture than in it."

"How did Eve find out about the policy?"

"She overheard a couple of the bit players gossiping about it earlier this evening."

"Why did she wait till now to tell you about it?"

"For a number of reasons. In the first place, she didn't much like the way the actors were raking Joyce over the coals, but she couldn't see herself as an informer, either, especially when she's not sure how much credence to give the story. As she pointed out, it could be supposition rather than fact, and even if it's true that Joyce carries insurance on Sonnet, it's not inherently sinister. In his position, it could be nothing more than a sound business procedure."

"So that type of policy isn't unusual?"

"No, not at all." Peter leaned forward, chin in hand. "Another thing Eve said is that she feels bad about eavesdropping on her guests. She didn't want to repeat the rumor and have Joyce trace it back to them. I think that's the main reason she hesitated about passing the tip along."

"That's Eve for you," Jenny murmured. "She's all heart. The mainstay of lost causes, champion of the underdog—"

"Even if the underdog happens to be a back-stabbing malcontent," Peter finished dryly. "What's weird is that I knew she was withholding something."

"She wasn't her usual cheery self this evening," Jenny agreed. "I thought maybe she wasn't feeling well."

"Chances are she wasn't, with this on her mind."

"What made her decide to call you?"

"Reed. She talked it over with him after we left, and he persuaded her the responsible thing to do was to fill me in."

Jenny studied Peter from beneath her lashes. "Now that she has, what are you going to do about it?"

"Confront Joyce with the story. Find out if it's true."

"And if it is?"

"He may have a legitimate explanation."

She rested her head against the back of the sofa. "He seemed awfully willing to share what he knows about Sonnet."

"Too willing?"

"I don't know.... Maybe." Her response was slurred by a yawn. She let her eyelids drift shut. "I don't trust him, Peter. After you shake hands with him, you want to count your fingers. And did you notice that he never blinks?"

"Never?"

She heard the amusement in Peter's voice and opened one eye long enough to confirm that he was grinning. Her own mouth quirked into a smile.

"He reminds me of a lizard," she said.

Peter laughed outright. "I'll grant you, he comes off as a cold-blooded character. He spun that yarn about Dick and Jane, milked it for all it was worth, and I'll bet a month's salary that he's Dick."

"Do you suppose that's one of the secrets Sonnet has on him?"

"If it was, he went public with it tonight."

"Well, I think his openness is a bluff. There were times at dinner I'd have sworn he was trying to direct suspicion toward everyone but himself." Jenny fought back another yawn. Her eyelids felt as if they had been glued shut. "It was creepy, the way he went on about Sonnet's fan mail."

"Vanessa and Leo went on about it, too." Peter took Jenny's hand and placed a kiss in the palm. His glance traveled over her tousled cap of hair, her brow, the feathering of gold-tipped lashes on her cheeks, the spray of freckles across her nose. His voice was husky as he asked, "Do you ever get letters like that?"

"Writers don't inspire that much passion," she answered drowsily.

Peter's gaze lingered on the graceful curve of her neck. He could see the delicate throbbing of a pulse beat in her throat, and his heart kept counterpoint as he bent his head and brushed his lips over the soft, scented hollow.

"Don't they?" he whispered against her skin. "I wouldn't be too sure."

Jenny threaded her fingers through his hair and melted into his embrace. She lifted her mouth for his kiss and thought, *the heck with being a good hostess.*

The messages on the answering machine would have to wait.

THE FOLLOWING MORNING, at Peter's request, Jenny tagged along for the meeting with Hal Joyce.

"I'd like you to have a look at Sonnet's dressing room before the cleaning people get to it," Peter explained. "A woman might notice details a man would miss seeing."

The cast and crew of *Foyle's Paradise* were staying at the Holiday Inn a few miles south of town. With taping suspended till Wednesday and most of the staff idle, the production company's vans, buses and motor homes circled the perimeter of the parking lot like a latter-day wagon train.

When Jenny and Peter arrived at the motel, the clerk at the front desk directed them along a corridor off the lobby, which led to a conference room Joyce had commandeered as a studio cum office.

The clerk must have notified Joyce that they were on their way. He was waiting for them in the hall, his bulk blocking the door. But it was the jeans-clad nymphet standing beside him who caught Jenny's attention.

"Good heavens!" she breathed. "For a moment, I thought you were Sonnet."

Joyce patted the girl's shoulder with his beefy hand. "Carla, you just passed your first test. And that's without makeup."

The producer didn't bother with hellos, but he moved to one side, which enabled Jenny to see into the room.

Desks and filing cabinets were crowded into the corner nearest the windows, while wardrobe racks and coils of electrical cable occupied another corner. The rest of the floor space was dominated by technical equipment: monitors and tapedecks, Betacams and battery packs, lights and reflectors, shotgun mikes on fishpoles and audio recorders.

A metal shelving unit held a variety of supplies. Stacks of video cassettes, an assortment of gels in a rainbow of colors, gaffer's tape and electrical tape, wireless mikes, lavaliere mikes and waistpacks bristling with tools, at the ready for every kind of emergency repair.

Joyce snapped his fingers and as a phalanx of assistants came running, he rattled off introductions.

"That's LaRue, our sound recordist, B.J. the P.A., Nelson, our assistant director, Tony, our lighting director, and Rachel, our costume designer. Rachel, hon, you found that scarf yet?"

"Sorry, chief. Still looking."

"If you don't come across it by noon, better order a replacement. We'll need it Wednesday." Joyce glanced around the room, taking census. "Where the hell's MaryAnn?"

"Yo, chief, I'm on my way."

A bosomy, middle-aged woman whose leopard-print jumpsuit and rhinestone-studded glasses were the epitome of vulgar chic squeezed between the fur coats on one of the wardrobe racks and as she approached, Joyce proclaimed, "Last but not least, this is my secretary, MaryAnn Largent, who keeps all of us organized and sane."

MaryAnn accepted his praise with a curtsy. "Don't forget humble."

Joyce favored his secretary with an indulgent glance. "Now that the gang's all here, these folks are Jenny and Pete. I want you to take good care of them."

"You're not staying?" Peter inquired.

"'Fraid not, Pete. Something's come up. I've got other fish to fry."

Peter frowned. "If this morning is inconvenient, we could come back later."

Joyce bared his teeth in what might have been a smile. "There's no need for that. MaryAnn's got those letters I was telling you about, and if you have any questions or there's anything else you'd like to see, all you have to do is ask. Someone'll take care of you."

With that assurance, Hal Joyce took Carla Niles in tow and sailed off down the hall, and once he was gone, his staff dispersed, with the exception of MaryAnn Largent.

Smiling impartially at Peter and Jenny, she jockeyed them toward her desk. "You'll have to excuse the chief. Since Sonnet disappeared, we're all in the pressure cooker, and he feels more heat than the rest of us combined."

"No problem," said Peter. "I'm sure Hal's left us in capable hands. How long have you worked for him?"

"Fifteen years this October. Twenty, if you count the time I worked in the steno pool. That was when he still had the partnership in Globe Studios, and when he left, I left with him."

"In that case, you must know Sonnet fairly well."

"None of us knows her well," MaryAnn answered with a vehement shake of her head. "She keeps people at arm's length."

"Yes," said Peter, "I understand. But you strike me as an astute judge of character."

MaryAnn offered them folding chairs and sat on the corner of her desk. "I like to think I am."

"Then you must have formed some opinion about where she went when she left the set."

"No, but I heard about the deal she had going with Kagan. We *all* heard about that."

"You overheard her fight with Hal?"

"Not so much the fight as what came after. She pitched a fit that measured seven on the Richter scale. They probably heard that in San Francisco. For a little girl, Sonnet has a great set of lungs."

"So she was angry when she left?"

"Actually, she seemed quite calm. Determined. Of course, by then, she'd had the chance to let off steam. You should see her dressing room."

"I'd like to," said Peter. "Later."

"But first you'd like to see those letters." MaryAnn slid to her feet and removed a manila folder from the center drawer of her desk. "I made two sets of copies last night, one for you, one for our files, and it's a good thing I did. The police came by this morning and picked up the originals."

She handed the file to Peter, then sat at her desk while he went through it. "Can I get you something to drink?" she asked Jenny. "Coffee? Tea?"

"No, thanks," Jenny answered, distracted by the buzz of activity in the room. To her left and slightly behind her, B.J. and Nelson were poring over a loose-leaf binder, entering data on a laptop computer and cueing up videotape on two monitors.

"Those segments were shot at the Russian River last Friday and early Saturday," MaryAnn said. "Before the big blowup. It's already been window dubbed to VHS to give us a time code."

Jenny's gaze never strayed from the monitors. "Is that what's in the bar at the bottom of the picture?"

"Umm-hmm. The numbers in the bar refer to the minutes, seconds and frames on the tape."

"But on one screen the numbers aren't consecutive."

"That's because they're recording shots from different tapes. Each frame on a tape has a number, and it keeps that number through the editing process. Do you see that notebook of Nelson's? Well, that's where he's logged descriptions of the tapes they shot at the remote. Right now, he and B.J. are editing Sonnet's scenes onto a tape for Carla to study."

One of the monitors faded to black for a few seconds, and then a picture reappeared on the screen. Jenny watched as one scene followed another, mesmerized by images of Sonnet in longshot and close-up. Sonnet laughing, Sonnet glowering, Sonnet pouting and playful. Sonnet running through the woods beside the river, dodging in and out among the trees in a game of hide-and-seek, leering through the pine boughs and mugging for the camera, twirling an imaginary mustache, like the villain in an old-fashioned melodrama.

Again the screen went black, and when Sonnet reappeared, the scene had shifted to the riverbank. She scrambled onto a boulder, played leapfrog over the rocks at the water's edge, and skipped from stone to stone, fording the stream. Halfway across, she landed off-balance. She tilted to one side, her arms making windmills in the air, and just when a fall seemed inevitable, she recovered.

But only for an instant.

Before she could secure her purchase, she tilted the other way. The windmills reversed direction, but she couldn't defy gravity forever. One sneakered foot slid out from under her and she made a five-point landing in the current, creating a backwash that rained down on the Betacam's lens.

The scene ended with an extreme close-up of Sonnet. Her face filled the screen, carrot-red curls dripping, her mouth an astonished O, and in her eyes, pure mischief. There was a quick cut to a wider shot as she scooped up a handful of water and deliberately splashed the videographer.

Jenny laughed. She couldn't help it, although laughter seemed out of place in the industrious atmosphere of the room.

Joyce's assistants glanced up from the screen. She had broken their concentration, but they didn't seem annoyed. The one named B.J. grinned at Jenny.

"You must be a fan."

She nodded. "I'm a very enthusiastic fan. I'm afraid I got carried away."

B.J. exchanged a glance with Nelson. "Come on over. We can use a little enthusiasm."

Jenny didn't need a second invitation. While Nelson referred to his notebook and cued up the next scene, Jenny folded her chair and moved within easy viewing range of the monitors.

"What you're about to see is Sonnet and Vanessa at a picnic," B.J. explained. "We're working on the reaction shot at the end of the scene."

"We've got fifteen takes to choose from," Nelson said. "But I see by my notes that nine of them are duds. We had flubbed lines and batteries failing and bees strafing Vanessa. Her perfume must've attracted them. And Sonnet got splinters off the table and her bracelet kept falling off. So if you're game to watch 'em, we've whittled the choices down to takes three, six, nine, ten, fourteen and fifteen."

"I'm game," Jenny replied.

B.J. raised his eyebrows. "We don't have to coax you?"

"I told you, I'm a fan."

"All *right!*" said Nelson. "We'll run the scene first, then show you the reactions."

Jenny leaned forward, intent on the screen.

The scene opened with a two shot of Vanessa and Sonnet sitting on the edge of a picnic table, with the leftovers from lunch scattered about them.

Sonnet, in her guise as Peggy Foyle, was wearing shorts and a faded T-shirt several sizes too big for her. Her hair was braided, her feet bare, and there was a Band-Aid on her knee.

Vanessa, as Tulip Foyle, Peggy's vivacious, scatter-brained mother, was wearing a frock better suited to a garden party than to a family picnic. A picture hat with a wide, lacy brim protected her porcelain complexion, and her feet were shod in stiletto-heeled sandals. A red silk scarf, trailing from the waist of her dress, fluttered in the breeze.

The dialogue concerned a dance at Peggy's school, and the dresses Tulip and Peggy had seen on a shopping trip that morning. Most of the lines were Tulip's. While she stored the leftovers in a picnic basket, she raved about a blue dress and how flattering its color was to her daughter's hair.

Peggy, in the meantime, was experimenting with Tulip's scarf. The scarf became a harem veil, a shawl, a bullfighter's cape. It seemed she wasn't listening, but when Tulip's gusher of superlatives ran dry, Peggy condemned the dress with three short words.

"It has ruffles."

Tulip slammed the lid on the basket. Iron in her voice, she replied, "Well then, sugar, we'll get you that pink dress. You looked awfully sweet in it."

Peggy made a gagging noise, but aside from this, she didn't object. She knew from experience, when Tulip used that tone, protests were futile.

With the scarf draped over her head, covering her face like a shroud, she gave in as gracefully as she could. "All right, Mother. I'll go to the dance. I'll wear the pink dress. I'll even dance with a boy, if I'm asked, but I *won't* have a good time."

"Oh, you won't, huh?" Laughing, Tulip grabbed the ends of the scarf and pretended to throttle Peggy with it, and then, taking her daughter by surprise, she turned the pretense of punishment into an embrace.

B.J. spoke in an undertone. "In the world of sitcoms, every problem is resolved with a hug."

That's not a bad resolution for a lot of problems in the real world, either, Jenny thought.

There was a slow zoom to a close-up of the two as Vanessa straightened one of Sonnet's pigtails. "Peg o' my heart, you'll be the belle of the ball."

B.J. hit the pause button, stopping the tape, and on the second monitor, Nelson cued up the shots of Sonnet's reaction.

In take three, she simply pulled away.

In take six, she played it for laughs, crossing her eyes at the camera.

In take nine, she looked petulant.

In take ten, she relaxed against Vanessa's shoulder and a look passed between the actresses that spoke of tenderness and affection. Vanessa was the first to turn away. She withdrew her arm from Sonnet's shoulders, and for an unguarded moment, Sonnet looked wistful, as if she might cry.

As slowly as it had drawn close, the camera retreated to a wide angle shot that echoed the distance between mother and daughter, the barriers of age and attitude and style and personality—all of the ingrained differences that the most fervent desire for intimacy could not bridge.

Sonnet scratched a mosquito bite. She fidgeted with the clasp on her bracelet and spread the scarf across her knees—anything to keep her face averted. She did not look at the lens....

"That's it," Jenny said.

"Don't you want to see the other two takes?" B.J. asked.

"I'll watch them if you want me to, but I can't imagine how they could be any better than this one."

"If you think the scene went on too long, we could cut with the shot of Sonnet and Vanessa looking at each other."

Jenny swallowed to dislodge the lump in her throat. "You guys are the experts. You do a super job with the show, so I'd have to defer to your judgment, but if I were editing the tape, I wouldn't change a thing."

Nelson bounced the eraser end of a pencil against his notebook. "It's a tough call, but to be on the safe side, I think we should go with the sixth take. Hal hates cheap sentiment. If I turn the scene into a tearjerker, I'll never live it down."

"I don't like tearjerkers either," Jenny said. "They make me feel manipulated, as if someone's tampering with my emotions. And I agree that this take was sentimental, but it wasn't cheap and it certainly wasn't contrived. It seemed real. It's warm and loving and natural, and there's a poignancy about Sonnet that moved me. She seemed lonely...almost forlorn."

"Yeah," said Nelson. "Sonnet has her faults. She's tough and pushy and rude, but she's one terrific actress."

B.J. scowled at the freeze-frame of Sonnet on the monitor. "I don't know, Nels. Sometimes I get the feeling she's not as confident as she seems. What if the tough girl's the act and the girl on the screen is the real Sonnet?''

"You think she's sincere?"

"If she isn't, how can she be so convincing?"

Nelson tucked the pencil above his ear and closed the binder. "You talked me into it, buddy. We'll go with this take, but I'm warning you, if Hal has any comments, I'll refer him to you."

B.J. shrugged. "That's fine with me. Whether or not Hal likes the way it's edited, this is one scene I'll be happy to take credit for."

Jenny cleared her throat. "Now that that's settled, is this where we hug?"

Nelson and B.J. laughed.

"Jenny," said B.J., "you're a natural. Have you ever considered a future in TV?"

"Only as part of the audience."

From across the room, Peter signaled it was time to move on, and Jenny thanked the assistants for showing her some of the work that went into the making of her favorite television show.

"This has been a fascinating experience," she told them, "like magic."

No small part of the magic was that B.J. and Nelson had restored some of her illusions.

In the last two days, she had heard only negative reports about Sonnet, but the tapes had blurred the demarcation between the make-believe of the actress's public image and the reality of her private life.

Energy, artistry, the capacity for laughter and tears—Sonnet possessed these qualities in abundance. They were as integral to her nature as her feuds and volatile temper. Sonnet was ambitious; she was also creative. She had a huge ego and tremendous talent. Millions of people knew her, yet no one understood her. She was self-contained and very much alone.

Jenny had learned all of this from watching the video-tapes, and she had discovered one thing more. Some ill-defined oddity she had observed, yet not completely regis-tered, had left an impression, and although it seemed un-related to Sonnet's disappearance, Jenny sensed that there was a connection.

She rejoined Peter and MaryAnn, who were on their way out of the conference room, preparing to pay a visit to Sonnet's Winnebago, and while they strolled through the parking lot, Jenny was haunted by the feeling that she was overlooking an important piece of information.

She recalled her conversation with B.J. and Nelson. She attempted to reconstruct, frame by frame, the tapes they had run, until they arrived at the Winnebago and walked into an overpowering cloud of scent.

MaryAnn made a face. "Whew! Smells like a funeral in here."

"You can say that again," Peter agreed. "Let's air the place out."

While they were busy opening windows, Jenny stood on the threshold, trying to bring half-forgotten details into focus.

MaryAnn sat at the vanity, surveying the ruptured con-tainers of makeup that littered the floor. From the midst of the rubble, she retrieved a shard of crystal.

"Here's the culprit. A broken bottle of perfume."

The secretary's mention of perfume triggered a rush of memories. Jenny recalled Nelson's comments about the takes of Sonnet's reaction shot. *Bees kept strafing Vanessa. Her perfume must've attracted them. Sonnet got splinters off the table and her bracelet kept falling off.*

In the take they had chosen, Sonnet had been fiddling with the clasp on her bracelet.

She always wore it, Jenny recalled. *Always*. It was the one constant in her wardrobe. And there was something familiar about it. Jenny was positive she had seen that identical bracelet somewhere else.

Where? she wondered. *Where have I seen it?*

She envisioned the bracelet, striving to remember, while MaryAnn assessed the damages and made notes for the cleaning staff in her steno pad and Peter explored the dressing room.

MaryAnn was sifting through the ruined makeup when Jenny noticed the pill bottle that had rolled to the back of the vanity.

Realization dawned with electrifying swiftness.

"That bracelet of Sonnet's—"

MaryAnn looked at Jenny expectantly. "What about it?"

"Is it by any chance a Medic-Alert bracelet?"

"Yes, it is."

Jenny swayed against the door frame, giddy with comprehension.

Peter caught sight of her in the mirror. "What's wrong?"

"Nothing." She managed a wan smile, hoping to reassure him.

He helped her to a chair. "For God's sake, Jenny! You're white as a sheet. Don't tell me nothing's wrong."

"I'm fine, Peter. Honestly, I am." But she sounded surprisingly weak. "It's just that I've figured something out."

"Drink this," he instructed, offering her a cup of water.

She bent over the cup and the giddiness passed. "The clasp was broken, don't you see? Her bracelet kept falling off and naturally, given her condition, she didn't want to be without it, so she went to the drug store to buy a new one. It's really quite simple, and it was all there on the tape. I don't know why I didn't see it sooner—"

"Slow down, Jenny. You're not making any sense."

Peter's voice rang with exasperation. To humor him, she took a sip of water.

"That's better," he said. "Now, take a deep breath and tell me, what is it you should have seen?"

Jenny closed her eyes, and a feeling of calmness settled over her. Her senses had never been more acute. "Sonnet went to Long's Drugs to buy a new bracelet for her Medic-Alert tag. That's why she stopped at the mall."

Chapter Eight

Jenny found a mauve chambray blouse in the back of Sonnet's closet. Although the garment looked brand-new, several buttons had been torn off. It was proof, said MaryAnn, of Sonnet's tantrum.

Aside from this, the dressing room yielded no further secrets.

By the time the search was finished, the smell of jasmine had given Jenny a headache. When Peter suggested that they adjourn to the coffee shop, MaryAnn begged off, pleading the pressures of work. Jenny, however, was ready for a break.

The breakfast rush was over and it was too early for lunch, so there weren't many customers in the coffee shop. They chose a booth overlooking the pool and watched a couple of ten-year-old boys roughhousing in the water.

The boys ducked each other and retrieved pebbles from the bottom. They did cannonballs and bellyflops with an exuberance that did more to ease the throbbing in Jenny's temples than the unscented blast of the air conditioner or the aspirin she found in her carryall.

The waitress brought Jenny's tea and Peter's pie and coffee and with her departure, it seemed apparent they could talk without interruption.

"Did you find anything of interest in the fan letters?" Jenny asked.

"Too much," Peter answered ruefully. "Yesterday at this time, I didn't have any leads. Today I've got too many to handle."

"Then Hal Joyce wasn't mistaken?"

"Not by a long shot." Peter angled the file folder toward her. "There's correspondence in here from five men, mailed from five different parts of the country. I'm no psychiatrist, but from the samples I've read, Joyce has good reason to be alarmed. These guys may or may not make threats—not openly—but in my opinion, they are obsessed with Sonnet."

"Do you think she was kidnapped?"

"These men are capable of it. I suspect they're capable of anything."

Jenny stared at the folder. Her mouth was suddenly dry, but she sought to emphasize the positive. "It's a good thing the police are involved."

"Finally," said Peter, unencouraged. "It may be too little, too late."

A chill of apprehension touched her spine. "What's the next step?"

"The first thing I'm going to do is get hold of Gus McAvoy. You remember him, don't you?"

Jenny looked out the window without really seeing the horseplay in the pool. Instead, she recalled the brawny ex-marine, ex-boxer, ex-cop, who handled investigations for Peter's law firm. McAvoy was street smart, unflappable and not easily impressed. A seasoned veteran of the LAPD, he'd seen all the seaminess life had to offer without letting it sour his ideals or his disposition.

"I'll never forget Gus," she replied, "or the hours he put in on my father's case. He was absolutely tireless."

"That's typical of McAvoy," said Peter. "Retirement hasn't slowed him down, but it's his instinct that makes him invaluable. Instinct and thoroughness and the fact that after thirty years in law enforcement, he has contacts from coast to coast."

"Are you going to ask him to look into the letters?"

"Sure am, as soon as we get back to your place." Peter ate the last of his pie and reached for the napkin dispenser. "Another thing I'd like him to do is dig up more information on Marty Riordan."

"The agent who introduced Dolf Kagan to Hal Joyce?"

"According to MaryAnn, he also represented Sonnet."

"That's an odd coincidence."

"Is it?"

Jenny met Peter's gaze above the rim of her cup. "Obviously you don't think so."

"No, and I'll tell you why. Riordan renegotiated Sonnet's contract last spring, and the terms were so unfavorable that she believed he was taking bribes."

"But that's the second time in two days that someone's accused Riordan of selling out!"

"Exactly. And in both cases, the sellout benefited Hal Joyce." Peter stirred sugar into his coffee with exaggerated care, his movements as deliberate as his contemplation of the evidence he had acquired. "It could be a coincidence," he said at last. "The incidents could be unrelated. If a guy makes a habit of playing both ends against the middle, eventually he's bound to get caught."

Jenny shook her head. "There has to be more to it than that. It's too—"

"Convenient?" Peter suggested.

"Yes. Convenient and . . . bizarre."

"I couldn't agree with you more." Peter put down the spoon and spread his hands. "I think Riordan works for Joyce, and Gus is the man who can confirm my suspicions.

And while he's at it, I'd like to know more about Joyce's financial position.''

"Because of the insurance?"

"That's right."

Jenny knitted her brow. "Maybe I'm missing something, but from the way Kagan talked, two million dollars is nothing compared with the profits Joyce could realize from a hit TV series.''

"That may be the reaction Joyce is counting on, but the last time I looked, two million was far from nothing, especially if the profits aren't his.''

"Why wouldn't they be?"

Peter glanced around the coffee shop, assuring himself of their privacy. "What if Joyce was in the middle of a divorce? And what if it wasn't a friendly divorce? He's been married a long time. He's been unfaithful, and he's been foolish enough to let his wife get the goods on him. Most of his assets would be community property—''

"Including his share of *Foyle's Paradise*.''

"You got it. Only if Joyce is as savvy as I think he is, before he'd split his percentage, he'd try to buy out his wife's interest. He'd begin by offering her real estate, stocks and bonds, holdings of equal value. But if his wife wanted to see him sweat, she'd probably insist on cash.''

"And that's why he'd need the insurance settlement.''

"That's why," said Peter.

Jenny gave him a quicksilver smile. "It occurs to me, if the ex-Mrs. Joyce is truly vindictive, she wouldn't go for the deal no matter what he offered, just to deprive him of something he wants so badly.''

Peter looked at Jenny with admiration, gold flecks dancing in his eyes. "God, you have a devious mind!''

Jenny wrinkled her nose. "Don't give me too much credit. I simply imagined myself in Mrs. Joyce's spot, and it seems to me, that's what she'd do.''

Peter's mouth curved into a grin. "You realize that'd be all the more reason for Joyce to want Sonnet out of the picture. At least temporarily, till his wife comes around. Television's an iffy business. This season's winner can be next season's cancellation, especially without its star."

"My, my," Jenny admonished him sweetly. "And you accuse me of being devious."

"Thank you, Jenny, but I'm not worthy of your praise. All I did was imagine myself in Joyce's spot...." Peter sobered and combed his fingers through his hair. He glanced at the file folder, then back at Jenny, his gaze suddenly distant and brooding. "Another explanation comes to mind, which has nothing to do with property settlements."

"Oh? What is it?"

"It's possible *Foyle's Paradise* will stay on top without Sonnet. If it does, Joyce can have his cake and eat it, too. He can hang on to his ratings and collect the insurance. Or he might plan on collecting from Kagan for releasing Sonnet from her contract. Either way, he's got a rosy financial future *and* a nice chunk of change to do whatever he wants with in the interim."

"Which might include buying off his wife."

"Sure. Why the hell not? Maybe all three of 'em are in on it."

"In on what? Which three?"

"Joyce and Sonnet and Kagan. This could be a scheme to rook Mrs. Joyce out of her share of the residuals from *Foyle's Paradise*. Or Sonnet, Kagan and Mrs. Joyce might be—"

Jenny threw up her hands. "No more, Peter. Please! Give me a minute to sort this out. It's getting awfully complicated."

"Yes, isn't it," Peter agreed.

How could he be so unperturbed when his talk of conspiracies had revived her headache? "It would help if you'd tell me which of your scenarios is based on fact and which on supposition.''

Peter signaled for the check. "You know as well as I do, Jenny, we've got plenty of rumors. We've got hearsay and educated guesses up the wazoo. But bona fide facts don't seem to be thick on the ground. That's why it's important to have Gus on the case.''

Jenny rubbed her temples. "But the situations you've outlined seem so plausible.''

"Of course, they're plausible. They're consistent with what we know about the people involved. But until we come up with some sort of proof, they're only theories.''

"Then what's the point of discussing them?''

Peter looked rather crestfallen. "The point," he answered patiently, "was to demonstrate the possibility of a connection between Hal Joyce's finances and Sonnet's disappearance.''

Jenny groped blindly in her bag for the tin of aspirin. While Peter took care of the tip and paid their bill, she swallowed one of the tablets with the dregs of her tea.

They were in the Maserati, just backing out of their parking slot, when B.J. hailed them from the entrance to the lobby. Peter straightened the wheels and let the engine idle while the production assistant trotted across the blacktop.

"Glad I caught you," he said, waving a couple of video-cassettes at Jenny. "The chief thought you might like to have these.''

Jenny glanced at the labels on the tapes. "Yes, I would," she replied. "I can't tell you how much.''

"They're copies of our edited tape of Sonnet," B.J. explained for Peter's benefit. "The extra's for Sonnet's family.''

"Thanks," said Peter. "This is very nice of you. I'm sure the Coles will appreciate it.''

"Hey, man, don't thank me. I'm just following orders. The copies were Hal's idea."

Before Peter could respond, B.J. trotted away from the car. At the doors to the lobby he called, "Enjoy the tape, and come again, anytime."

"Well," Peter said in a musing tone, "what do you make of that?"

They were on the freeway, miles away from the Holiday Inn, before Jenny answered. "Maybe Hal Joyce isn't such a villain, after all. He saw to it that his staff was helpful and hospitable, and it was considerate of him to send along the cassette for Sonnet's family."

Peter slanted a smile her way. "One humane act doesn't mean he's a saint. The most bloodthirsty hit men have been known to send wreaths to their victims' funerals."

Jenny was about to acknowledge the wisdom in this comment when Peter chucked her under the chin.

As if I were a five-year-old, Jenny thought. *A not-too-bright five-year-old. Of all the condescending—*

She slid the tapes into her carryall. Her hands curled into fists. "Look, Peter, I realize you've got a lot on your mind. You're worried about Sharon, and you feel obliged to find Sonnet, and you've knocked yourself out following leads. You've hardly slept since you got here, and I haven't been at my best. The weekend's been a disaster. Nothing's lived up to your expectations, and I don't blame you for being disappointed, but don't take it out on me."

Enough said, she decided. She was seething inside, yet she'd managed to remain calm, focused, understanding, polite, and she certainly had made herself clear. She would have felt that she had acquitted herself well if a pall of silence hadn't descended on the driver's seat.

She kept her gaze fixed on the highway ahead. The only sounds she heard were the growl of the engine, the whizz of southbound traffic on the other side of the median and the wind rushing past her ears.

After a minute or more had gone by, Peter cleared his throat. "I'm sorry, Jenny. Evidently I've offended you."

"I suppose you think that entitles you to a blanket pardon."

"No, but it might help if you'd tell me what I said."

She darted a glance at him. "It's not what you said. It's what you did."

"Then tell me what I did."

"This," she said, delivering a mock blow to his chin.

Peter looked startled, perhaps even mystified. "I was teasing."

"And you think it's unreasonable to complain. Well, it may not seem like much to you, but it pretty effectively stifled any argument."

"Seems to me it triggered one."

Her fists tightened. "If you don't take me seriously, I'd rather you'd tell me so straight out."

"But I do take you seriously."

"Of course, you do. That's why you treated me like some brainless bimbo you picked up in a bar. That's why you stopped talking to me, one adult to another, and started messing around."

"It was a way of easing tension."

"It was a put-down. An insult."

"I'm sorry you took it that way. It's not what I intended."

"What did you intend?"

"I wanted to show my affection."

"In the middle of our conversation?"

"Yes, dammit! In the middle of our conversation, in the middle of the day, in the middle of the lousy freeway, in this blasted Maserati with its bucket seats and stick shift. You were lost in thought, holding on to those cassettes as if someone had just handed you the Pulitzer Prize. Your hair was blowing around your face, and you scowled and pushed it out of your eyes. You looked so darned cute, I had the urge to kiss you, but given the circumstances, that cuff on the chin was the best I could do." A road sign loomed a quarter mile ahead and Peter swerved into the exit lane. "You'll probably say that's a sexist remark."

"No. I wouldn't say that." *Oh, God,* she thought. *I shouldn't have said anything.*

As soon as they were off the cloverleaf, Peter pulled onto the shoulder of the frontage road. He cut the ignition and turned to her, one arm propped across the wheel. *The better to watch me squirm.*

This notion brought with it a sense of shame. Indignation spent, she studied the half-moon gouges her nails had left in her palm, wondering how they'd come to be there.

"Look at me, Jenny."

"I can't. I'm too embarrassed." She moistened her lips and edged closer to the passenger door. "I owe you an apology."

"I'd rather have an explanation."

"I don't have one, Peter. I could tell you it was all a misunderstanding, but even if I hadn't misinterpreted things, I shouldn't have come on so strongly."

"Why not? You have a right to be angry."

"But you were only teasing, and it's not like me to make a major battle out of a minor incident. With anyone else, I wouldn't have."

Only Peter could provoke such an extreme reaction. Only with him did her emotions veer out of control.

He touched her face, testing the shell-pink flush beneath her cheekbone. It was a gentle caress, yet it gave her the strength to meet his gaze.

"Maybe I should be flattered," he said.

"Maybe you should."

The flush in her cheeks deepened, their warmth as revealing as her admission, and as entrancing to Peter.

"What I mean is—"

He placed a silencing finger against her lips, charmed by her confusion. "It's okay, Jenny. You don't need to say any more. You bring out the beast in me, too."

She saw the laugh lines that fanned from the corners of his eyes, and sought refuge in his arms.

"I can't believe I did that, Peter. I screamed at you like a fishwife."

"Yes, you did."

She pinched him in an acutely sensitive spot. "You really are a beast. If you were a gentleman, you'd tell me I look beautiful when I'm angry."

"You do," said Peter. "You're gorgeous when your nostrils flare and your eyes get all squinty."

He made a face, mimicking her expression, and she tried to pinch him again. This time he captured her wrists and after a brief, uneven struggle, pinned her hands against his chest. She rested her head against his shoulder, catching her breath.

"Can you forgive me?"

Peter drew her closer. "There's nothing to forgive. You're allowed to make an honest mistake now and then. Besides, there's some truth in what you said. We have been under stress, and I am disappointed that we haven't had more time together, just the two of us."

"So am I."

"There's a remedy, you know. Have you thought about moving to Sacramento?"

"Yes. I've given it a lot of thought."

"Any decision?"

"Not yet. Would you care to persuade me?"

"That'd be fun, but I can't do it here." Peter bent down to kiss her ear. "Why don't we go on to your place and I'll show you how convincing I can be?"

"Mmm. What a good idea."

Peter's hand grazed her knee as he shifted into first. "Fasten your seat belt," he said.

He broke all the speed limits on the way to her apartment, but as luck would have it, when they got to Sutter Court, they discovered that a stretch limousine took up most of the block.

Jenny's heart sank when she saw the vanity plates on the limo: H T'BOW.

There were a dozen or more Thiebaults in Santa Rosa who could afford a Cadillac limousine, and several of them might have wanted the phonetic spelling of their surname on their license plates. But there was only one Thiebault whose first name began with *H*....

Chapter Nine

In the early 1940s, people often told Helene Thiebault that she looked like Marlene Dietrich.

Most young matrons of that era would have taken this as a compliment. Helene most emphatically did not. "You are mistaken," was her unvarying response to would-be flatterers. "Marlene Dietrich looks like me."

As the forties turned into the fifties, Helene's glamour began to lose its luster. In the sixties her honey-blond hair turned gray. An invasion of age spots and wrinkles spoiled her complexion. The seventies exacted a toll from her body. Gauntness replaced voluptuous curves and her fine, shapely legs began to look like sticks. In the eighties, bags and pouches rimmed her eyes, while her strong facial bones stretched her skin so tightly, it seemed there was scarcely enough flesh to cover the rest of her skull.

By 1990, people often thought that Helene Thiebault looked like an aging sparrow hawk, but no one told her this. As Eve Vandiver said, "No one would dare."

"I don't know why," Reed Vandiver replied. "Your mother might take it as a compliment."

And laughing, Eve admitted, "Yes, she jolly well might."

Reed's comment could have implied that he neither respected nor sympathized with his mother-in-law. But Jenny knew better. Reed had remarked more than once that he was saddened by the changes the passing years had made in Helene's appearance.

"It's like watching a monument decay," he'd said.

By the time Jenny came to Santa Rosa, Helene Thiebault had lost her resemblance to Marlene Dietrich, but she had lost none of her arrogance. Jenny supposed she never would—not if she lived another fifty years.

When Jenny and Peter got back to the duplex that day, Helene's chauffeur helped her out of the limousine. She ignored the arm he offered, and with an imperious stab of her forefinger, indicated that she preferred to use her cane. Her classic Chanel suit was sizes too big for her and decades older than Jenny, yet Helene wore it with a majesty worthy of the designer. Low-heeled walking shoes, a rope of matched pearls and a mangy fox-fur neckpiece—the jaws of one fox clamped onto the tail of the other—completed her fashion statement.

The overall effect should have been ludicrous, but Helene contrived to give it elegance. Even leaning on her walking stick, she cut an imposing figure.

She preceded Jenny and Peter up the walk with a jauntiness that belied her age, as if she were queen and they her loyal subjects, and once inside she made straightaway for the most comfortable chair in the living room and occupied it like a throne.

"That will be all, George," she declared, redistributing the neck piece across her narrow chest. "You may return for me in half an hour."

The chauffeur touched the brim of his cap, acknowledging her instructions, and made his escape.

Peter said, "I'm going to see if I can get hold of Gus," and vanished into the kitchen, closing the door behind him.

"So that's your young man," Helene observed, still adjusting her furs. "Eve told me about him, but she didn't say he was quite so abrupt. Some sort of detective, isn't he?"

"Peter's a lawyer," Jenny said. "He has some urgent phone calls to make."

Helene removed her spotless white gloves and laid them across her lap. "Regarding Sonnet Cole, no doubt. Curious business, that."

"Yes, it is," Jenny replied. *But not nearly as curious as your presence in my living room.* "What can I do for you, Mrs. Thiebault?"

"To begin with, you can sit down— No, not over there. Here, on the sofa, where I can see you without getting a crick in my neck."

The spot Helene indicated was in a splash of sunlight that spilled through the screen door—the one sunny spot in the room. Jennifer winced as the edge of the sofa cushion scorched the backs of her knees. With her literally on the hot seat and the beady-eyed little foxes arranged, Helene fastened her hands about the silver head of her cane and affected a judicious air.

Oyez, oyez. Court is now in session. The honorable Helene Thiebault presiding, Jenny thought.

"Now then, Jennifer, you must be aware, this is not a social call."

Thank heaven.

"My time is limited," Helene went on. "Apparently, yours is, too, so if you will pardon my bluntness, I will dispense with the niceties and come directly to the point."

"By all means," Jenny answered quickly.

Helene raised her cane as if it were a gavel, then let it slide through her fingers so that the rubber tip thudded against the carpet. "There's a job I'd like you to do."

"A job?"

"A neighborly act." *Thud* went the cane. "A charitable act." *Thud, thud.* "An act which might properly be considered your duty." *Thud, thud, thud.* "And speaking personally, if you agree to assume this responsibility, I would take it as a great favor."

The *neighborly* was the giveaway. "I gather this job has something to do with Edwina Farber's . . . passing?"

"With her death, Jennifer! With her death! I abhor euphemisms."

So much for diplomacy, Jenny thought. If Helene wanted bluntness, that's what she'd get. "What is it you want me to do?"

"I'd like you to sort through Edwina's belongings. Not the large items, you understand. Not the furniture and appliances, but her personal effects. Her clothing and mementoes, any objets d'art or jewelry she may have owned, her correspondence and financial records. The latter will be most important for purposes of settling any unpaid bills and for filing Edwina's income-tax return for this year." Helene's mouth twisted to a brittle curve that might have been a smile or a grimace. "It seems the IRS does not consider death sufficient cause not to pay one's taxes."

"I understand perfectly," Jenny said, repentant, "and I want you to know, you have my condolences. I had no idea you and Mrs. Farber were friends."

"Friends?" Helene's tone was faintly horrified. The tip of her cane skated across the floor. "Edwina and I were hardly friends. We lived in the same community. We were members of the same church. I saw to it that she had transportation to services on Sunday. From time to time, we served on the same committees, but we never gravitated toward the same social set. At most, we were acquaintances."

"Then why have you taken an interest in settling her affairs?"

"Edwina's will names Russell Loomis, the pastor at Calvary Lutheran, as executor of her estate. Unfortunately, Edwina made this designation without consulting Russell.

He is a busy man, Jennifer, but he will do everything in his power to fulfill this obligation. If one is realistic, however, one must admit that the Reverend cannot be expected to oversee each and every detail. Therefore, he has asked me to represent him in this matter, and naturally, I said that I would. It is, after all, the Christian thing to do."

"And now you're passing the buck to me."

The penciled lines that substituted for eyebrows arched higher on Helene's forehead. The pouches about her eyes receded, and her facial bones sprang into prominence. She swooped toward her cane and cocked her head to one side, studying Jenny as a hawk might study its prey.

"I'd sooner do it myself," she hissed. "If you think otherwise, you're a fool. I would rather walk barefoot over burning coals than beg anyone's favor. I cannot tell you how distressing it is to find that the choice is out of my hands!"

Helene sighed and slumped over her cane. Her eyebrows slackened and the rest of her features sagged into place. But before Jenny could wonder if she regretted her outburst, the cane beat a tattoo on the carpet.

"Make no mistake." *Thud.* "My mind is still sharp." *Thud, thud, thud.* "I am in possession of all my faculties."

No one would ever question that, thought Jenny.

"What I don't have," Helene continued, "is the capacity for physical exertion, and that being the case, the next best thing is a division of labor. I'll take care of the paperwork and leave the sorting and packing to you." She set her cane aside and sank back in her chair. "Now, I ask you, what could be fairer than that?"

"Nothing," Jenny answered. "It's extremely fair. The only thing is, why me?"

"For the simple reason there is no one else."

"I'd assumed Mrs. Farber's son would take charge of her affairs."

"Theodore? Good grief, no! He couldn't possibly do that."

"Why not? Was there some sort of rift with his mother?"

"No, nothing like that."

"But he never came to see her."

"Of course he didn't, but not because they didn't get along." Helene gave Jenny a probing glance. "The truth is, Teddy Farber is severely retarded. He lives in a group home and requires constant supervision. Without a great deal of coaching, he can't even tie his shoes."

"I had no idea," Jenny murmured.

"No reason you should have, although it is common knowledge. I suppose it speaks well of you that you didn't know. It's proof that you're no gossip."

"It's also proof that I'm nothing to shout about as a neighbor."

Helene snorted derisively. "With a neighbor like Edwina, you were wise to keep your distance. That's the best defense against a blabbermouth like her."

Jenny shook her head. "I can't honestly say it was her gossiping that put me off. I mean, gossiping is part of life. Just about everybody does it. You get together with friends and you all let your hair down, and before you realize what's happening, the rumors start to fly, and the wilder the rumor, the more entertaining it is. But when the party's over, no one spreads the rumors. No one really believes them. They're not—malicious."

"Malicious... Yes... That's the word for Edwina Farber. Even in her salad days she was not Miss Congeniality, and from what I saw of her, she did not improve with age."

Helene rearranged her furs and brushed a speck of lint off her skirt. "Edwina was a jug wine, a Burgundy, perhaps. Hearty and flavorful, vastly underrated, splendid with good plain fare. But she wasn't content with meat and potatoes. She developed ambitions, a yen for caviar. She wanted to be a sparkling wine, and she squandered her resources on dreams. She pretended that her earthenware jug was actually a crystal decanter...."

"What happened then?" Jenny prompted when it seemed that Helene would not go on.

"What generally happens to sparkling wine once it's opened. She had a taste of triumph, a time of celebration, but when it was over, all of her bubbles burst. And then she turned to vinegar."

"That's an interesting analogy."

Helene dismissed the compliment with a chopping movement of her hand. "It's nonsense comparing people with wines, a habit from my girlhood."

"But you must've come by it naturally. Didn't you grow up in the wine country?"

"Yes, and my father was a vintner."

"So in a way, your habit's inevitable."

Helene's smile revealed an array of discolored teeth and an expanse of pallid gums. "Be that as it may, it accomplishes nothing except to tickle my fancy. Eve, for instance, is a crisp, woodsy Chardonnay, and Reed has the mannered grace of vintage port. As for you, Jennifer, you are a very young Madeira. You're versatile and homespun, but if you cultivate a stronger sense of yourself, there's a promise of opulence to come."

Jenny eased into the shade, the better to see her visitor. "And Peter? What about him?"

"Well, I don't really know him, but he impresses me as Chianti. Robust and earthy, unpretentious, more complex than he appears. He'll never be mellow, but if he remains true to his principles, he ought to improve with age."

"And you, Mrs. Thiebault? Which wine are you?"

"I've stood the test of time, Jennifer. I've survived compromise and corruption, and become the wine most treasured by connoisseurs—a rare old Bordeaux."

"Ah, yes. What every young Madeira wants to be."

"Not if the Madeira is smart." Helene gathered her furs about her throat as if, suddenly, she felt cold. "Envy does monstrous things to people. It makes them ugly, grasping, mean. It warps their perspective, blinds them to the value of the very things they should hold dear."

"Is that what happened to Mrs. Farber?"

"Yes. That's precisely what happened. She had a perfectly nice husband. He was the salt of the earth, an honest cooking sherry. Not what I'd call a world beater, mind you, but he was not afraid of hard work."

Helene gave the neck piece a quarter turn and let her hand fall to the arm of the chair. Her clawlike fingers dug into the upholstery, the knuckles deformed and arthritic. "Lloyd Farber was associated with Citizens Bank, so I can attest to his employment record. He started out as a teller and wound up in charge of the accounting department. He wasn't rich by anyone's standards, but he made a comfortable salary. He gave Edwina a beautiful home, saw to it that she wanted for nothing. What's more important, he loved her. God knows why, but he genuinely loved her! And she ruined everything she touched."

"Including her marriage?"

"Especially her marriage," Helene replied, her voice harsh with indignation. "Edwina drove Lloyd to despair. He was a good man, a decent, God-fearing man, but he couldn't keep up with her demands. Everything she owned had to be top of the line—the latest, the showiest, the best."

"She must have changed drastically in that respect," said Jenny. "Except for the new locks she had installed, there's no evidence of extravagance in her apartment now."

The penciled eyebrows made another climb. "Looking back, I suppose it's possible her spending sprees were a means of affirming her identity. Either that, or they may have been an outlet for her maternal instincts. At any rate,

Edwina turned over a new leaf as soon as she found out she was pregnant."

"Had she been married long?"

"Fifteen years. And for a while after Teddy was born, she seemed happy. Both she and Lloyd were wrapped up in their son. I've never seen a couple more proud of a child. You'd have thought they'd invented parenthood. And I must say, they had good reason. Teddy was an adorable little boy. Smart as a whip, full of the dickens, always laughing—"

"He wasn't born with a disability?"

"Heavens, no! He was completely normal until he was five or six, and then shortly after he started kindergarten, while he was at a friend's birthday party, he choked on a piece of hard candy and stopped breathing. As I recall, his friend's mother managed to dislodge the candy and start him breathing again, but by then, he'd been deprived of oxygen so long that the damage was done—not just to Teddy, but to all three of the Farbers."

"Did Edwina revert to her old ways?"

"Quite the contrary. It might have been better if she had."

"Why? How did she react?"

"With denial. Teddy was in a coma at first, and that made it easy for her to discount the doctor's prognosis. And even when Teddy came out of the coma, it took Edwina a year or more and consultations with a half dozen specialists before she accepted the fact that mentally her little boy would never grow up. And once she accepted the truth, there was anger."

"That's understandable," Jenny said softly. "If I were in that position, I'd be outraged."

"Certainly you would. I would be, too. But where would you direct your outrage?"

Jenny shrugged. "I expect I'd be angry at the world in general. I'd be looking for someone to hold responsible and gradually, I'd narrow it down from God or fate to doctors and hospitals to candy makers and candy stores to all those parents of normal children who don't seem to appreciate how lucky they are—''

"And when you'd defined your anger, where would you fix the blame?''

"On myself, most likely. I'd probably be convinced that I'd let my child down, that I'd let my husband down, that I'd let myself down, and I'd think of all the if-onlys. If only I hadn't let my son go to the birthday party, this would never have happened. If only I'd gone to the party with him, I could have kept him safe.''

"Would you punish your husband? Would you let your feelings of guilt spill over onto him?''

"No! At least, I hope not." Jenny's throat felt tight; she swallowed to ease the constriction. "Is that what Edwina did?''

"It seemed so to me.''

"Did she ever forgive him?''

"Not that I noticed. I know that she never forgave herself. And predictably enough, the root of the problem was money.''

"Didn't they have insurance?''

"Yes, through the bank. The hospitalization itself was covered, but once Teddy was released from in-patient care, Edwina started hauling him about the country to see all those specialists, and the traveling expenses and medical bills ate up their savings. If any of the doctors had offered so much as a glimmer of encouragement, I'm sure Lloyd would not have objected, but the verdict was always the same. With intensive therapy, they might see minor improvements in motor skills and coordination. Teddy might learn to bathe himself, to brush his teeth, feed himself, put on his jeans, button his shirt—in other words, he might relearn the basics of personal grooming. But intellectually, emotionally, he would not advance beyond the level of a two-year-old."

"So there was no hope?"

"None at all. The consensus of medical opinion was that Teddy should be institutionalized, but Edwina wouldn't hear of it. She would not commit her son to the custody of strangers, she said. She would devote herself to his care and in the end, she'd prove that the doctors were wrong."

"But they weren't," said Jenny.

"No, they weren't, but Edwina did not admit defeat easily. She kept Teddy at home and after several years with no visible progress, she turned over Teddy's therapy and the majority of his care to Lloyd. But she still refused to hospitalize the boy. It wasn't until Lloyd's health began to deteriorate that she gave up. They were deeply in debt by then, and both of them were obsessed with providing some sort of security for Teddy's future. The upshot was that Lloyd began embezzling money from the bank. He took small sums at first, enough to cover the mortgage payment or an installment on one of his debts. He said he regarded the money as a loan and that he intended to pay it back, but once Teddy was in a group home, the expenses went up like a skyrocket. By the time the auditors discovered the irregularities in the books, Lloyd had 'borrowed' more than a hundred thousand dollars."

"Did the bank press charges?"

"It had to. Lloyd scraped together as much cash as he could and gave it to the bank as a gesture of good faith. It seemed to come as a relief to him that he'd finally been caught, and Reed was willing to let it go at that. He would have kept the whole sorry mess quiet if it had been up to him, but someone at the newspaper got hold of the bank examiners' report, so he was forced to seek legal redress."

"That must have been difficult for Reed."

"Few people realized how difficult. Reed had known Lloyd all his life. Reed looked up to him. There was a reservoir of mutual affection between them, and aside from that one very human aberration, Lloyd had always been worthy of respect."

"He was a gentleman," said Jennifer.

"That he was, in the finest sense of the word. Even after he'd been arraigned, he kept the proceedings as painless as possible. He pleaded guilty and made what restitution he could. He managed to avoid a trial. And for his part, Reed met with the judge and argued for leniency. By then, you see, Lloyd hadn't long to live. As his doctor testified, even the shortest sentence was tantamount to life in prison. But the judge was bound by the statutes. There was precious little he could do."

"So Lloyd went to prison?"

"Yes, and six months later, he died there."

A shadow blocked out the streamer of sunlight. Helene's chauffeur had returned. Punctual to the second, Jenny realized, glancing at her watch.

She rose to open the screen door, aware that in the last half hour, she'd had the dubious privilege of watching a master manipulator at work.

Perhaps she ought to resent this new demand on her time. She had her own move to contend with, and once she was settled, she had to get back to work on her book. But her conscience argued that it shouldn't take long to sort Edwina's belongings. A day or two at most. And instead of feeling resentful, she was resigned.

She asked, "How long would I have to get Mrs. Farber's things packed?"

Helene collected her gloves and walking stick. The joints of her vertebrae creaked as she hoisted herself out of the chair. "The rent's paid till the first of August, but I'd like to have my end of it wrapped up before then. There's no sense putting it off.''

"I'll try to take care of it by the end of next week." *The sooner the better,* Jenny thought.

"Very well, then. Next week it shall be. I'll have George deliver some boxes for you to use and drop off the key. Would Wednesday morning be convenient?''

"Wednesday will be fine. I'll give you a call when I've finished.''

"I'm counting on that,'' said Helene.

Chapter Ten

Jenny was standing at the front window, watching the chauffeur help Helene into the limousine, when Peter came out of the kitchen.

"There's a message on the answering machine from Claude LeFevre. He's anxious to speak to you. He'd like you to call him back as soon as possible."

Claude was her editor at Aldrich & Hayes. Jenny bit her lip and decided she'd wait till Wednesday to return his call. If he was anxious now, he'd be more anxious if he figured out how much of the de Silva biography she had left to write. Why ruin his holiday?

"Were you able to reach Gus?" she asked.

Peter nodded. "Sharon, too." He wrapped his arms about Jenny's waist. "I also contacted a friend of mine, Jim Bratten. He and his wife own an inn north of Bodega Bay."

"It's beautiful over there."

"I'm glad you think so. Jim's saving a room for us, if you'd like to drive over for the night."

"Could we?"

"I don't know why not. I've talked to everyone in the area who might have information about Sonnet. Gus is on the case. There's nothing to do now but wait."

"Then there's nothing I'd like more than a night on the coast," Jenny said.

Peter rested his chin against the top of her head while the limousine circled the cul-de-sac and swept out of sight. "Helene Thiebault is quite the queen bee," he remarked.

"I take it you were listening to our conversation."

"I heard the part about the wine. After that, I tuned her out."

Jenny gave him a quicksilver grin. "Have some Madeira, m'dear?"

"Don't mind if I do," Peter replied, kissing the back of her neck. "Sweet, but not insipid." The tip of his tongue darted about, teasing, seductive. "Interesting. Provocative. And I believe I detect a hint of impertinence."

Jenny made a purring sound deep in her throat and turned her head to a slightly different angle, presenting new delights for him to sample.

"Mmm, delicious. You have an irresistible bouquet."

"Thank you," she said. "I like your bouquet, too."

"Even though I'll never be mellow?"

"Even though."

"Even though I'm vin ordinaire?"

"You're Chianti," she said.

"Same difference."

"There is nothing ordinary about you, Peter Darien. You're much too complex."

"Honestly?"

"In vino veritas."

Peter nuzzled the curve where her neck joined her shoulder. "I love it when you talk Latin."

"Because it's like shoptalk?"

"Because your voice is so sexy."

"Ipso facto?"

He nibbled his way toward her ear. "Careful. You're turning me on."

"Sine qua non. Ars Gratia Artis."

"Have mercy! A man can only take so much."

"Veni. Vidi. Vici. Vice versa."

His hands were trembling with anticipation as they tunneled beneath her T-shirt to explore the smooth, bare skin of her midriff. "How about a little *quid pro quo?*"

"Ad lib," she murmured. *"Ad infinitum."*

"Let's adjourn to the bedroom."

As Peter's caresses roved higher, Jenny wisely said nothing. She was more than content to let him have the last word.

BONNYBROOK INN, AS PETER told Jenny, was the best-kept secret on the California coast. "The nicest thing about the place is its privacy," he explained. "The Brattens purposely chose not to publicize it, so the only advertising is word-of-mouth."

"I'm surprised they can stay in business that way," Jenny said.

But after one look at Bonnybrook, she understood how the inn could best serve its clientele by disdaining hype.

Built of rose-colored brick and pewter-gray shingles, set on a windswept promontory high above the sea, the inn might have been transported, brick by brick and board by board, from the moors of England.

There was a serenity about the place; a sense of timelessness that invited visitors to escape the workaday world.

They arrived at Bonnybrook a few minutes past six, along with the first tendrils of evening fog, and Jim Bratten showed them to a room tucked cozily beneath the eaves. He beamed with pride when Jenny admired the four-poster bed with its snowy counterpane. She sat on the mattress, bouncing a bit to test it for comfort, while she surveyed the rest of the room.

There was a fieldstone fireplace with a gleaming brass fender, and in front of the fireplace, a love seat upholstered in powder-blue velvet. There were matching nightstands fitted with flower-sprigged reading lamps, a tall rosewood bureau, a pair of lounge chairs drawn up to a graceful pedestal table, and the pièce de résistance, mullioned windows that framed views of ocean and sky, pine-studded hillsides and rock-ribbed bluffs that plummeted to the shore.

"I hope you'll enjoy your stay," Bratten said. "Restoring the inn has been a labor of love for me and my wife, but I realize it's not everyone's cup of tea."

"It's exquisite!" said Jenny. "Who wouldn't like it?"

Bratten glanced at Peter. "There are those who accuse us of being terminally quaint."

"It's a matter of taste," said Peter.

"Or no taste, in the case of those who prefer neon cacti."

Peter turned to Jenny. "My cacti make me smile, which is one reason I happen to like them better than doilies and doo-dads. But the way Jim carries on, you'd think I'd done something to disgrace myself socially. He won't let me live it down."

"Not in this lifetime, old buddy," said Bratten. "But our preference in wall hangings aside, we don't offer much in the way of diversions. The inn's fairly remote and very quiet. No swimming pool. No gift shop or newsstand. No telephones. No radio or TV."

"No intrusions," said Peter.

Jenny smiled. "That sounds like the height of luxury to me."

Bratten pointed out an old-fashioned bell pull. "Our specialty is service, so don't hesitate to ring if there's anything you need. I've reserved a table for you for dinner, but take your time. The kitchen's open till ten. There's no need to rush."

That would be another luxury, Jenny thought. *If only it were true.*

Tomorrow night the weekend would be over. She would go back to packing and moving and writing, and Peter would return to Sacramento, to his law practice, to his investigation of Sonnet's disappearance, to the glass-and-steel ambience of his condo—and to Sharon?

But a day remained before they went their separate ways. They had twenty-four hours to do whatever they pleased, and because their time was limited, they did their utmost to make each of those hours memorable.

They had dinner in a brick-walled alcove off the courtyard where roses bloomed and hollyhocks nodded. Holding hands beneath the table, they talked of many things, but the conversation was notable for the things they left unsaid. Jenny was careful not to mention Edwina Farber or the biography of Jaime de Silva, and Peter said nothing about Sonnet Cole. Neither of them brought up the topic that was foremost in their minds: Jenny's upcoming move and Peter's suggestion that she relocate to Sacramento.

Peter was afraid that further attempts to influence Jenny's decision might backfire, and Jenny was afraid that he was experiencing misgivings.

She wouldn't blame him if he had his doubts; she had a few of her own.

The shadows lengthened, and they lingered over coffee, listening to the records that played on the phonograph, dancing when the spirit moved them.

At sunset, they left the inn for a stroll among the pines at the edge of the bluff. They sat on the grassy verge, watching the waves roll into the cove far below, while the sun went down and the moon played hide-and-seek through the drifts of fog that rose from the sea.

With the coming of darkness, the evening grew chilly, but Peter's arms were warm, and when they kissed, Jenny tasted the tang of the ocean on his lips.

The next morning, they slept late. It was half-past ten before they made their way downstairs for breakfast. By then, the fog had lifted and the sky was a dazzling, cloudless blue. After breakfast, lured by the sunshine, they wandered down the path toward the beach.

The ground was slippery with pine needles and the trail steep. Jenny broke into a trot and after giving her several seconds head start, Peter gave chase. She heard his pursuit and ran even faster. Near the bottom of the trail, where the incline leveled off, she was running so fast, she felt as if she were flying. Her feet scarcely disturbed the hard-packed sand as she dodged the waves.

Without slowing down, she glanced back at Peter and laughed, the boom of the surf muting her joy. With his much-longer stride, he was gaining on her, just as she had expected he would, and although getting caught by him was the purpose of this game, she pretended reluctance and picked up speed.

On and on she ran, leaving the cove behind, skirting driftwood logs and swags of seaweed, until she rounded a rocky headland. She darted behind an outcropping of boulders, and in this secluded spot she stopped, leaning against the sun-drenched stone to catch her breath.

She was about to move on when she heard scuttling noises on the far side of the rocks.

Obviously, Peter was up to something, but what? What was he doing?

She tensed as the clatter climbed higher, closer.

"Aha!" Peter leapt from the top of the boulder, trapping her in the narrow grotto between the stones. "Now I've got you, me proud beauty."

Heart pounding wildly, Jenny tried to sidestep him. He spread his arms and braced his hands against the boulders, blocking her escape.

"You're a pretty good runner," he said. "You should take up jogging."

She shook her head. "I'm not athletic."

Despite her rest, she sounded breathless, whereas Peter was not the least bit winded. She smiled to throw him off guard, then tried to duck under his arm, but before she could elude him, his arms closed around her.

"Had enough?"

"Never, but I surrender." She met his gaze and found that she could not look away.

They hurried out of their clothes, fumbling a bit in their eagerness, then Peter bore her gently downward until she lay with him in the cavelike shelter of the rocks.

Submerged in his embrace, she felt the texture of the sand beneath her back, felt the grains of sand give way, molding themselves to the curves of her spine as he covered her body with his.

She welcomed his strength, the boldness of his kisses, the tantalizing friction of skin against skin as they moved to a rhythm as old as time.

A wave broke on the headland, and as the fine salty spray rainbowed above them, Jenny glimpsed a gull soaring high overhead, white wings arcing against the sky.

In that instant she knew that years from now, if she lived to be a hundred, when she thought about Peter, she would remember this place, this day, this *moment*.

And remembering, she would rejoice.

Chapter Eleven

All dressed up and no place to go—except a funeral.

Jenny ran a comb through her hair, stepped into her sling-back heels and checked her appearance in the mirror.

For the last twelve hours she had been playing catch-up, attending to the chores she should have done over the holiday weekend. She felt harried, hurried, hopelessly snowed under, but she hadn't had time to miss Peter.

At nine o'clock that morning, the moving van had pulled into the cul-de-sac, and at nine-thirty, while the driver and his helper were loading her belongings into the truck and she was disassembling her PC, Helene Thiebault's chauffeur had delivered a supply of boxes and the key Helene had promised.

Jenny had interrupted her work long enough to store the boxes in the opposite end of the duplex, and at eleven-thirty, with the last of the computer components crated and stowed in her car, she had followed the moving van to the house on Juniper Street.

In the hour and a quarter since then, she'd unloaded the Toyota, had a quick shower and changed out of her shorts and T-shirt into a navy-blue cotton dress. Now, while the movers carted her possessions into the house, she was taking a brief time-out to pay her last respects to Edwina Farber.

Calvary Lutheran was only a ten-minute drive from the house, but she was running late. The services were under way when she arrived.

She stood at the back, just inside the main doors, while Reverend Loomis offered the opening prayers, waiting for a less-solemn moment to slip into a pew.

The church was surprisingly crowded, the air heavily spiced with flowers. Once she was seated on the hard wooden bench, Jenny had to crane her neck so that she could see over the heads of the people in front of her. She focused on the casket, and thought that Edwina would have been pleased by the size of the turnout.

Aside from a few former neighbors from Sutter Court, Jenny saw no one she knew during the services, but afterward, as she was leaving the church, she ran into Betty on the steps.

"How's it going?"

"It's all over but the unpacking," Jenny replied. "Stop by later and see for yourself."

"Maybe I will. Seems like ages since we talked." After pausing to scan the mourners filing out of the church, Betty inquired, "Was Eve Vandiver close to Edwina?"

"Not that I know of. Why do you ask?"

"She was awfully upset. Didn't you notice?"

"I didn't even notice she was here. Where was she sitting?"

"Down front, near the bier, between Reed and her mother. The two of them were glaring at each other, and Eve looked as if she'd been crying."

Jenny searched the crowd, but didn't see Eve. She glanced toward the street and saw that the pallbearers were sliding Edwina's coffin into the hearse. The procession was forming for the trip to the cemetery. She spotted Helene's limousine near the head of the cortege, but the car's tinted windows prevented her seeing the passengers inside.

"They must've gone out one of the other doors," she said.

"So it would appear." Betty answered absently, descending the stairs, one hand on the railing. "I wonder if there's trouble in paradise?"

Jenny stared after her friend, taken aback by the suggestion that marital difficulties might account for Eve's woes.

In the year she'd known the Vandivers, she had never heard them exchange a cross word. They seemed so affectionate, so perfectly attuned to each others feelings, she regarded them as proof that happiness and marriage were not incompatible.

No, she decided, shaking her head. Reed couldn't have been responsible for his wife's tears. At least, not directly.

It was possible, however, that Helene had heard about Reed's deal with Hal Joyce. And if Helene knew about the plans for the house, she could be giving Eve a bad time.

Jenny worried about Eve all the way home. Once there, discovering the movers gone and the house in chaos, she changed from her dress to her work clothes and set about organizing the kitchen.

She should have called Claude LeFevre.

She would have called Eve.

She wanted to call Peter.

But she couldn't call anyone till she remembered what she'd done with the phone.

By late afternoon she was weak with hunger. She was about to make an emergency run to the closest McDonald's when Betty came to the rescue with Chinese takeout.

Jenny hadn't eaten since dinner the previous night. She was too hungry to do much talking until the spring rolls, pork-fried rice and butterfly shrimp had taken the edge off her appetite.

Sensing this, Betty chattered about how she'd spent her holiday, about her excursion to the Monterey Peninsula and mutual acquaintances at Ringer-Dent Academy, until Jenny reached for her fortune cookie.

Betty poured the tea and propped her elbows on the table. "Tell me about the Vandivers' party for Hal Joyce. I've been dying to hear about it."

"What would you like to know?"

Blushing like a schoolgirl, Betty confessed, "I've got a crush on Leo Prince. Is he as handsome in real life as he is on the screen?"

"He's more handsome in person."

"And is he really Prince Charming?"

"The image fits," Jenny allowed. "He's very suave and polished, and he has an amazing tan. He's a walking endorsement for Grecian Formula."

"You can't mean he dyes his hair!"

"No, not exactly. He just sort of blends in the gray."

Betty's face fell.

"It could be worse," Jenny hastened to add. "Leo's roots may be gray, but at least he *has* hair, which is more than I can say for Hal Joyce."

Betty plugged her ears with her forefingers. "Stop it, Jenny. That's enough. You've tarnished my last illusion. I'm in no mood to be philosophical."

Neither was Jenny. She wasn't in the mood to tackle the living room, either, but that was what she did. The quicker she found the telephone, the quicker she'd be able to call Peter.

Betty cleared away the supper things, then stayed to kibitz about the placement of the furniture.

Jenny toted cartons out of the center of the room. She didn't find the phone, so she turned her attention to the entertainment center and three massive sectional book cases, trying them as an L-shaped room divider, and more traditionally, against the wall.

"The first arrangement's cozier," Betty said.

Jenny switched them back.

"That's almost perfect," said Betty.

Jenny choked back a groan. "What's wrong with it?"

"Nothing, if you like a room that looks the size of a postage stamp. Grouped together, those pieces are so weighty...."

The pieces were individually weighty, too, and getting heavier by the minute. Puffing and panting, sweating and straining, Jenny wrestled them back against the wall.

After that, she moved the sofa and love seat from one side of the room to the other. She tried various arrangements with end tables and lamps, and while she worked, she filled in details Betty hadn't heard about Sonnet and Edwina.

Betty listened attentively and ventured an occasional opinion. When the position of the sofa met with her approval, she fluffed the throw pillows and aligned them along the cushions. Other than that, she watched Jenny move the furniture and never offered assistance, but before she left, she volunteered to help Jenny sort Edwina's things.

"I'm free next Wednesday, if you can wait till then," Betty said.

"I can wait."

"Wednesday it is, then. Shall we meet at the duplex?"

Jenny nodded.

"One o'clock?"

"One's fine." Jenny flopped down on the sofa. "Does this mean I'm forgiven for telling the truth about Leo Prince?"

"No. It means I'm curious." Betty's smile took the sting out of her answer. "Don't get up. I can let myself out."

Jenny didn't argue. Fatigue made a coppery taste in her mouth, and her arms and legs felt like worn-out rubber bands. She toppled full length on the sofa and lay there, too weary to move, one arm shielding her eyes from the glare of the unshaded lamps.

She supposed she ought to go to bed—but her bed was buried by a mountain of boxes.

That's what happened when you took off in the middle of moving day, even if you marked every packing crate in huge block letters. Boxes meant for the bathroom got carted to the office; the office got carted to the kitchen; the kitchen got carted to the living room.... "The knee bone connected to the thigh bone; O hear the word of the Lord."

All afternoon, she hadn't been able to get the tune to "Dry Bones" out of her mind, and no wonder. She had assumed it was some sort of morbid reaction to the funeral; now she realized that she'd been reacting to the movers' haphazard distribution of her belongings. But the fact that at this very moment, her bed was occupied by a half ton of books that should have been left in the living room, was nothing to sing about.

Tomorrow, she resolved. *I'll get to the bedroom first thing tomorrow, and I'll find the phone and call Claude and Eve and Peter....*

She yawned and stretched. Her eyes drifted shut.

It was barely ten o'clock and she tended to be a night owl, but she hadn't slept much the past few nights.

She smiled, thinking of Peter, wondering what he was doing, wondering if he was thinking of her.

It occurred to her that probably he had seen Sharon today. In fact, he might be with Sharon right now—

Rest, Jenny told herself. *Don't dwell on that possibility. Worry about Sharon tomorrow.*

She rolled onto her side, wincing at the ache of overtaxed muscles. Her hand brushed one of the throw pillows, and she hugged it to her chest; then, realizing the pillow was no substitute for Peter, she used it to cover her eyes.

In her worst nightmare, she had never imagined moving could be so complicated, and if she moved to Sacramento, the complications would multiply.

She'd have to pack much more carefully, for one thing, or trust the moving men to pack for her. She'd have to trust her computer to them, too. She'd have to get used to a new phone number, file another change of address with the post office, and she would definitely need referrals to a doctor and to a dentist. And once she was moved, she'd have to get acquainted with a new supermarket. She'd have to find a bookstore, a bank, a dress shop, a pharmacy. She'd have to find an office-supply store and a mechanic who could keep the Toyota in tune.

In comparison with all that, coming up with a tenant to sublet the house seemed like child's play.

Of course, Peter had promised to help, but she had certain requirements he couldn't begin to appreciate.

She had feminine needs a man would dismiss as frivolous, unessential. Where should she get her hair done, for instance? Which stores carried the brand of lipstick she preferred? Where could she buy a double-dip butter-almond raspberry-ripple ice-cream cone?

She had professional needs, as well. What about public libraries? Who would service her computer? If her software developed a glitch, who could deglitch it? If she had a fantastic day at the keyboard, wrote ninety-two pages or one brilliant sentence, if she made a breakthrough in technique, who could she talk to about it?

Here in Santa Rosa, she relied on Betty, whose objectivity, honesty and background in journalism made her comments pure gold. How could she replace that valuable a critic? How could she replace that loyal a friend?

And then there was Sharon.

How did Peter really feel about her? Was their involvement limited to Sonnet's disappearance? Was Sharon a rival for his affection?

"If she is, heaven help me," Jenny muttered.

With her sleek good looks and aura of glamour, if Sharon were a wine, she'd be champagne. She'd be scintillating and very expensive—Dom Perignon, perhaps. How could a homespun Madeira who didn't know her own depths hope to compete with sparkle and glitz, no matter how shallow? How could she compete with a magnum of bubbles that would never go flat?

"You can't," Jenny concluded, and then, "don't think about Sharon."

Instead she thought about how she should handle the call to her editor.

Before the ink was dry on her first contract with Aldrich & Hayes, she had learned that if she questioned the effectiveness of some aspect of a manuscript, the last person she should discuss it with was Claude LeFevre. Claude would worry at her uncertainty the way a dog worries a bone. Once confessed, her concerns invariably came back to haunt her, so although she didn't intend to lie, she wasn't about to admit that the subject of her current biography remained a mystery to her.

Jaime de Silva was her problem; one she would solve in her own way and, God willing, in time to meet her deadline.

Jenny flipped onto her stomach and buried her head beneath the pillow.

Was Claude the reason she had misplaced the phone? A Freudian would say her memory lapse was no accident. He would say it was her subconscious at work, providing her with an excuse for not returning Claude's call.

But if she couldn't call Claude, she couldn't call Peter. Or Eve. Or her mother.

And, Jenny thought, Phyllis can't call to complain that she hasn't received a letter from me since the middle of June.

Maybe there were advantages to being incommunicado after all.

Jenny turned onto her back with some difficulty, hemmed in by the narrow sofa and muscle cramps. Her bed was unusable, but she could open the hide-a-bed. If she had the inclination. If she had the energy.

She considered this and decided she hadn't enough energy to open her eyes. What she wanted most was sleep, but her last waking thought was that, in the morning, she would find the phone.

BY THURSDAY AFTERNOON, the last dish was in the cabinet, the last towel in the linen cupboard, the last book on the shelf. Jenny had only to install her computer and hang a few pictures and the move would be complete. But the telephone hadn't turned up.

At three-thirty, she loaded cleaning supplies in the Toyota, preparing to tidy up the duplex. On the way to Sutter Court she stopped to rent a Mr. Suds so that she could shampoo the carpets, and while she was at the hardware store, she got five dollars in change and used the pay phone.

She tried Claude's number first and got one of the editorial assistants. "Mr. LeFevre's out of the office," she was told. "May I take a message?"

"This is Jennifer Spaulding. I'm returning Claude's call."

"Oh, yes, Ms. Spaulding. I know that Mr. LeFevre was trying to reach you, but he won't be back till the eleventh."

Five days' grace. Jenny breathed a sigh of relief.

She tried Peter's office and got a similar response. "Mr. Darien's left for the day," the receptionist said. "May I take a message?"

"No, thank you," Jenny replied, and hung up without leaving her name.

She tried his condo and got his answering machine. Again she left no message, except for a sigh of disappointment.

She dialed Eve's number and got a busy signal. When she hung up, the phone kept her quarter. She jiggled the disconnect button. Still no quarter.

Sighing with consternation, she fished another quarter out of her change purse and tried her mother's number in New Haven. She let the phone ring fifteen times. Not only did Phyllis not answer, but Jenny lost another quarter. She pounded the heel of her palm against the telephone box, hard enough that her hand went numb. The equipment responded with a metallic gurgle, but it didn't cough up her quarter.

Back in the car, she told Mr. Suds, "I've been out of touch with the rest of the world for the better part of two days, and nobody's noticed I'm missing."

Mr. Suds did not disagree.

Some days you can't win.

When she arrived at the duplex, she pulled into the driveway and parked near the kitchen door to unload the Toyota. The first thing she noticed when she let herself in was the telephone, sitting on the counter.

"Let that be a lesson to you," she advised Mr. Suds. "Just when you're about to lose hope, your luck takes a turn for the better."

The carpet shampooer didn't answer. It really wasn't much of a conversationalist.

She disconnected the phone, coiled the cord neatly around it and took it out to the car, then went inside and spent the next several hours vacuuming and dusting, scrubbing and polishing, and trying to recall whether any other details had slipped her mind. Before she left the duplex, she went through the closets and cupboards to make sure she hadn't overlooked anything.

When she got back to the house on Juniper Street, she found a pleasant surprise on the step. A bouquet of flowers had been delivered while she was gone. She left the phone on the step, carried the flowers into the living room and removed the green tissue wrapper, revealing three perfect calla lilies in a smoked crystal bowl.

A florist's card was tucked into the greenery. "Jenny," the message read, "where the heck are you? I miss you. Call me. Peter."

He missed her!

Oh, yes, she thought. *Things are definitely looking up.*

She tried the lilies at either end of the coffee table, on a lamp table and finally settled on the mantelpiece. Although the flowers seemed out of place there, it was the best spot she could manage.

For all their waxy perfection, the blooms were stiff and formal, too modern for the room. They were, she realized, more reflective of Peter's taste than her own. Calla lilies were not her favorite flowers. If it had been left to her, she would have chosen daisies or roses—something more casual—but it was the thought that counted.

She looked at the card, reread the message and hugged her arms with delight.

Call me.

Not quite "I love you." Not even close. But for now, it was enough.

She retrieved the telephone, connected the plug to an outlet near the sofa and got a dial tone. She tried Peter's condo and got the answering machine again.

"This is Jenny," she said. "Thank you for the flowers. They're stunning. I, uh..." She hesitated, cleared her throat, listened to the silence echoing through the receiver then added, "I miss you, too."

To say that she missed him didn't begin to express the way she felt about Peter. But for now, it would have to do.

Chapter Twelve

Eve stopped by that evening just as Jenny was about to step into the tub.

"Keep your distance," Eve cautioned, holding up the box of tissues in her right hand. "I've caught a miserable summer cold, which explains why I look so yucky and why I've come equipped with my favorite remedy." She held up the grocery sack in her left hand. "Burritos with guacamole and sour cream. There's nothing like 'em to clear your sinuses, and these should be especially potent. They're from that new Southwestern Deli at the plaza."

Jenny waved Eve into the entry hall, knotting the belt on her robe. "They smell delicious."

"Do they? I wouldn't know. My nose is so stuffed up, I can't smell a thing." But Eve's cold had not affected her other senses. She took in Jenny's attire and heard the bath water Jenny had left running. "Is this a bad time?"

"No, Eve, not at all."

"I tried to call ahead, but I couldn't get through."

"Same here," said Jenny. "I tried to phone you earlier this afternoon, but your line was busy."

"That's not surprising. Hal's crew showed up Monday morning and ever since then, the place has been a madhouse. We're literally inundated with painters and roofers and carpenters. They're replacing the planking on one of the porches and resurfacing the drive and God knows what-all. And with the workmen running in and out and the noise and the dust and the pounding and hammering, I haven't been able to hear myself think."

"It'll be worth it, though. The house'll look great when they've finished."

"I know it will, but somehow, tonight, I couldn't take it anymore. Reed had to go to a business dinner, and I told him I'd rather stay home and try to knock out this virus. I intended to go to bed early and catch up with some reading I've been meaning to do, but the crew decided to work overtime. The house is like Grand Central Station, and I couldn't concentrate. I simply couldn't take it anymore, so I thought, if you wouldn't mind some company—"

"Your company is always welcome." Jenny nudged Eve toward the living room and headed for the bathroom. "Make yourself comfortable. Enjoy the quiet. I'll be with you as soon as I turn off the water."

"Don't rush on my account," Eve replied. "The burritos will keep. Why don't you go ahead and have your bath? Soak as long as you like, and while you're in the tub, I'll watch *Foyle's Paradise*."

"It's a rerun."

"I don't mind. Besides, I'm pretty sure it's an episode I missed last fall."

Jenny walked into the bathroom, leaving the door ajar. "If it turns out you've seen it, you might want to run that videotape on top of the TV. It has the latest footage of Sonnet."

"Now, that's an offer I can't refuse." The television came on in the midst of a raucous commercial, but the noise level faded as Eve adjusted the volume. "By the way," she called, "I love what you've done with this room."

Jenny dropped her robe and tested the temperature of the water. Before she could say thank-you, Eve inquired, "Where on earth did you get this tape?"

"From one of Hal Joyce's assistants."

"You went over to the Holiday Inn?"

"Yes, on Monday."

"My goodness! You and Peter must've been terribly busy."

"No stone unturned, that's Peter's motto."

"Do you realize it's been five days since Sonnet vanished?"

"Five and a half," said Jenny.

"A week this Saturday," said Eve. "Did you dig up any clues as to what could have happened to her?"

"A few." With a blissful "Ahh," Jenny lay back in the bath. The water sloshed against the sides of the tub so that she didn't hear Eve approaching along the hall until her footsteps stopped at the bathroom door.

"Jenny, please don't leave me in suspense. Tell me what you and Peter learned."

"Nothing definitive, I'm afraid. Sonnet's whereabouts are still a matter of guesswork. At least, they were when Peter left here on Tuesday."

"You haven't spoken to him since then?"

"How could I, Eve? I've been busy moving. Till an hour ago my telephone wasn't connected."

"Oh. Well, I gather official interest in Sonnet's disappearance is gaining momentum. She's all over today's paper. The latest news is, the FBI has entered the picture."

Jenny chased a drip from the faucet with her big toe. "If you've been following the papers, you know as much about the case as I do."

"Nonsense," said Eve. "You've got inside information."

"Do I?"

"Yes! Peter had three days' head start on the police. He questioned virtually everyone who'd had recent contact with Sonnet, and you were with him every step of the way. But if you say you have no idea where Sonnet is, I believe you. What I can't believe is that Peter hasn't formed an opinion."

"Maybe he has, but he didn't share it with me."

"And you didn't ask?"

"Peter's a lawyer, Eve, working for a client. He has to keep some things confidential. Anyway, what's the use of speculation?"

"None, aside from its entertainment value. *Everybody* loves a mystery."

Jenny sank deeper in the water and spread the washcloth over her face. "Not me," she said.

After a moment of incredulous silence, Eve laughed. "Knock it off, Jennifer. You're a writer. Even if you don't like mysteries, you must be curious."

"I wouldn't be human if I weren't," Jenny agreed. "But mysteries raise too many questions."

"Of course, they do," said Eve. "That's why they're called mysteries."

"Precisely. And as a writer, I'd rather have answers than questions."

JENNY WAS STILL SEARCHING for answers on Sunday, when Peter called.

"We just got back from L.A.," he said.

We? Jenny wondered. Did that include Sharon? "You and . . . ?"

"Gus," said Peter. "Seems a neighbor spotted one of Sonnet's wacko fans hanging around her apartment. When the police picked him up, he claimed he'd kidnapped her. For a while they thought he might be for real, but it turns out he spent Saturday, the First, in jail on a drunk-and-disorderly charge.''

"So he couldn't have had anything to do with Sonnet's disappearance,'' said Jenny.

"Not unless he had an accomplice.''

"Is there any chance he did?''

"Slim to none,'' said Peter. "The guy's a certifiable flake. He might see conspiracies all around him, but it's not likely he'd be able to organize one.''

Peter went on to report that, thus far, Gus McAvoy's inquiries into the obsessed fan angle had led to a series of dead ends, "With one exception. A college student named Richard Detweiler from Erie, Pennsylvania wrote Sonnet a batch of love notes last March. He said he was coming out to California to see her over spring break, but those letters were about the last anyone heard from Rickie. He didn't go home, and when spring break ended, he didn't go back to Penn State. As far as Gus's contacts could find out, he hasn't been in touch with any of his family.''

"If he's dropped out of sight, he could be anywhere,'' said Jenny.

"Or he could be dead,'' said Peter.

"But he might have made the trip.''

"Gus hasn't ruled it out. Don't worry, Jenny. If the Detweiler kid's in California, Gus'll track him down.''

McAvoy's investigation of Marty Riordan had confirmed the rumor about Sonnet's firing him. "She felt he wasn't protecting her interests,'' Peter said. "She told anyone who'd listen that she was positive Riordan was taking bribes.''

"How did that go over?''

"About like you'd expect. Her accusations haven't helped his agency. Other clients have walked, and apparently he's talked about starting litigation to keep her quiet and recover lost income.''

"And has he?"

"Nope, and those in the know see this as proof that her accusations are justified."

In addition to Detweiler and Riordan, Dolf Kagan was prominent on the list of suspects because of his running feud with Hal Joyce and by virtue of his history of vindictiveness.

"Kagan's motto is, Don't get mad, get even," Peter said. "He has a reputation for stopping at nothing. It's the story of his life."

But in Peter's judgment, Kagan's motives were less compelling than those of Hal Joyce. Gus McAvoy's probe of the producer's financial dealings had exposed some startling details.

Although there was no divorce in the works, Joyce's wife had locked him out of the house and demanded a separate maintenance agreement. "Aside from that," said Peter, "there wasn't much truth in the story Hal told at the Vandiver's party. The marriage was window dressing, constructed to hide the fact that Hal Joyce is gay."

"You can't be serious," Jenny scoffed. "What about the divorcée?"

"She doesn't exist. According to Gus's informant, Joyce had a long-term liaison with a would-be actor. And then a few months ago, he got involved with an eighteen-year-old beach boy and ended the affair. Now the actor's preparing to file a palimony suit, and he's formed an alliance with Mrs. Joyce. Unless Hal can come up with hefty cash settlements, both his wife and his former lover are threatening to go public."

"If I were Hal Joyce, I'd beat them to it."

Jenny's caustic reply made Peter chuckle. "It's easy to see you're nobody's patsy."

"This isn't the Victorian era," she replied. "Thank heaven we've made some advances since then. Some of us have actually learned to live and let live, at least about sexual practices between consenting adults. Hal might be gay, but what does that make them?"

"You don't have to convince me," said Peter, "your reaction is very logical. It's the rational response to blackmail. Evidently, though, Hal doesn't see it that way. If he did, he wouldn't have taken such pains to keep his sexual preference a secret."

"How big a secret can it be? Gus McAvoy found out about it easily enough."

"Yeah, but Gus is unusually resourceful. And perhaps instead of secret, I should've said private. The idea could be not to flaunt his homosexuality. Don't forget, Jenny, Hal Joyce is of another generation."

"You mean one that's less tolerant than our own."

"Right. And as a producer, he has to raise venture capital to make his films. He has to work with bankers—"

"And when it comes to investments, bankers are notoriously conservative."

"Which leaves him between a rock and a hard place," Peter finished. "His last movie flopped, and he sank every cent he could lay his hands on in it, which wiped out most of his savings. He used what was left to buy time to come up with the cash to pay off his wife and his boyfriend, but the time he bought is running out. With all the pressure he's under, Hal might have seen collecting the benefits from the insurance policy on Sonnet as the only way to avoid personal and professional ruin."

Jenny frowned and rubbed her temple while the import of Peter's observations sank in. "It doesn't look good, does it?"

"No, Jenny, it doesn't."

"Is there any hope?"

"That Sonnet's alive? No, I don't think so."

Jenny sat on the arm of the sofa, absently coiling the telephone cord around her fingers. "How's Sharon holding up?"

"She's . . . coping."

Peter's hesitation, the uneasy clearing of his throat, were freighted with things he had left unspoken. His wary use of understatement revealed more to Jenny than his reply.

Without stretching her imagination, she could envision Peter offering Sharon consolation, support, a sympathetic ear, a shoulder to cry upon. And Sharon, distraught, must be doing a lot of crying—prettily, no doubt.

Unlike me, Jenny thought.

Sharon's nose wouldn't get red. Her eyelids wouldn't get swollen or her complexion blotchy. She might suffer, but her appearance would not. The more she cried, the more fetching she would seem, and the more obvious it would become to Peter that she needed him—

Stop it! Jenny scolded herself.

With the memory of her father's death still painful and fresh, how could she envy a woman in Sharon's position? It must be hell, not knowing what had happened to her sister. If Peter was available, willing to provide comfort, wasn't that all to the good? Instead of succumbing to jealousy, shouldn't she be charitable?

"Is there any way I can help?" Jenny inquired.

"I don't know if there's anything you can do for Sharon," Peter answered, "but I'd feel a whole lot better if I could see you. Is it possible you could come over to Sacramento next weekend?"

"I wish I could."

"Look, I realize you've got a deadline—"

"But I'd like to see you, too," Jenny broke in.

She scuffed up the nap of the carpeting with her sandal, then smoothed it out again, and she thought about her manuscript and about Claude LeFevre, weighing her responsibility to him against her responsibility to Peter.

There was no question what she wanted to do.

At last she promised that she would see what she could work out.

"That's all I ask," Peter said gruffly. "Just that you'll try."

JENNY SPENT THE REST OF THAT Sunday and most of Monday going over what she'd written of the de Silva biography, preparing to discuss it with Claude.

After a week away from the manuscript, she had hoped it might be better than she'd thought, but a few pages into chapter one, she recognized that it was worse. Her usage was precise, her technique passable and her style appropriately unobtrusive. Each piece of data was correct, yet de Silva remained two dimensional. She had portrayed the cold, calculating facets in his character without capturing the color or depth. The overall effect was dry, scholarly and incredibly boring.

On the bulletin board in her office was an index card on which she had typed Elmore Leonard's admonition to "leave out the parts readers skip."

If she kept to that advice, she would have very little left of her rough draft, and time was growing short. She had only two and a half months till the end of September. Even if a miracle happened and she developed a sudden understanding of de Silva, she couldn't finish the book on schedule.

Should she admit that she would need an extension? Should she confess that, in her hands, a life story dramatic enough to translate into a genuine page turner had become pedestrian and dull? Should she be direct with Claude, or pave the way for disillusionment with hints?

Jenny went over her chapter outlines and studied her notes, looking for clues to de Silva's character that might have eluded her in prior readings. She glanced through his journals and played the tapes of her interviews with de Silva's brother and his grade-school teacher.

At one o'clock, when she broke for lunch, she had come up with nothing new.

She put together a cheese sandwich and a glass of iced tea, and took them out to the patio, leaving the back door open so that she could hear the phone. She sat in a lawn chair, chin in hand, sandwich forgotten on the table beside her, recalling her own meetings with de Silva.

She had seen him twice, in the guise of Milo Jaffre.

The first occasion had been her father's funeral. Milo was driving Max Darien's Rolls, wearing his brass-buttoned uniform with the authority of a general reviewing his troops, and although neither Peter nor Max had bothered to introduce the chauffeur, she, as a passenger, had noticed him watching her in the rearview mirror.

Mystified by his interest, more disturbed by his scrutiny than she cared to let on, she had come away from that meeting impressed by his military bearing.

Two months later, at Max Darien's house, she'd chanced to observe a scene between Jaffre/de Silva and Felicia and sensed an intimacy between Max's wife and the chauffeur. She had been surprised by their closeness—and promptly dismissed it as none of her business.

In retrospect, recognizing the clarity of her insights, Jenny wondered what other details noted in those brief encounters might lie buried in her subconscious even now.

"I should have trusted my instincts," she murmured.

When LeFevre telephoned a few minutes after two, she had nothing positive to tell him about the de Silva manuscript. As luck would have it, however, he had called to get her approval of the revised author's bio for *Diary of a*

Journalist. "You should have your galleys by the first of next month," Claude said, "but it's not too late to make minor changes."

From the author's bio, their conversation veered to potential book club and paperback sales. "There's a good deal of interest in this trilogy of yours," Claude said. Almost as an afterthought he inquired, "How's de Silva's biography coming along?"

"Slowly," she answered truthfully. "I haven't accomplished much lately because of my move."

"Well, these things happen. Life goes on. But we've got time to play with. I'm sure the book will be smashing."

"I hope so," said Jennifer.

Claude was silent, waiting for her to go on. Uneasily, she did.

"I'm thinking of starting each chapter with a quotation from his journal, and contrasting his actions with his philosophy."

"Sounds a bit cerebral," said Claude. "Still, it just might work if you don't shortchange the personal angle."

Aye, there's the rub, thought Jennifer. With hardly a pause to mourn the loss of her standards, she heard herself saying, "Speaking of de Silva's personal life, I may be able to arrange an interview with his former mistress."

"Brava, Jenny, that's more like it! That ought to lead to material marketing can promote! When will you be talking with this woman?"

"Soon," she answered. "Next weekend."

After Claude rang off, Jenny dialed Peter's office and asked if he could get her an appointment with Felicia Darien for the following Saturday.

"Does this mean you're accepting my invitation?" Peter asked.

"I am if it's still open."

"Fantastic! Let me check with Felicia and get right back to you."

Peter was as good as his word. At three-thirty, he called to inform Jenny that Felicia had agreed to see her at eleven o'clock on Saturday morning.

"If that's too early for you, we can change it," he said, "but I thought if you got your interview out of the way, we'd have the rest of the weekend to ourselves."

"Eleven's perfect," Jenny replied.

It seemed she would stop at nothing to see Peter, including abandoning her scruples. She hadn't forgotten the role Felicia had played in her father's death, but in that moment, Jenny was grateful to her for providing a ready-made excuse for the trip to Sacramento.

TO APPEASE HER CONSCIENCE, Jenny spent Tuesday excerpting passages from de Silva's journals to use as chapter headings. She had mentioned the idea to Claude in passing without stopping to think about it, but as long as she'd brought it up, she might as well give it a try and see if de Silva's rhetoric did anything to sharpen her focus.

On Wednesday, as planned, she met Betty at Sutter Court. With typical foresight, Betty had brought her portable radio, but the upbeat rhythms of classic rock-and-roll didn't make the task of packing a dead woman's personal effects any less depressing.

Betty took charge of the living room and kitchen. Jenny took the bedrooms and bath. They worked steadily, efficiently, filling stacks of boxes with clothing and linens, dishes and utensils, books and magazines and the ceramic cats that covered every tabletop.

Jenny was clearing out the middle drawer of the desk in Edwina's room, separating junk mail and store coupons from unpaid bills and other correspondence, when she came upon a sheaf of newspaper clippings that chronicled the embezzlement of funds from Citizens Bank. Skimming the articles, she saw that they told essentially the same story she had heard from Helene Thiebault.

She set the clippings to one side, unsure what to do with them, and went on to the next drawer. It was stuffed to the brim with bank statements and cancelled checks, rent receipts and copies of income-tax returns that went back at least ten years.

After arranging these items chronologically, Jenny bundled them, along with the unpaid bills, into an empty carton, then found a felt-tip marker, labeled the box with the name Farber, and listed the contents in bold letters. She was about to seal the flaps with mover's tape when it occurred to her that Edwina's current checkbook hadn't yet turned up.

A hurried glance into the other drawers revealed the checkbook wasn't in the desk. Except for old family photographs, some finger-paintings and crayon drawings signed in a childish scrawl "Teddy F.," and a savings-account passbook, the bottom drawer was empty, and the center drawer held a supply of paper, a cache of pencil stubs and dried-out ballpoint pens, a sheet of postage stamps, and a profusion of rubber bands, paper clips and thumbtacks.

The paper and postage stamps were the only things worth salvaging. Jenny rescued them, then eased the drawer out of its slot, wrinkling her nose with distaste when her fingers encountered a sticky substance on the bottom.

When she upended the drawer over a trash bag, she found a strip of adhesive tape pasted onto the wood, and several inches away, paralleling the tape, a grayed, gluey oblong where another strip had been removed. Recently, from the looks of it.

Jenny knelt down and peered at the innards of the desk, then checked the other drawers and found that they were clean. She peeled off the remaining tape, puzzling over her find.

The underside of a desk drawer wasn't a very good hiding place, but gossipy and garrulous as she was, Edwina had never struck Jenny as being terribly imaginative. Nor had Edwina seemed the sort of person who had anything to hide.

But she did, Jenny thought.

What had been hidden there? A letter or document? A picture or photocopy? And whatever it was, why had Edwina removed it?

For that matter, had she removed it, or had someone else?

Jenny frowned, remembering the Sunday Edwina had gone from door to door around the cul-de-sac, raving about a break-in.

Had she been telling the truth all along? Had someone entered the duplex while Edwina was at church? Had the intruder searched her apartment and found...

What? Jenny wondered. What had been hidden in the desk?

Whatever it was couldn't have been big or bulky, and it couldn't have been valuable. At least, not in the monetary sense. Edwina hadn't hoarded cash in a sock or under her mattress. Like any reasonable person, she had kept her money in the bank. She'd had a checking account and a savings account.

Jenny replaced the drawer and turned her attention to the passbook.

She was not surprised to see that Edwina's account was at a nearby branch of Bank of America rather than Citizens. There would have been too many unhappy associations there.

What was surprising—amazing, in fact—was the six-digit balance.

Jenny wiped the back of her hand across her eyes. Had she misread the figures? Overlooked a decimal?

A count of the zeros revealed she had not.

She studied the rows of numbers, following the columns upward, and saw that, in the years since the account had been opened, Edwina had made regular deposits and a few modest withdrawals.

Even allowing for wise investments, how had an elderly widow with no apparent means of support aside from Social Security managed to accumulate so much cash?

From what Helene Thiebault had said, Jenny had assumed Edwina was left destitute after her husband's death; now it appeared she'd been well taken care of.

Where had she gotten those monthly deposits? Had Lloyd Farber held out on his employer? Was there a secret stash of his ill-gotten gains? Or was there a simpler, more innocent explanation for the size of the savings account?

The money could have come from life insurance. It could have come from an annuity. An inheritance. The sale of property. The state lottery. The Irish Sweepstakes. Rich relatives. Rich friends. A wealthy benefactor.

Had Edwina declared the deposits as income on her tax returns?

The answer to that was less than three feet away. If Jenny wanted it, all she had to do was look through the box of financial records and abandon another principle or two. No one would know. No one would censure her for prying into matters that were none of her concern.

No one but me, she thought.

And if it turned out that Edwina had welshed on her taxes, what then?

She couldn't inform the IRS. She was no stool pigeon. Besides, what purpose would it serve? Instead of continuing as a private resident in his group home, Teddy Farber would be dependent on public funds. His expenses would be paid by the county and state. Any back taxes owed by Edwina's estate would go into the pocket of one government agency and come out of the pocket of another, which was akin to robbing Peter to pay Paul.

Senseless, Jenny thought. Utterly senseless.

And frightening.

If she insisted on wrestling with temptation, the day was bound to come when temptation would win. And the next time she found herself in a moral dilemma, it would be easier to give in. Eventually, she would become an inveterate snoop, like Edwina—and all because she had indulged the demands of idle curiosity!

As much as she hated unanswered questions, the answer to this particular question carried too high a price.

Her decision made, Jenny tossed the passbook in with the other records and hastily sealed the box, but as the morning wore on, she discovered it was much more difficult to seal off her imagination.

Toward noon, Shelley Augustine stopped by to invite Betty and her to lunch. Referring to her eight- and ten-year-old sons, Shelley told them, "The boys are just finishing up. They'll be leaving for their swimming lessons soon, so if you'd like to come over about twelve-thirty, we'll be able to hear ourselves think."

Half an hour later, after a short stroll across the cul-de-sac, Jenny and Betty were seated in the refreshingly pleasant clutter of the Augustines' kitchen.

Smiling at Shelley, Betty said, "This is very thoughtful of you."

"It's self-preservation," Shelley said wryly, rolling her eyes. "By this point in the summer, my guys are bouncing off the walls, bored out of their squirrely little minds, and I'm dying for some honest-to-gosh adult conversation."

Jenny laughed, not unsympathetically. "I know the feeling," she admitted.

"That's right," Shelley exclaimed. "You used to be a teacher."

"Umm-hmm, and Betty was my boss. She's the dean of girls at Ringer-Dent Academy."

Shelley turned to Betty. "Maybe you can tell me why the school year only lasts nine months."

Over generous servings of pasta salad, Jenny lapsed into a companionable silence while Shelley and Betty got better acquainted. They had reached the coffee stage when Teddy Farber's name came up.

"Seeing him at the funeral really shook me up," Shelley confided.

"You know him?" Betty inquired.

"I used to," Shelley answered. "When I was a little girl, my folks lived next door to the Farbers. Teddy and I were in kindergarten together. But then he had his accident, and you know how kids are. I didn't keep track of what happened to him. After all these years, I was shocked to find out that he's still alive."

"I never realized Edwina had a son till I read her obituary," Jenny said. "She never spoke of him or her husband."

"She never talked about the past," said Shelley. "But I suppose that's understandable, considering everything she'd been through. She'd had so much and lost it, poor thing. And the way she lost it was tragic—that business about Lloyd, for instance. He was the *nicest* man, and he seemed so honest. I still can't believe he stole that money."

"Did Edwina believe it?" Jenny asked.

"She must have. She never defended him, never denied that he was guilty. She didn't even bother to put in an appearance at his trial."

"Maybe that was the way Lloyd wanted it," Jenny said.

"Maybe, although that's not the way my folks saw it. I felt sorry for Edwina, but my mom and dad didn't. I can still hear them talking about coldhearted Edwina, abandoning Lloyd when he needed her most. And the sad thing was, she wasn't the only one. Lloyd was a joiner. He belonged to Rotary, the Lions, a bunch of other clubs, and he was deeply involved in community affairs. He was always working for one cause or another, so he was fairly popular. Everyone seemed to like him. He knew scores of people and had scads of friends, yet none of them stood by him. The only visitors he had in jail were business associates—Reed Vandiver, my dad, a couple of the other directors at Citizens Bank, and that lawyer of his—I've forgotten his name."

Jenny thought of the newspaper clippings. "Benjamin Rush," she said.

"Yes, that's him! As I recall, he and Lloyd grew up together, and when he heard about the trouble his old chum was in, he postponed retirement to represent Lloyd. Not that there was much he could do."

"Did Edwina see Lloyd after the trial?"

"I wouldn't know. By then I'd met Hank and I was too wrapped up in him to notice what Edwina was up to."

"Do you know whether Lloyd carried life insurance?"

"No, I don't. I know Edwina received small monthly payments from his pension fund, but if he had insurance, I don't think it would have been worth much. He'd begged, borrowed and stolen as much as he could to keep up with Teddy's doctor bills. Anyway, it seems to me if Edwina'd had hopes of coming into any amount of money after Lloyd's death, she would've been kinder to him. As it was, she behaved as if he never existed. It wasn't just that she refused to talk about him. If anyone mentioned him, she'd change the subject. It was as if she couldn't bear remembering Lloyd, so she tried to erase him from her memories."

Edwina may have tried, but she didn't succeed.

Jenny thought of the mementos she had found that morning. The clippings and drawings and photographs in the desk, a box of baby clothes in Edwina's closet, a scruffy teddy bear missing an eye, in the drawer of her nightstand.

Surely these things were evidence that neither Lloyd nor Teddy had ever been far from Edwina's mind.

THAT AFTERNOON EVE CAME BY the duplex to see how they were doing. She stayed to lend a hand and by five o'clock, the worst was over. Both bedrooms and the living room had been stripped of Edwina's personal possessions, and nothing out of the ordinary had shown up.

Betty was packing the last boxful of items in the kitchen, and Eve was in the entry hall stacking the cartons destined for the St. Vincent de Paul thrift shop, preparing for the arrival of the truck that would haul them away.

Jenny was in the bathroom taking down the shower curtain, when she spotted Edwina's string shopping bag and her shapeless cotton knit sweater hanging from a hook on the back of the door. She dropped what she was doing so that she could pack the sweater with the rest of the clothing before the wardrobe box was taped shut. She had to stand on her tiptoes to reach the handles of the shopping bag, and as she pulled the sweater off the hook, Edwina's key ring fell out of the pocket and along with the keys, weighted down by them, a scarf.

She bent down and untangled the crumpled bit of silk. When she shook out the wrinkles, a faint whiff of fragrance drifted up from it. She inhaled deeply, trying to identify the scent. It was delicate, exotic—

Jasmine, she realized with dismay.

The shower curtain forgotten, she took the scarf into the kitchen to show to Betty and Eve.

"Look at this," she said, holding it out for their inspection.

Eve rubbed the fabric between appreciative fingers. "Giorgio," she said. "Silk jacquard, fine as a cobweb. I love that paisley weave, and what a scrumptious color!"

Betty nodded. "Reminds me of a candy apple. Where'd you find it?"

Jenny told them. "What do you make of that?" she inquired, eager for their reaction.

"Nothing," said Betty.

"Me, either," said Eve.

Jenny stared at her friends and held the scarf higher. "This must have cost more than any two of Edwina's dresses. Not only that, it's red. Don't you think it's unusual that she should have owned something so extravagant?"

Betty shrugged. "Maybe it was a gift."

"A gift from whom? Who gave it to her?"

"I don't know," Betty answered, "and I don't particularly care. What difference does it make where Edwina got the scarf?"

Jenny's eyes widened, registering disbelief. Before she could think of an adequate response, Eve spoke up. "Maybe Edwina found it."

"There you are, Jenny. The voice of reason." Betty shoved the wiry curls off her forehead with poorly concealed impatience. "I'm not sure why you're making such a big deal over that scarf, but I can tell you're upset. Problem is, it's been a helluva day. I'm tired. You're tired. Neither of us is at her best. Let's just finish this job and get out of here."

Jenny's face grew hot with annoyance, but she didn't argue. In that moment, not trusting her voice, she simply turned on her heel and left the kitchen.

But later that night she discovered she couldn't sleep. When she closed her eyes, she saw red. Literally. Visions of candy apples danced in her head. Not because of her near squabble with Betty; they had patched up their differences before they left Edwina's. It wasn't irritation that jangled her nerves and kept her tossing and turning.

It was the blasted designer scarf that kept her awake. She was haunted by its color, its fragrance, its tone-on-tone paisley weave. But most unsettling was that the scarf was familiar. She had seen it before that afternoon, in Sonnet's videotape.

As soon as she got home that evening, she had run the tape and rerun it until she'd memorized each frame and could recite the dialogue. And with each replay of the scene between Sonnet and Vanessa, the conviction had grown that the scarf that trailed from the waist of Vanessa's dress, the scarf Sonnet had appropriated and used so effectively as a prop, was identical to the scarf she had found in the pocket of Edwina's sweater.

And not just identical, but one and the same.

Somehow or other, that bright square of silk linked Edwina's death and Sonnet's disappearance. That much was certain. What bothered Jenny was that in the hours since she had arrived at this conclusion, she hadn't been able to figure out how.

Crossroads Plaza had seemed a natural place to look for a point of contact. Edwina had gone to Long's Drugs to get her prescriptions refilled. A broken clasp on the Medic-Alert bracelet had given Sonnet a reason to visit the drugstore. It seemed apparent to Jenny that their paths had crossed at the mall, but what happened next, how the scarf changed hands, remained pure conjecture.

The simplest explanation—that Edwina had found the scarf—did not explain why she had left the mall without her medicine. But suppose she had taken ill and Sonnet had rushed to her assistance. And suppose, instead of requesting the pharmacist's help or calling for an ambulance, Sonnet had driven Edwina home. Once there, if she'd recognized the gravity of Edwina's condition, if she'd been afraid that she would be held responsible for Edwina's death, would Sonnet have left a dying old woman alone?

No, she wouldn't, Jenny decided.

Sonnet had the reputation of being a tough cookie, but it was hard to believe she would do anything that heartless. And if she had, how had her scarf wound up in Edwina's pocket?

But suppose Sonnet had been kidnapped by a deranged fan. She would have put up a struggle and in the course of the struggle, she might have dropped her scarf. What if Edwina witnessed the struggle? What if she picked up the scarf and shoved it in her pocket? What if she gave chase and the kidnapper forced her along with Sonnet into his car? Would the kidnapper have taxied her home? Before he took off with Sonnet, would he have gone to the trouble of hanging Edwina's sweater and her shopping bag on the hook on the bathroom door?

In a pig's eye! Jenny thought. But she couldn't imagine Edwina putting them there. Not in the midst of a heart attack.

Edwina might have dumped them in the living room or draped them over a kitchen chair. She might even have thrown them into the hall closet, but she wouldn't have taken them into the bathroom.

Neither would Sonnet. From the looks of her dressing room, she was not especially tidy. But if for some unknown reason, she had wanted to put the sweater and shopping bag away, she wouldn't have chosen the bathroom.

In the first place, Sonnet wasn't tall enough to reach the hook and in the second place, no woman would hang a sweater and shopping bag there.

But a man might.

In fact, the more Jenny thought about it, the more it seemed the sort of thing a man might believe a finicky old woman would do....

What if Edwina and Sonnet happened to witness a crime? What if they had seen enough to identify the criminal?

No matter how Jenny racked her brain, she couldn't imagine any other connection between Edwina and Sonnet and the unknown assailant who had made them victims.

It was as frustrating as fitting together pieces of a jigsaw puzzle without having the slightest inkling how the finished picture should look. None of her theories seemed plausible. None of them accounted for all the facts or addressed all the issues. And so she lay with her arms folded behind her head, staring into the darkness and seeing shades of red.

The carrot-red of Sonnet's hair. The red of her car. The red of the scarf.

Red was the color of celebration. Hal Joyce had been wearing red socks the night of Eve's dinner party. The centerpieces on the tables had featured red roses and red candles, and the canapés had been garnished with chunks of pimento.

Red was associated with love and with real and counterfeit passion. Chianti was red. Valentines were red. But redlight districts were at the opposite end of the spectrum, on the shady side of the emotional tracks.

Sometimes it wasn't easy to tell the genuine from the fake. The battle scenes in *The Red Badge of Courage* were acclaimed for their realism, yet the author, Stephen Crane, had never been in combat. And Dolf Kagan's study was like the inside of a jewel box, but he'd called its color "cat-house red."

Which was real and which the fake?

Nowadays people went to great lengths to stay "in the pink," but nobody wanted to find themselves "in the red."

To keep from drowning in a sea of red ink, Lloyd Farber had stolen money and paid for the theft with a prison term.

"Red sky at morning, sailor take warning..."

Red symbolized Danger. Anger. Death.

Stop signs were red. So were the cherry lights on police cars. Hospitals used red plastic bags to dispose of hazardous waste.

Blood was red.

The scarf was red.

How could Betty believe it had belonged to Edwina? How could anyone? The scarf was blatantly out of place among the drab browns and grays of Edwina's belongings. It stuck out like a sore thumb, so easy to see, a person would have to be blind—

For the space of a pulsebeat, things clicked into focus. Jenny glimpsed the puzzle from a new perspective, and suddenly, the pieces fit.

Edwina's watchfulness.

Her spells of paranoia.

Her bank balance.

The expensive new locks she'd had installed.

The break-in.

The desk drawer.

The abrupt way she'd left the mall.

Her sweater and shopping bag. And the scarf. Sonnet's scarf...

Horrified, Jenny punched the pillow. "No! No, it can't be."

Or could it?

She flung back the covers and sprang out of bed. "It's unthinkable. Preposterous."

Her suspicions were unfounded, a bad dream, a product of the late hour, an overactive imagination, the leftover ravioli she'd had for supper.

She was mistaken. She *had* to be.

Unless this was one of those times when it was hard to tell the genuine from the fake.

She might be wrong about some of the specifics, but she hadn't dreamed up the scarf. It was real. It was incriminating. It was proof of murder.

"I shouldn't have left it at the duplex."

Instinct told Jenny not to dawdle. She hadn't a second to spare.

She switched on the bedside lamp and squinting against the light, pulled on whatever clothes came to hand, then grabbed her carryall and dashed out of the house.

Chapter Thirteen

The front page of Thursday's papers carried the news that Hal Joyce and the cast and production crew of *Foyle's Paradise* were offering a fifty-thousand dollar reward for information leading to the arrest and conviction of the party or parties responsible for Sonnet Cole's kidnapping.

A sidebar accompanying the article featured comments from Sonnet's costars. Leo Prince was "grief-stricken," and Vanessa Wayne "devastated that Sonnet's still missing."

"Sonnet's more than a gifted actress," Joyce was quoted as saying. "She's everyone's favorite, everyone's pet, the heart and soul of this show. She's been like a daughter to me."

"Bull!" said Peter.

Gus McAvoy, seated across the desk from him, chuckled. "USDA prime. Great for the image."

Peter lowered the paper and studied the investigator, trying to read his expression. Gus hadn't been to bed last night. He was rumpled and bleary-eyed, but his broad, battered face gave away nothing.

He almost always phoned in his reports. Why had he requested this early-morning meeting?

"You think the reward was Joyce's idea?" Peter asked.

"I'd lay odds on it, boss. Wouldn't you? That announcement's got Joyce's signature all over it, and more loopholes than my Aunt Tillie's knittin'. No kidnapping, no payoff. No arrest, no payoff. No conviction, no payoff. I can tell you right now, the only thing that reward will do is flush out every nut in the state. The police'll be workin' overtime following up all the tips, and five'll get you ten, none of 'em pan out."

"So basically it's a hollow gesture."

"You got it. Even supposin' a miracle happens—say the perpetrator is arrested and brought to trial—Joyce'll come outta this smellin' like a rose. If he has to pay the reward, he's got himself publicity worth a million bucks, all it's costin' is fifty grand, and not all of that's coming outta his pocket."

"The guy's a vulture." Jaw hardening with disgust, Peter skimmed the folded newspaper toward the wastebasket in the center of his office. It hit the rim, then fell into the target with a thunk.

Gus licked his forefinger and chalked up two points in the air. "Not bad, Pete. Glad to see you haven't lost your touch."

"As long as you haven't lost yours," Peter replied. He opened the paper sack on his desk and removed two Egg McMuffins and two cups of coffee and after handing one of each to McAvoy, aligned his own breakfast on the windowsill at his elbow. He crumpled the sack and tossed it at the wastebasket. "Whatever you've got to report this morning, I hope it's good news."

"I wouldn't've caught the milk run up from L.A. if it wasn't. Looks like we've got our first real break in the case."

Peter washed a bite of sandwich down with coffee while he rummaged about for a legal pad and pencil, preparing to take notes. "Let's hear it."

"It's about the Detweiler kid," said Gus. "All along I had a hunch there might be an angle there."

"And you believe in playing your hunches."

"I wouldn't be much of a detective if I didn't, and my digestion would be shot. Somethin' seems off-key. Maybe I can't say what. Sometimes it's nothing I can put my finger on, but I get a cramp in my gut that won't go away till I dig a little deeper. I don't always hit pay dirt, but it keeps me from gettin' ulcers."

"What bothered you about Rickie Detweiler?"

"That's hard to say, except I'd get a bellyache whenever I'd think of him not keeping in touch with his folks. I mean, Rickie's no prize. He's been in and out of trouble since he was eight and a neighbor caught him peeking in the window of his daughter's bedroom. And bein' a Peeping Tom is just the tip of the iceberg. Since then, Rickie's graduated from stealing lunch money to stealing cars, from beating up on littler kids on the school playground to assault and battery."

Gus paused for a swallow of coffee. "This kid's hostile, Pete. He's disturbed. He's a borderline sociopath, but he's also his mama's only child. Even with a hard case like Rickie, those apron strings cut pretty deep. And they cut both ways. Even so, if mama says she hasn't heard from her baby boy, okay, I'll buy it. But Mrs. Detweiler went further than that. She said she has no idea where her son is, and that I couldn't believe."

Peter smiled. "When you put it that way, neither can I."

Gus set his coffee cup on a corner of the desk, then unfastened the button on his suit coat and relaxed against the cushions of the visitor's chair, his thumbs hooked beneath his suspenders, fingers splayed across his ample stomach. "Anyways, it just so happens there's an operative in Cleveland who owes me a favor, and since Cleveland's only a hundred miles from the Detweiler home in Erie, I decided to do some digging. And guess what."

"You hit pay dirt."

"Better than that. I hit the mother lode—no pun intended." McAvoy's battle-scarred features split in a wolfish grin. "Seems Rickie used to commute to college in an old VW Beetle. Now Rickie's gone and the Volkswagen's gone, and his roommate at Penn State says Rickie had at least one gasoline credit card. The local police contacted the airlines and buses, and came up empty. Assuming Rickie's alive, that leaves two possibilities. Either he hitchhiked cross-country, or he drove."

Peter glanced up from his notes. "If he hitchhiked, there's no telling where he is."

"Right, boss. But I figured, if Rickie's running true to form, he's gotta be driving the VW."

"Do you have the license number?"

"'Course, I do. So do the police. But if you ask me, there's not much hope of tracing the car. Not when all it takes to switch license plates is a screwdriver. On the other hand, though, if Rickie's driving, there's a good chance he'd use his credit card."

"If he did that, he'd be billed."

Gus nodded agreement. "That's why my friend from Cleveland went to see Rickie's mother last week. He saw her every morning, brought her coffee and donuts. He was sympathetic, said she must be worried. Now and again he asked questions, but he didn't press for the answers."

"He won her confidence," said Peter.

"Sure as hell did. And when he sensed she was dyin' to talk, he turned up the heat. He told Mrs. Detweiler, if Rickie's involved in Sonnet Cole's disappearance, he's in trouble over his head. He told her he understood why she'd been trying to protect her son, but it's time she protected herself. He reminded her, if she's withholding information about Rickie's whereabouts, she's an accessory after the fact. He told her he wants to help Rickie and her any way he can, but there's nothing he can do for Rickie until he knows where Rickie is, and he can't help Mrs. Detweiler if she won't help herself.''

"Sounds like your friend can be very persuasive."

"Best damn interrogator I ever saw. What's more important, he gets results."

"I gather Rickie's mother produced the bills."

"She did," said Gus. "And like I expected, the kid left a paper trail straight to L.A. But on top of that, we got a bonus. Seems as how on June 28, Rickie got a parking ticket, and following procedure, a copy of the ticket was sent to his home."

"So he hasn't switched license plates."

"Hadn't then," Gus qualified. "Had no reason to."

"Not yet," said Peter. "Where was the ticket issued?"

"Petaluma."

"But that's not far from Santa Rosa!"

"Less than twenty miles," said Gus. "Practically the scene of the crime."

BY ELEVEN THAT MORNING, Peter had put in a full day's work. After hashing out logistics, he had approved of the approach McAvoy suggested for tracking down Rickie Detweiler. He'd cautioned the investigator to coordinate his activities with those of the Santa Rosa police to avoid stepping on official toes and seen Gus to the elevator, then returned to his office to phone Sharon and let her know what was going on.

He was dictating the last page of notes from his conference with McAvoy when his secretary, Mrs. Larch, rang him on the interoffice line to inform him, "Ms. Spaulding is here."

Peter rooted through the overflow of papers from his In basket, looking for his calendar. He wondered if too many late nights and skipped meals were catching up with him. Was it Saturday already? Had he misplaced two days? He found the calendar and saw that he hadn't. It was only Thursday, after all. Either he hadn't heard correctly, or his secretary had misspoken.

"You mean she's on the phone."

"No, Mr. Darien," the secretary answered, her voice pitched discreetly low. "Ms. Spaulding's here, in the waiting room. I wouldn't have disturbed you, but she says it's urgent that she speak to you. Should I give her an appointment for this afternoon?"

"No, Mrs. Larch. I'll be right out."

Peter was already on his way to the door, scowling at the Egg McMuffin box and the row of coffee cups on the windowsill. As he passed the wastebasket, he stopped to scoop up the wadded-up sheets from the legal pad that littered the floor, disposing of the evidence that his hook shot had a tendency to fall short.

Urgent, he thought. *What could be urgent enough to bring Jenny to Sacramento two days early?*

When he reached the hall, he saw that Jenny was pacing back and forth in front of the receptionist's cubicle as if she could not sit still.

"Jenny," he called, "this is a surprise."

She looked up, forced a tremulous smile and rushed to meet him. He sensed her agitation, her thinly veiled excitement, even before she ran into his arms and clung to him as if he were a lifeline.

"Oh, Peter, I shouldn't have come here. I feel so foolish. You're probably busy, and I apologize if I'm taking you away from a client, but I'm so mixed up. I had to talk to someone and I didn't know who to turn to."

He drew her closer, stroked her hair. "Easy, honey. It's all right. I'm glad you came to me."

"But it's not all right! Nothing's right! You don't—"

He touched his fingers to Jenny's lips. The receptionist was staring. She blushed when Peter caught her gaze, and asked, "Is there anything I can do, sir?"

"Hold my calls," he instructed.

He turned and coaxed Jenny along the corridor, shielding her from prying eyes until he had closed the door to his office behind them.

He could feel Jenny trembling, and his legs were none too steady as he guided her to a chair. Once she was seated, he got his first good look at her. He was alarmed by what he saw.

She was pale, shaken, almost dazed. Her hands were icy to touch, as if she were in shock.

He went to the credenza and poured Scotch into a tumbler, then sat on his heels in front of Jenny, holding her free hand, warming it between his own, while she drank the liquor in obliging sips and soft color washed into her cheeks.

"Feeling better?" he inquired.

"Not really."

"Maybe it would help if you tell me what's going on."

She knit her brow. "There's so much to tell and it's all so confusing. I don't know where to begin."

"There's no hurry, Jenny. Take your time."

She pulled in a ragged breath and haltingly, uneasily, began sketching in the details of Teddy's accident, his injury, and Edwina's search for a miracle cure. She talked about the Farbers' rising medical bills, the theft of funds from Citizens Bank and Lloyd Farber's confession to embezzlement, then went on to tell Peter about sorting Edwina's personal effects. She told him about the items she had found in the desk, and finally described the scarf.

"Are you sure it was the scarf you saw in the videotape?" Peter asked.

"I'm positive," Jenny answered. "It not only looked the same, it smelled of her perfume. Last night, when I realized how important it is, I went back to the duplex to get it, but the truck from St. Vincent de Paul must've come out yesterday evening. By the time I got there, Edwina's stuff was gone. The only things left were these.''

She removed the sheaf of newspaper clippings from her carryall and gave them to Peter. He glanced through them, slouching against the corner of his desk.

''I stopped by St. Vincent's this morning,'' Jenny continued. ''I was there when they opened at eight. I thought if Edwina's things were still in the boxes, I'd be able to find the scarf. So I spoke to the store manager. I made up a story about being close to Edwina and wanting a memento of our friendship.''

''Did the manager buy it?''

''I don't know, Peter. It's hard to say. He took me back to the storeroom and showed me the bins where they dump the donated clothing till it's sorted and priced, and he told me if I could find my friend's scarf, I was welcome to it.''

''And?''

''And nothing. I think the manager was having a joke at my expense. There were maybe fifteen or sixteen bins, about four feet long, three feet wide and another three deep, and every one of them was chock-full of old clothes, but there was nothing I recognized as Edwina's. And beside the bins, they've got stacks of clothing all over the floor—'' Jenny wrinkled her nose, recalling the condition of some of those garments. ''After an hour of searching, I'd scarcely made a dent in the pile. Then it dawned on me that, if B.J. and Nelson were still in town, I might learn something more if I could see the outtakes from Sonnet's tapes.''

Peter frowned and laid the newspaper clippings aside. ''Did you go to the Holiday Inn?''

''No, I telephoned ahead. The desk clerk told me the *Foyle's Paradise* crew went back to L.A. last Sunday.''

"So you didn't come up with anything to confirm your theory that the scarf establishes a connection between Edwina and Sonnet."

"It's not just a theory, it's a fact!"

"How can you be certain? You only saw Sonnet's scarf in the videotape. Besides, even if they are the same, what does it prove?"

Jenny laced her fingers together, gripping them tightly, as if she were struggling for composure. Her response, when it came, was barely audible. "Last night, even after I knew that Edwina's death was linked to Sonnet's disappearance, I couldn't see how they were related until it dawned on me that we've been focusing on the wrong crime."

"There's only one crime I'm aware of," Peter replied gently. "Edwina died of a heart attack."

"But what brought on the attack? Was it natural causes? Or did someone deliberately scare her to death?"

His shrug dismissed these questions. "You're reaching, Jenny."

"Am I?" she challenged. "Then answer this, if you can. Why did Edwina leave the drug store without her prescriptions? And what happened to her purse?"

"Didn't you find it among her things?"

"No. I didn't find her checkbook, either. Don't you think that's strange?"

"Yes, but it doesn't necessarily indicate foul play."

Jenny huddled deeper into the chair. "Maybe you're right, Peter, but just for sake of argument, suppose you're not. Suppose Sonnet's disappearance is secondary to Edwina's death."

"I don't see how it could be."

"Neither did I, till I took another look at my false assumptions. For three years I saw Edwina sitting at her front window, and I assumed she was a nosy old snoop. But perhaps she kept watch because she was frightened."

"Frightened? Of what?"

"The can of worms she'd opened. Did you know that the Sunday before she died, Edwina claimed someone had broken into her apartment? At the time, I assumed she'd imagined it."

"With good cause," said Peter. "You didn't have to be an appraiser to see that she had no valuables. There wasn't much incentive for burglary there."

"That's what I thought until it occurred to me there are things people prize that don't have a monetary value. Intangibles like reputation and public standing can be priceless."

"So?"

"What if Edwina had access to damaging information that someone wanted suppressed?"

"About the embezzlement, for instance?"

"That's one possibility that comes to mind. If Lloyd Farber wasn't guilty, he might've had proof that someone else was, and before he died, he would have given that proof to Edwina, and she could have profited by it, which would explain where she got the money in her savings account."

"Lloyd's guilt would explain the money, too, and much more simply," Peter said.

"That's true," Jenny allowed wearily. "I'd have accepted that explanation, if it weren't for two things. Everyone I've spoken to who knew Lloyd Farber, from Helene Thiebault to his lawyer, makes a point of mentioning what an honest man he was."

Peter was taken aback. "When did you talk to his lawyer?"

"This morning. I phoned Benjamin Rush just before I left Santa Rosa."

"And he discussed the case with you?"

"Within the bounds of ethics."

"How'd you manage that?"

"He recognized my name," said Jenny. "He'd actually read my book."

The accusing look she shot Peter made it clear she'd bet that was more than he'd done. Peter opened his mouth to defend himself. He wanted to tell Jenny that he intended to read *Justice Denied* as soon as he had the time, but before he could offer excuses, Jenny went on.

"Do you know what Mr. Rush told me? That he never believed Lloyd was capable of embezzlement."

"Well, that's what I'd expect him to say. If there's any truth in those newspaper articles, Farber and Rush were old friends. But Farber confessed, Jenny, and the evidence supports his guilt. He was hard-pressed financially. He was dying. His medical bills had exhausted his savings. He had a second mortgage on his house, a wife who'd never worked outside the home and a son who needed total, long-term care. He must've been desperate!"

"I'm not saying he wasn't," Jenny replied, "but as Mr. Rush remarked, there's a big difference between desperation and thievery."

Peter bit back a groan. His mouth turned down at the corners. "What else did this guy tell you."

"That in his opinion, Lloyd took the fall for someone else."

"And you don't think he's biased?"

"What if he is? It doesn't change the fact that Edwina had hidden something—a key or some sort of document—on the underside of a desk drawer. I think that raises the specter of blackmail, and if she *was* blackmailing someone, when you consider that she was also a gossip—"

"It makes her much more dangerous than your average garden-variety busybody," Peter finished, resigned but not convinced. "All right, Jenny. You've covered the why, let's get on with the how."

Jenny moistened her lips with a nervous flick of her tongue. "Last night, while I was trying to make sense of all this, I got to wondering. What if the person Edwina was blackmailing broke into her place while she was at church and found the evidence she'd hidden and took it?"

"If something like that happened, she'd probably lock herself in the house and never come out."

"Maybe she'd want to, but living alone, she'd have to go out sometime. It would be more practical if she tried to re-assure this person, so what I think she did was arrange to meet him somewhere she'd feel safe, someplace public—"

"Crossroads Plaza," said Peter. "Specifically, Long's Drugs."

"Either Long's or the food court just outside the entrance to the drug store. It's usually crowded, and I don't think the embezzler knew that Edwina was having her prescriptions refilled. Otherwise, he wouldn't have left without them."

"Of course," said Peter. "He'd have wanted everything to seem as normal as possible."

Jenny nodded agreement. "What Edwina didn't reckon with was that the embezzler would stop at nothing to keep his secret. She didn't foresee that he'd resort to violence, or that he'd force her to leave the mall. And what the embezzler didn't foresee was that, on their way out of the mall, they would run into Sonnet Cole. As for Edwina..."

She faltered briefly, wondering how Edwina had reacted. Had there been a moment when she might have warned Sonnet? If she'd shouted, "Look out! He's got a gun," would tragedy have been averted? Would she be alive today?

"Yes?" said Peter. "What about Edwina?"

"I suppose at first she thought this was a stroke of good fortune, because Sonnet was acquainted with the embezzler. She may even have called him by name. But instead, the encounter was Sonnet's misfortune because the embezzler was determined to get rid of Edwina."

"Why then?" Peter demanded. "If he'd been paying her for years, wouldn't he be more likely to go on paying her?"

"The situation had changed. Edwina was getting old and senile. He probably felt he couldn't rely on her silence anymore, and he knew about her heart condition. He knew she didn't have long to live, and he decided it should be relatively easy to speed things along. He must've thought it through a hundred times, and when Sonnet showed up, he didn't hesitate. He'd already tipped his hand. If he'd backed out then, Edwina would've gone to the police, and a man in his position couldn't afford that. He had to carry out his plan. But he couldn't leave a witness behind. He realized no one must know about his meeting with Edwina. There must be nothing suspicious about her death, which meant he had to get rid of Sonnet, too, so he forced her to go with them. And that's where he got lucky, because Sonnet was on her way to a business lunch. She was wearing dark glasses and she'd tied a scarf around her head—a red, silk-jacquard Giorgio scarf she'd borrowed from the set—so when they left the shopping center, they made it to his car without anyone recognizing her."

"And then he drove to Edwina's— No, wait a minute." Peter strode to the windows. "He couldn't drive the car and keep the gun trained on both of them. The minute she wasn't covered, Sonnet would've tried to escape. But he couldn't shoot her while they were in the parking lot. It'd be too noisy, too likely to attract attention. So he must've subdued her somehow, maybe knocked her out."

"Maybe," said Jenny. "But my guess is, he made Edwina tie her up before they left the mall. Only he hadn't planned on a second hostage. He had to improvise, so he used his belt to bind her hands and the scarf for her feet, and when they got to the duplex, he ordered Edwina to untie Sonnet's feet until he got her inside.''

Peter turned from the windows to look at Jenny. "That's when the scarf changed hands, but what about the purse?"

"Edwina could have left it at the mall or in the embezzler's car. In the excitement, he didn't notice...."

Jenny paused. Visualizing what must have happened when they arrived at Sutter Court, she swallowed to ease the tightness in her throat. "On a holiday weekend, most of the neighbors aren't home, but I think, to be on the safe side, he parked on the next street over and brought them in the back way. By then, Edwina must have been terrified, but once they got to her apartment, all he had to do was wait for her to die and figure out how to deal with Sonnet."

"He also had to make a clean getaway," Peter added. "How the devil do you suppose he managed that, with you next door keeping an eye on the place?"

"That part was simple. He created a diversion. And all it took was a phone call from a friend." Jenny's eyes shied away from Peter's as she remembered the call she had received that fateful, fatal Saturday afternoon.

At the time it had seemed innocent, mere happenstance, an impromptu invitation to a dinner party in honor of Hal Joyce. But the call had come through about two o'clock, while she had been anticipating Peter's arrival.

While Edwina lay dead in the hallway of her apartment.

While the man who killed her hung up her sweater and shopping bag and planted an empty pillbox in her hand and plotted how he would dispose of the only witness to his crime.

While Sonnet Cole pleaded for her life.

"Trust no one," Gareth Spaulding had said. For most of his adult life, his actions had been guided by that rule.

In the months before his death, while he was working on the exposé of Judge Eaton, Gareth had been so cautious, he hadn't even trusted Jenny with his address.

And Sonnet was equally guarded, equally bitter, equally practiced at brinkmanship, and fond of living on the edge. In the last few weeks, she had filed suit against her parents, fired her agent, fought with her producer, upstaged her costars, treated her best friend shabbily, ignored her sister and threatened to walk off the set.

And where had her lack of faith gotten her?

Most likely the same place it had gotten Gareth.

Dead.

That was the irony.

Mistrust required too much energy. It was emotionally draining. It guaranteed loneliness, but it didn't guarantee safety. It made no sense to live that way. Not to Jenny.

She had trusted the embezzler. He was personable, outgoing, the essence of charm. The idea that his congenial exterior disguised a murderer seemed absurd.

But in the small hours of this morning, she had recalled one small detail, and that recollection had revealed him for what he was.

He couldn't tell pimentos from olives. He'd said, "They both look brown to me." Just as Sonnet's red scarf would have looked brown and would not have seemed out of place in the pocket of Edwina's sweater.

Reed Vandiver was color blind. He was blind in so many ways. He couldn't tell red from green, right from wrong, good from evil.

He'd seen embezzlement as a shortcut to wealth. He'd seen a good and decent man as a way to hide his crime. He'd seen a sick old woman as a threat. He'd seen a talented young actress as an obstacle.

And he saw me, Jenny realized, *as a means to an end. I provided a way for him to keep tabs on Edwina Farber.*

"This friend," Peter said, "the one who called you. Do you want to tell me who it was?"

"It was Eve," Jenny answered. "But I don't think she knew what Reed was up to. All he'd have had to do was drop a hint that she call me, and Eve would've done it. She'd do anything he suggested—or almost anything. She's always been anxious to please him."

Even now, when she was convinced of Reed Vandiver's guilt, to suspect Eve of being a willing accomplice seemed a betrayal. How could she doubt a woman who had offered her friendship at a time when she'd needed it most?

Reed used her, Jenny thought. *Just as he used me.*

She felt outraged at his duplicity.

She felt ashamed of her own naiveté.

She felt conscience stricken, as if a share of responsibility for Edwina's death, for Sonnet's death, should be hers.

Part of her hoped Peter would disagree with the conclusions she had drawn. If he didn't agree, that would be a kind of absolution.

But, oh, God! What if he did?

Chapter Fourteen

Peter, as usual, kept her guessing.

The first thing he did was reach for the telephone and place calls to Gus McAvoy and Hal Joyce, neither of whom was in. He left his name and phone number and a message for Joyce to call him back, and told Jenny he'd try to reach Gus again later.

"I want to hear his reaction to your story as soon as possible," Peter explained.

Jenny might have followed up on that if she had been fully functional, but she hadn't slept in thirty hours, and now that she had confessed her suspicions, she felt unburdened, lighter than air, almost dizzy with relief.

She wondered if her reconstruction of events seemed as logical to Peter as it did to her. She wanted to ask if he believed her, but her tongue felt thick. An odd spinning sensation filled her head, as if the room were swimming about her. It was all she could do to drag herself from the chair to the sofa that lined one wall of the office.

She sprawled on the sofa, using her arm as a pillow. The leather cushion cover felt soothingly cool against her skin.

Peter was lounging in his swivel chair with his feet on the edge of his desk, amending the notes he'd made on a legal pad. When she looked at him, she saw him through a haze of exhaustion. The sunlight streaming through the windows at his back hurt her eyes. They refused to focus, and she closed them.

"I'll just rest here for a minute," she said.

"Sure, honey. You do that."

Peter's voice seemed distant, worlds away. She felt herself floating, drifting. Finally, she slept, but her sleep was fitful, broken by dreams.

She dreamed she was searching a deserted old house, going from room to room, and when she came to one particular room, she was filled with sudden panic. No matter how hard she tried, she couldn't make herself open the door and confront whatever terror waited inside.

She dreamed that Reed Vandiver was wearing a mask, and when he removed it, there was another mask...and another...and another...and another...each more frightening than the one before. And when he took off the final mask, she saw that he had become a monster.

She dreamed she was in the Vandivers' garden, helping Eve cut a bouquet of roses when, for no apparent reason, Eve plunged into a bed of crimson hybrids and began clipping all the blossoms from every bush she passed, leaving Jenny to pick up the flowers.

"My shears need sharpening," Eve complained. "These stems aren't long enough."

Careless of the thorns, she began uprooting bushes and casting them aside, until the ground was pockmarked and cratered, littered with mangled plants.

"You're killing them!" Jenny cried.

"Never mind," said Eve. "They're only roses."

But they weren't.

Blood was oozing from the cut surfaces of the stems, gushing from the soil where the roots had been torn out. The craters in the earth resembled open wounds.

"Stop!" Jenny cried. "Please, Eve. I'm begging you."

"Very well, since you're so squeamish, but I must have one more."

Before Jenny could protest, Eve hacked off a candy-apple red rosebud that was just coming into bloom.

"There now, silly. Didn't hurt a bit. And isn't this a lovely specimen?" Eve fondled the bud with a blood-smeared hand, then lifted it to her nose. "Mmm, it smells like jasmine."

Horrified, Jenny sought escape. She tried to run away from Eve, but before she had taken a half-dozen steps, the ground turned to quicksand beneath her feet. She heard taunting laughter and sensed that Eve was following her. She felt a hand on her shoulder and tried to fight it off—

"Jenny. Wake up, honey. Time to go."

She woke with a start to twilight, and Peter's face above her and the reassuring knowledge that the hand on her shoulder was his. She sat up, groggy and slightly disoriented, and wound her arms about his middle, hugging him close while the terrors of the nightmare faded.

"I was having a bad dream," she said by way of explanation.

Peter kissed the back of her neck and cradled her cheek in the hollow of his shoulder. "Want to tell me about it?"

She shook her head, assessing her surroundings. She noted an overflowing wastebasket, a pair of club chairs, shelves of books and athletic trophies, and in a circle of lamplight, a heavy oak desk.

Beyond the desk, tall windows framed a dusky sky.

Remembering where she was and why she had come there, she exhaled on a sigh. "What time is it?"

"A little after eight-thirty. I've been working in the conference room so I wouldn't disturb you."

She had slept eight hours, yet she didn't feel rested.

"Are you hungry?" Peter asked. "Want to get something to eat?"

His question caught her midyawn. "If you do," she answered. "After I pull myself together."

Peter helped her find her shoes and showed her to the ladies' room. She washed her face and combed her hair, straightened her clothes and put on some lipstick, and by the time they left the office, she felt more alert.

They walked to a steak house a block from the capitol; the night air helped revive her. While they waited for a table, she asked Peter if he'd gotten hold of Gus McAvoy.

"Yes, I did. I spoke to Hal Joyce, too."

"Any new developments?"

"One or two. Nothing that won't keep. Let's talk about it after dinner."

Peter expected an argument from Jenny, but got only an apathetic shrug, which he interpreted as a barometer of her mood. She was dry-eyed and stoic. She went through the motions and produced a smile for the waitress, but she showed little interest in the menu; even less in the food.

She was grieving, Peter realized, and the last thing he wanted to do was add to her distress. When they were finished with their entrées, he gave her a reluctant summary of Gus's report on Rickie Detweiler.

Jenny perked up when he told her Rickie had been traced to Petaluma. On a note of rising hope, she said, "Then it's possible Rickie's responsible for Sonnet's disappearance."

"It's possible," Peter agreed. "For a couple of hours this morning, I'd have said it was a sure thing."

"And now?"

Peter shifted uneasily in his chair. "It's beginning to look as if this thing with Rickie may be a coincidence."

"But Gus is still looking for him, isn't he?"

"Absolutely. If Rickie isn't guilty, he may have information we can use. Either way, it's important that we find him."

"You mean he might be a witness."

Peter nodded. "The operative who interviewed Mrs. Detweiler faxed us a picture of Rickie. Gus is going to show it around the Holiday Inn, and the police are actively investigating. There'll be plenty of manpower on the case, so we ought to find some sort of trail."

Jenny fidgeted with her coffee spoon. "When we find this trail, where do you think it will lead?"

"I don't know, Jenny. Offhand I'd say your guess is as good as mine." After a moment of silence, Peter admitted, "The truth is, your guess is the best thing we've got going for us. At first your story seemed farfetched, but everything else I've heard today supports it. Edwina's pocketbook, for instance. Gus checked with the bus line and the manager at the mall, and it turns out one of the maintenance people at Crossroads Plaza found the purse in the employee's lounge."

"Why wasn't it returned?"

"They didn't know who it belonged to till today. The billfold was gone, and so were the credit cards."

"Well, then, how did Gus know the purse belonged to Edwina?"

"Helene Thiebault identified it."

Jenny's coffee spoon clinked against the saucer. Peter covered her hand with his, stopping the clatter. He felt her despair as keenly as if it were his own, but he had one more piece of information to tell her about, and he was determined to get it over with. Jenny couldn't begin to cope with the facts until all of them were at her disposal.

"There's also the matter of the missing scarf. It's been recovered. A busboy at the Holiday Inn found it in his locker yesterday evening."

Jenny paled and turned her palm toward his.

"I'm sorry, honey," Peter said. "I know this is difficult for you, but there's a flaw in your theory I'd like to clear up. That scarf was physical evidence that connected Sonnet and

Edwina, and now, of course it's worthless. So I have to ask whether you told anyone else you recognized it.''

"No. Only you," Jenny answered in an anguished whisper, carefully averting her face.

"Then how the devil did Reed Vandiver find out about it so quickly?"

"Eve saw the videotape."

Peter let out a long, low whistle and signaled for the check. "That makes her a coconspirator."

"Yes, it does." Painful as this admission was, Jenny felt compelled to make it.

She respected loyalty. She prized objectivity. She valued honesty. But her affections were neither lightly given nor easily withdrawn, and a clear conscience was cold consolation for lost friendship.

It hurt to acknowledge that Eve's friendship had been an illusion, a will-o'-the-wisp.

It hurt even more to admit that she had been fooled by the illusion, so taken in by false friends and false hopes, she had overlooked the fact that only Eve could have realized the importance of the scarf; its timely recovery implied that she was a willing accomplice to her husband's crimes. That she had been all along.

As they left the steak house, Jenny wondered how Reed had gone about conning Eve into becoming an accessory to murder. Had he begun by asking her to make small concessions, to fudge on the expense account, tell little white lies? Had petty misdemeanors led to major offenses? Had he worn down her resistance, day by day, year by year?

And why hadn't Eve seen how unscrupulous Reed was? Was she afraid he would leave her if she didn't accede to his demands? Did she love him so much, need him so desperately that she would do anything he asked?

Like Felicia, Jenny realized. It occurred to her there were certain parallels between these two women. Both had loved not wisely but too well; both had forfeited the ability to think for themselves.

Was loss of self-reliance one of the dangers of love? If so, it seemed an awful price to pay.

During the walk to the parking ramp adjacent to Peter's law office, Jenny considered his request that she move to Sacramento. If she went along with him, if she relocated, would she be taking the first step toward losing her own independence?

Preoccupied with these questions, Jenny waited in her car while Peter retrieved his, then followed him through town, driving by rote.

You're overreacting, part of her said. *Peter isn't Reed, and he jolly well isn't Jaime de Silva.* But another part, the cautious, self-protective part, wondered what Peter would demand of her next.

They had crossed the American River and arrived at the high rise that housed Peter's condo before Jenny could come up with an answer.

She felt caged in, riding the elevator to Peter's floor, edgy and ill at ease as he hurried her along the corridor, and when he unlocked the door and urged her inside, she moved slowly, warily, as if she were walking into a lion's den. In the living room, while he fixed a nightcap, she wandered about getting her bearings, noticing the personal touches he had added.

The last time she'd stayed with Peter, his place had been gray and white, glass and steel, high-tech and sterile. In the year since then he had filled the barren spaces around the modular sofa with art-deco *torchères* and a low, teak table shaped like an artist's palette. A mound of floor cushions in bright orange and chrome yellow provided accents of color, and woven wall hangings echoed the sharp citrus shades.

And then there were the neon cacti she had heard about. Three of them in varying sizes, arranged to give the impression they were vanishing into infinity.

"You're smiling," said Peter, coming up beside her. "That must mean you like 'em."

Head tipped to one side, Jenny studied the blank space near the top of the wall. "I was thinking what you need now is a neon desert."

"What I need is an oasis. I've got my eye on this really neat waterfall."

"And maybe some tiny date palms?"

Peter laughed, and she laughed with him, willing herself to relax. "This looks refreshing," she remarked, accepting the drink he'd prepared.

"It's my specialty. Light on the gin, heavy on the tonic, twist of lime and lots of ice."

They clinked glasses and sipped their drinks.

Peter glanced toward the sliding doors that occupied one wall. "It's nice on the balcony this time of night. Why don't we sit out there?"

"I'd like that," Jenny murmured.

It was peaceful outdoors, and balmy. The sweet summer breeze touched her skin as softly as a lover's caress. Three stories below, the American River flowed into the darkness, smooth as black satin and as silent. The lights from the marina across the channel made gleaming pathways on the surface of the water.

Jenny stood at the balcony railing, entranced by the view. Peter sat in a lounger behind her. She could feel him watching her. There was an expectant quality about his silence, but neither of them spoke until the tranquility of the night had worked its magic.

She lifted her face toward the sky, letting the breeze ruffle her hair. "It's really lovely here," she said quietly. "Even nicer than I remembered."

"There's a vacancy on four," Peter answered. "They've got the keys in the office, if you're interested in seeing it this weekend."

"I'm tempted," she said, "but I don't know how practical that would be. Just now we're in the first flush of romance and everything's wonderful, but what if it doesn't last? A few months down the road, if either of us decides to call it quits, I don't imagine you'd want me living right on top of you."

"I can't figure you out, Jenny. Are you saying you're not sure of your feelings for me?"

"No, I'm not saying that. The truth is, I care for you more than I've ever cared for anyone else." *More than I should. More than I want to.* Her feelings for him ran so deep, they were frightening.

"I feel the same way about you," Peter replied gruffly, as if he'd read her thoughts. "So what's the problem?"

"Feelings change, Peter."

"Mine won't."

"What if you meet somebody new?"

"There are no guarantees, Jenny. All I can tell you is, I played the field last year. I met quite a few women—and compared 'em all to you. I tried my damnedest to forget you, honey. It didn't work. I couldn't get you out of my mind."

Moved by his declaration, she turned to look at him. "But there must be lots of things about me you'd like to change."

"No," he said without hesitation. "Just your address."

And the length of my hair. "Are you certain that's all?"

"That's it, except I wish you weren't so far away." Peter leaned forward and set his glass on the deck, then extended his hands toward her. "Come here, Jenny."

Powerless to resist, she put her hands in his and let him pull her down beside him.

"There, now. That's more like it." He sighed and folded her close. "I've been wanting to kiss you all day."

As his lips claimed hers, Jenny acknowledged that she, too, had wanted this, and as his kiss deepened, passion replaced worry. Desire overcame doubt, and her heart overruled her head.

Being with Peter, kissing him, holding him in her arms, might be the closest she would ever get to heaven. It might be the most she would ever know of love.

For the moment, that seemed enough.

ON FRIDAY, WHILE PETER WAS at the office, Jenny prepared a list of questions for Felicia Darien. At eleven o'clock Saturday morning, notebook and pen in hand, she was standing at the front door of Felicia's house with a serious case of the jitters. Although she had done her homework, this was the last place she wanted to be.

She rang the doorbell and heard chimes pealing inside. The door was opened almost immediately by a woman who was belting a thigh-length kimono over a maillot-style bathing suit. Instead of shoes, she wore rope-soled flip-flops, and her long, slender legs were bare.

Tanned, fit and clear-eyed, this woman bore little resemblance to the Felicia Jenny had met last summer, and despite Peter's warning, Jenny was astonished.

"How delightful to see you again!" Felicia said.

Jenny glanced down at her own blouse and skirt. She felt gauche and overdressed. "Am I early?"

"No, you're precisely on time. It's I who's running late— or I should say swimming late. I meant to shower and change before you got here, but I lost track of the time." Laughing, Felicia stood aside and beckoned Jenny to come in. "Would you prefer to sit in the living room or out by the pool?"

"The pool's fine."

"Marvelous!" Smiling at Jenny over her shoulder, Felicia confided, "In recent months I've become a devout sun worshiper."

"It seems to agree with you."

"Thank you, Jennifer. It's sweet of you to say so."

Felicia's faint British accent had a musical lilt. There was a spring in her step as she led the way to the kitchen, where she collected drinking glasses and a carafe of iced tea.

"Now then, if you'll just bring that tray of cookies, we'll be all set."

Jenny tucked her notebook into her carryall, gathered up the plate of cookies and followed the older woman through the patio door to poolside.

"I hope you like chocolate chips," Felicia said.

"They're my favorite," Jenny answered, "but you shouldn't have gone to all this trouble."

"It's no trouble, I assure you. On the contrary, it's a pleasure. I seldom have company, you see. Not because I've become a hermit, but because my schedule is so full."

"What are you doing these days?"

"I'm going for my master's in psychology at Sac State, and working as an AODA—that's alcohol and other drug abuse—counselor. Between classes and studying and my thirty hours a week at the rehabilitation center, I'm not often home."

Jenny slung the shoulder strap of her bag over the back of a chair, admiring the graceful economy of Felicia's movements as she arranged the refreshments on a glass-topped table and poured the tea.

"Help yourself to the cookies," she invited. "Heaven knows I don't need the calories. Not till I get rid of my spare tire." As proof that her figure could stand improvement, she removed her robe to display the slight thickening of her waistline. "When I was first released from detox, meals were the one thing I looked forward to. After years of not eating properly, I was starved for nutrients and I went overboard with food, till one day, about six weeks into treatment, I got on the scales and discovered I'd gained twenty pounds—none of it in the right places!''

"That's not unusual, is it?"

"Far from it. Recovering alcoholics are notorious for eating everything but the pattern on the dishes, and of course, a balanced diet is essential to recovery. But carried to excess, overeating can be a symptom that you're replacing one addiction with another." Felicia lifted one shoulder in a shrug. "At any rate, these days I'm on a health kick. Sleep, fresh air and exercise, work and play, a balanced diet— But I try not to be a fanatic about it. Everything in moderation, that's the secret."

"Sounds as if you've got your life in order," Jenny observed.

"It's about time, wouldn't you say? If I'd gone on the wagon at twenty-six rather than forty-six, things might have worked out very differently."

"With Max, you mean?"

"Yes, and with Jaime."

Jenny opened the notebook and uncapped her pen. "It can't have been easy for you."

"No, but I'm through blaming the things that happened to me in Santa Marta for the choices I've made since then. An alcoholic will seize any excuse to take a drink."

Felicia removed a bottle of sunscreen from the pocket of her robe, then circled the table and sat at the front of a chaise, applying the lotion to her arms and shoulders.

"That's something it took me a long time to learn, and even longer to confront," she continued with disarming candor. "It's something Max never understood. He thought I drank to escape unhappy memories, and Jaime thought I was punishing myself."

"So did I," said Jenny.

"You were wrong," said Felicia, "but I went along with the myth until I hit bottom. Then, like it or not, I came face-to-face with the truth that the reason I drank is simply because I'm an alcoholic."

"It must've taken a good deal of courage to admit that."

"Perhaps, but it wasn't half as difficult as doing something about it." Felicia smoothed a dab of sunscreen across the bridge of her nose. "To this day, I don't know where I found the strength to sign myself into the hospital. In a way, Jennifer, I have you to thank for that."

"Me? What did I do?"

"You insisted on investigating Gareth's death and in the process, you brought things to a head. Do you remember the night I asked Peter and you to come to dinner?"

Jenny nodded. "Peter told me Jaime was behind the invitation. He said it was Jaime's way of luring us into the open."

"Did Peter also tell you that Jaime gave me his promise that neither of you would be harmed? His last words to me were, 'No one's going to get hurt but Eaton.'"

Again, Jenny nodded. "What surprised me is that you'd believe him."

"I had no reason not to. In all the years I'd known Jaime, he'd never lied to me before. I sensed he wasn't telling the whole truth, but I didn't know what he was up to till Peter came by to see his uncle and me, just after the explosion."

Felicia slanted a glance toward Jenny, then dropped her gaze to the bottle of sunscreen and replaced the cap with more care than was necessary.

"I was sober when Peter arrived that night. I hadn't had a drink for two days, and when Peter told us Jaime was dead, it was as if my worst nightmare had come true. I can still see the expression on Max's face when he realized he'd been harboring a fugitive and that I'd kept Jaime's identity a secret. I can still hear the fury in his voice when he accused me of betraying him, of being unfaithful. I'd never seen anyone so angry, Jennifer. I'd wounded him so badly. Hurt his pride. I knew our marriage was over and that Max would never forgive me." Felicia raised her head and regarded Jenny, her eyes dark with pain. "I wonder if you can guess how I reacted."

Jenny wanted to look away, and found she couldn't. "I suppose you wanted a drink."

"Yes, but I didn't take one. Gareth was dead. Jaime was dead. And I was partially responsible. I'd disillusioned Max. I'd jeopardized Peter's safety, and yours, as well. I'd ruined everything I cared about, and I couldn't fool myself any longer. I had to bring something positive out of all the destruction, and the only way I could do that was to stay sober. So I checked into the hospital. That was over a year ago, and I still haven't had that drink. I'm proud of that, because it hasn't been easy. And now I take life, and sobriety, one day at a time. I hope, eventually, to make peace with the past."

"Does it bother you to talk about Jaime?"

"No," said Felicia. "It's therapeutic. If anything I say increases your understanding, if I can make some contribution to your book, that will be my memorial to him."

"You feel he deserves a memorial?"

"Yes. Oh, yes. However misguided his methods, Jaime de Silva was a man of high ideals."

"He killed my father!"

"He also killed himself."

Jenny frowned. "Are you saying he killed himself because he'd killed my father?"

"I'm saying it's possible, Jennifer. Jaime and Gareth were friends, but more important, they were allies. The two of them made a pact to get Eaton, no matter what the cost, even if it meant they had to sacrifice their lives."

"That doesn't justify murder."

"No, naturally it doesn't. Jaime would have been the last person to claim that it did. But his death may have been intended as expiation."

Jenny's frown deepened. "That would imply a capacity for remorse, and I don't think he felt the least bit guilty. I don't think he felt *anything*."

"May I ask on what you base that opinion?"

"People who knew him, the articles I've read—"

"Don't be misled by the public image," Felicia broke in. "Jaime didn't display his emotions, but that doesn't mean he had none. He was deeply sympathetic with the Santa Martans."

"Not according to the students I've talked to."

"Where did you find these students?"

"AT U.C., Berkeley."

"Then they represent the one percent of Santa Martans who own ninety-five percent of the island. They're the 'haves,' Jennifer. The privileged class. You can't expect them to be unbiased about the man who would have forced them to share the wealth."

"I took that into consideration," Jennifer replied.

"Did you consider making a trip to Santa Marta to speak to the peasants? Because that's what you'll have to do if you want more than propaganda."

Jennifer responded to this observation with a skeptical shake of her head.

"Listen," said Felicia with sudden intensity, "back in the early seventies, the majority of Santa Martans looked upon Jaime de Silva as a sort of latter-day Robin Hood. He lived in the mountains under conditions more primitive than you can imagine. Sanitation was nonexistent, illiteracy endemic, and the infant mortality rate was a national disgrace. There were no schools, no hospitals or clinics. At times, even food was scarce. The only thing there was plenty of was poverty. The peasants who lived in the region had almost no resources. They were accustomed to being exploited by the landowners and neglected by the government, yet Jaime treated them with dignity. He advocated human rights, and he talked about decent housing and better roads and public education and health care—things we take for granted in this country. He agitated for reforms, for fairness and equality—revolutionary ideas to the Santa Martans! He became the peasants' spokesman. He helped organize protests, and when the Mercado regime sent in the militia, Jaime taught the peasants to fight. He gave them pride and discipline, encouragement, hope—"

"What did he get in return?"

"Nothing," said Felicia. "He asked for nothing."

"He didn't want power?"

"No, Jennifer, he didn't. And this was the most revolutionary thing of all. It's what made him dangerous to his fellow Librists."

"I find it hard to believe he was so altruistic."

"Believe it," said Felicia. "He was. But nowadays it's easy to question his motives. I'd wager the students you talked to described him as a power-hungry subversive who only pretended to care about the welfare of the people, but I'm here to tell you, if the popular rebellion had succeeded, Jaime de Silva would be regarded as a hero."

Chapter Fifteen

Success led to heroism; failure to infamy.

There might be an angle in that.

And the notion that Jaime had condemned himself to death for the murder of her father came as something of a revelation.

But with these exceptions, Jennifer took the things Felicia told her about Jaime de Silva with a grain of salt.

At Peter's insistence, on Saturday afternoon she took a look at the condo on the floor above his. The unit was memorable for its views of the river, and far too modern for Jenny's taste. She said as much to Peter, but she didn't tell him that, even if she'd loved the place, she wouldn't have made an offer.

That night, after a telephone conference with Gus McAvoy, Peter brought up the subject of the Vandivers.

"The one thing we've got going for us is that Reed doesn't know we're on to him," he told Jenny. "It'd be a big help if you could carry on as if nothing's changed."

"I'll do my best," Jenny promised, "but I'm not much of an actress."

Peter muttered something beneath his breath that sounded suspiciously like, "I noticed."

Did he know she was stalling? Did he know that, although there was no question in her mind what she wanted to do, she was nowhere near a decision about moving to Sacramento, and that she was not at all certain she ever would be?

For the rest of the evening, she studied him covertly, looking for signs that he was upset, but if Peter was disappointed, he gave nothing away. He talked with her easily and laughed readily. On Sunday, when the time came to say goodbye, he gave her a farewell kiss that warmed her from head to toe and kept her heart skipping all the way back to Santa Rosa.

She missed Peter that night.

The house was unbearably quiet and, after being closed up all weekend, stagnant and hot. The air conditioner soon took care of the temperature, but it didn't fill the silence.

Peter's calla lilies had withered, but she couldn't bring herself to throw them out.

She went through three days' accumulation of mail, unpacked her suitcase and started a load of wash, then showered and got into a sleeveless cotton nightshirt. She put a frozen dinner in the microwave and ate a solitary supper, with a letter from Phyllis for company. She was transferring her laundry from the washing machine to the dryer when Peter phoned.

"Just wanted to make sure you made it home okay," he said.

Touched by his concern, she replied that she was fine; the drive from Sacramento had been uneventful. Neither of them had much else to say, but before Jenny hung up, she asked Peter to let her know the minute Gus McAvoy unearthed any new information.

"Sure thing," Peter agreed. "If Gus learns anything, you'll be the first one I call. I'll be in touch later this week, either way."

Jenny said she'd look forward to hearing from him, and instead of saying "good night," Peter wished her "sweet dreams."

By the time she put the laundry away, it was eleven-fifteen. She checked the locks and switched off the lights, preparing to turn in. She was yawning as she folded back the covers, but when the room was dark, she lay in bed unable to fall asleep.

She thought about issues Felicia had raised; and about success and failure.

Last summer, she remembered, Peter had told her, "Life's a gamble, but it's not winning or losing that matters. It's how you play the game. The clock is running, and there are no time-outs. Whatever you're doing at any given minute might be the last thing you'll ever do, so you'd better make the most of it."

Jenny envied Peter's adventurous spirit, his spontaneity, his openness to new experiences. She wished she had the tiniest fraction of his zest for life.

If he wanted something, he didn't mess around. He let the devil take the hindmost and went for his goal wholeheartedly. If he encountered an obstacle along the way, he made corrections and took another tack.

Unlike her, Peter didn't waste time second-guessing his choices. He didn't equate retreat with defeat. He didn't weigh the odds, count the costs, dwell on the worst-possible consequences. He didn't try to plan for every contingency. He wasn't plagued by doubt, nor was he saddled with fear that a less-than-stellar performance would leave him out in the cold. The possibility that he might be outdistanced never entered his mind. He gave an endeavor his best shot, and if he made a mistake, so be it. He was human, therefore entitled to his share of goofs.

His flexibility gave him the advantage of confidence, not to mention a head start. He'd be racing across the finish line while she was stuck at the gate, plotting her first move and thinking of all sorts of reasons she shouldn't make it.

How could she overcome the habits of a lifetime? It was her nature to be cautious, just as it was Peter's nature to throw caution to the winds. Thinking either of them would change was about as realistic as believing a leopard could change its spots.

But sooner or later, Peter was bound to become impatient....

Jenny hopped out of bed and left her room. She didn't want to think about what would happen when Peter got tired of waiting for her to make up her mind.

In the living room, she turned on a lamp and curled up on the sofa with an Elmore Leonard novel. Somewhere in the middle of chapter two, her eyelids started to droop. She was almost asleep when it occurred to her, if she lived in Sacramento, she could be with Peter right now.

Jolted awake by this truant thought, she grabbed the remote control from the coffee table and turned on the TV. She watched the last few minutes of the weekend sports roundup and the beginning of a movie. Alfred Hitchcock's *The Birds*. Tippi Hedren had delivered the lovebirds to Rod Taylor's kid sister and was in her skiff, racing Rod's car back to Bodega Bay, when Jenny finally dozed off.

She wound up sleeping on the sofa all night, with the TV tuned low to fill the silence.

The next morning she plunged into work on her manuscript. She didn't come up for air till Wednesday, when Betty phoned to invite her to lunch.

"I tried to reach you last weekend," Betty said.

"I was in Sacramento," Jenny replied, and abruptly changed the subject. "Where would you like to eat?"

"I'm in the mood for a burger."

They met at McDonald's, and over Big Macs and fries Betty inquired about Peter.

"He's fine," Jenny answered. She might've gotten away with this generic response if she hadn't blushed.

"Something's up," Betty remarked. "If you feel like talking about it, I'd be happy to listen."

Jenny hid behind her napkin on the pretext of wiping her mouth. "He wants me to move to Sacramento."

Betty grinned. "He's a fast worker. I like that in a man. But I guess I should ask what you want."

"I want to be with him, Betty. I want that more than I can tell you."

"If you feel that way, what's stopping you?"

Jenny fidgeted with her soft-drink straw. "You know me—I get into a certain routine and I stick to it. Maybe I'm too complacent. Maybe I'm too conservative—"

"Or maybe you're in a rut?"

"Maybe I am, but it's my rut and I'm comfortable with it. Peter, on the other hand, thrives on change. He goes through life like he's supercharged, and I can't keep up with that kind of pace. I have to take things slowly. I need the time to adjust. Not only that, but he's into sports, and I'm not athletic. I prefer maple and chintz and Grandma Moses, and he has neon cacti all over one wall of his living room."

"You're joking," said Betty.

"No, I'm not. I swear it. Even if I wanted to, I couldn't make up something like that. The truth is, I can't imagine Peter living in a world without Lycra."

"I hear what you're saying, Jenny. You and Peter are opposites. He's modern, you're traditional. He's an optimist, you're a pessimist—"

"Yes, that, too."

"And let us not forget that he's a man and you're a woman. To which I have the definitive response." Betty waved a French fry as if it were a banner. *"Vive la différence!"*

Jenny leaned across the table, earnest and intent. "I'm serious, Betty. Please don't tease."

"What makes you think I'm teasing? You pointed out a number of ways in which you and Peter are poles apart, and all I've done is agree. But I honestly don't see your problem."

"What if it turns out we're incompatible? What if it doesn't last?"

"I'm no authority on romance, Jenny, but there's one thing I can promise you. Your relationship with Peter almost certainly won't last if you're not willing to compromise."

"I'm willing," Jenny declared. "I told you I want to be with him, and I do. But I'm aware that this concession won't be the last. If I move to Sacramento, someday Peter will ask me to compromise about something else, and I can't help wondering where it will end. What happens if he asks me to do something I can't? What if he expects more than I can give?"

Betty dunked a French fry in ketchup and popped it in her mouth. "Exactly what is it you're afraid of, Jenny? That you'll get hurt? That you'll hurt Peter? That you'll lose him? That you'll lose your identity? Or that you don't have what it takes to sustain a relationship?"

"All of the above," Jenny said.

"Well, if it's safety you're after, you'd better not fall in love."

"What if it's too late for that?"

Betty subjected her to a searching glance. "In that case, your choices are limited to the frying pan or the fire. You can either move to Sacramento and be prepared to take your lumps, or stay in Santa Rosa and kiss any chance for a future with Peter goodbye. Of course, if you stay here, you'll be settling for quite a bit less than you want. It seems to me that would be the real loss, but then, I'm prejudiced.

The older I get, the more I find that my deepest regrets are for the things I didn't do."

Jenny's smile was bittersweet. "There's no simple solution, is there?"

"I wouldn't lose any sleep over it," Betty said. "If it's any comfort, there are lots of women who'd give five years off their lives to be in your shoes."

ALTHOUGH HER TALK WITH Betty didn't yield much in the way of practical advice, it helped ease Jenny's mind. Instead of anticipating trouble that might never develop, she decided to adopt a wait-and-see attitude. One way or another, when the time came to make a decision, she would *know* what she had to do.

That afternoon she applied her new laid-back philosophy to her writing, and it led to a breakthrough of sorts.

There were no simple solutions to Jaime de Silva, either. She didn't understand him. She doubted she ever would. Anyone who could murder a friend, however lofty his purpose, had to be cold and unfeeling, an egomaniac who considered himself above the law. How could she understand a man like that?

But in reviewing her notes of Felicia's interview, Jenny realized her mistake had been writing as if she knew what drove de Silva. That pretense dulled the edges of his character.

If she could remain detached, if she presented de Silva's actions clinically, unemotionally, without letting her personal value judgments creep in, wouldn't the facts speak for themselves? Wouldn't de Silva's nature be self-evident? Wouldn't understatement heighten the drama and objectivity make the book more passionate? More powerful?

For the first time in weeks, Jenny felt a revival of interest in the manuscript. She worked through dinner, and by the time she quit for the night, she had actually made some progress. Not much, it was true, a few lines short of two pages, but that was better than nothing.

She was back at the keyboard at eight the following morning. By five-thirty that afternoon, she had written another four pages. If she could keep going at this rate, she might meet the deadline.

She had an early supper and was back at work at seventhirty that evening, when Peter phoned.

"How's the writing?" he asked.

"Not bad," she replied, settling into a corner of the sofa. "I think I'm beginning to get a handle on this beast."

"That's great," said Peter. "Happy to hear it."

Jenny kicked off her shoes and rested her feet on the coffee table, scowling because Peter didn't sound the least bit happy. "You sound different." *Tired,* she thought, *and more than a little grumpy.*

"Yeah? Well, I'm trying out a cellular phone to see how I like it. I've been thinking of getting one for my car."

"Where are you?"

"Headed east on I-80, on my way out of San Francisco. I spent most of the day at St. Francis Hospital."

"H-hospital?" she stammered. "Are you all right?"

"Good as can be expected under the circumstances."

Her heart catapulted into her throat. "Peter, are you sick? Have you been in an accident?"

"No, nothing like that. I was strictly a visitor—" A familiar voice at the other end of the line called Peter's name. "Hang on a sec," he said to Jenny. There was a muffled exchange, as if Peter had covered the mouthpiece with his hand. In less than a minute, he was back.

"Was that Gus McAvoy?" she asked.

"It was," said Peter. "I just dropped him off at his car. He located—"

"Sonnet!" Jenny cried, breathless with excitement. "You found Sonnet."

"No. It's Rickie Detweiler. Gus traced him to the hospital last night."

"And you drove over to question him?"

"Not directly. His doctor wouldn't permit that."

"Why? What's wrong with him?"

"He's hallucinating, Jenny. He abandoned his car on the Golden Gate Bridge, and when the police checked it out, they found the vents had been stuffed with bread. When they asked Rickie about it, he said he had to do that to keep the spiders out. He was calm enough, but they figured they ought to have him examined, and as soon as he hit the emergency room, he freaked out and started screaming that the wolf was going to get him, so the resident on duty in the E.R. admitted him to the psychiatric service."

Jenny swung her feet to the floor. "When did all this happen?"

"Tuesday morning. By the time Gus saw him, he was confined to what they call the low-stimulus area of the ward. He was quieter, but still seeing spiders. He told the nurse who took his history he was being punished because he hadn't protected Red Riding Hood and her grandma from the wolf."

A chill of foreboding touched Jenny's spine. The fine hairs on her forearms stood on end. "Could Red Riding Hood be Sonnet?"

"Gus thought so, and from Rickie's description, grandma sounded like a ringer for Edwina. Anyway, going on the assumption that Rickie had witnessed a crime, I figured I ought to hear the whole story, so I drove over from Sacramento this morning, and after hours of negotiations and miles of red tape, I got permission to see him in the presence of his doctor."

"Was it worth it?" Jenny asked.

"The story fits."

"What about the wolf?"

"Reed Vandiver. Rickie identified his picture."

"That's it, then! We've got corroboration."

"Wrong!" said Peter. "What we've got is nothing. The consensus here is that Rickie's had an acute psychotic break, brought on either by schizo-affective disorder or d.t.'s. The staff'll know more in a couple of days after they've run more tests. But whatever the diagnosis, Rickie's identification won't stand up in court. A lousy defense attorney could discredit his testimony in about five minutes, and a good one would send the kid into mental meltdown."

"But Reed's guilty. You know he is."

"Sure I do, but there's a difference between knowing he's guilty and proving it." After a moment of silence, Peter erupted. "Dammit all, Jenny! That monster killed Edwina Farber. There's an excellent chance he killed Sonnet, and unless somebody comes up with hard evidence of what he's done, he's going to walk away from it all."

Chapter Sixteen

By the end of July, the media circus that surrounded Sonnet Cole's disappearance had run its course. Although the police had received countless tips that Sonnet had been sighted in locales ranging from Maine to California, none of the leads panned out. The investigating officers believed she was dead, and responsible newspeople shared that opinion.

The first week in August, the headlines were dominated by a plane crash in Iowa, the onslaught of drug-related violence in Colombia, the coal miners' strike in the Soviet Union. By the middle of the month, even the trade papers were burying articles about Sonnet in the back pages.

On August 17, amid speculation that *Foyle's Paradise* was about to be cancelled, Hal Joyce called a press conference and announced that production was going forward.

His prepared statement read, ''Reports of the show's demise are grossly exaggerated. This fall, *Foyle's Paradise* is going to be livelier than ever. We've got the best ensemble on TV, dynamite scripts and a couple of tricks up our sleeves. We'll be shooting on location in Santa Rosa at the end of the month, and we intend to kick off the new season on schedule.''

In a display of unity, the stars of *Foyle's Paradise* were on hand, and at the end of the question-and-answer period,

Joyce requested that they join him at the podium. He embraced Vanessa Wayne and Leo Prince, and after introducing them to the press, he said, "Also with us today is a very talented young lady who needs no introduction. Everyone knows who plays Peggy Foyle."

Flashbulbs exploded and cameras whirred as the young lady in question made her entrance. There was a collective gasp when the assembled reporters caught sight of her carrot-red hair and pixie face. She was tiny, especially by contrast with the mountainous Mr. Joyce, but her charisma, her energy, her thousand-watt smile, made her seem larger than life.

She said, "Hi, everybody. It's wonderful to be back—" She had no opportunity to deliver a longer speech. After those seven words, a wave of applause rocked the auditorium.

The moment was electric. It was ecstatic. It was touched by magic. It was captured on videotape and telecast coast to coast. The most poignant close-up was a still photograph that showed the actress smiling yet misty-eyed, waving at the camera, with her Medic-Alert bracelet easily visible.

This was the picture most favored by the wire services.

The Santa Rosa *Clarion* ran it in its afternoon edition. The *Los Angeles Times* ran it with a feature that debated whether the alleged abduction of the prominent young actress had been a hoax. In newspapers throughout California, editorials posed the question, "Is this news or the punch line of a publicity stunt?"

That evening Jenny phoned Eve Vandiver to ask what she thought of Sonnet's return. Eve said she didn't know what to make of it, and Jenny admitted she didn't, either.

"But you must have been expecting this," Eve replied.

"No," said Jenny. "I'm as surprised as you are."

"Didn't Peter take you into his confidence?"

"I haven't spoken to Peter for quite some time," Jenny answered stiffly. "We've both been so busy. You know how it is."

"I'm sorry to hear that. He's such an attractive man. Now that this business with Sonnet is over, you really ought to call him."

Jenny said, "Yes, perhaps I will."

In the days following Sonnet's appearance at the press conference, rumors began to circulate. The *National Tattler* insisted that she had been kidnapped by aliens from outer space. Various gossip columnists and TV correspondents, each of whom claimed to have the inside scoop, declared that Sonnet had eloped, that she had been on a secret mission for the government, that she had spent the month and a half she was missing in jail, that she had been hospitalized for major surgery.

On Monday, the twenty-first, Eve phoned Jenny. "I wondered," she inquired casually, as if it were of passing interest, "have you been in touch with Peter?"

"As a matter of fact, I talked to him last night."

"What did he have to say about these incredible stories?"

"Apparently there's some truth to the one about the hospital, but Sonnet didn't have surgery, and she was an inpatient for less than three weeks."

"Where was she the rest of the time?"

"That's still a mystery."

"She wouldn't tell anyone?"

"She can't, Eve. She has amnesia."

"*Amnesia?* Good heavens! What caused it?"

"Her doctors suspect some kind of trauma. I gather the poor little thing was in a frightful state when she was admitted, but her last clear memory is driving to Crossroads Plaza."

"That's it? She doesn't remember anything else?"

"Not till the day she wandered into the hospital in Crescent City."

"I don't get it," said Eve. "Crescent City's more than three hundred miles from here. It's practically on the Oregon border. How did she get all the way up there? And why didn't the hospital notify the authorities?"

"The police were informed on July twenty-second. So was her family."

"Did Peter know?"

"Yes, he did."

"Well, he must've known how worried you were. Why did he leave you in the dark?"

"He's her lawyer, Eve. It was privileged information. The hospital...the police...Sonnet's relatives...everyone concerned respected her right to privacy. As to how she got to Crescent City, no one knows the answer to that. It's another thing Sonnet can't recall. At least, not yet."

"Does that mean she'll regain her memory?"

"Her doctors are hopeful she will," said Jenny. "So far she's only remembered bits and pieces, but that's an encouraging sign. It may be a long, slow process. Then again, everything she's blanked out could come back to her all at once."

"How fascinating," Eve murmured, and then with some urgency, "Jenny, if you hear anything more about Sonnet, will you tell me right away?"

"Of course, Eve. That goes without saying."

After that conversation, Jenny prowled about the house, too wound up to sit still. When Peter phoned two hours later, she answered on the first ring.

"You shouldn't underestimate yourself," he said. "You're a much better actress than you think."

The release of tension made Jenny feel light-headed. She collapsed into a chair.

"She took the bait," Peter continued. "I just heard from Crescent City. About half an hour ago a woman who identified herself as a claims representative with Blue Cross called about Sonnet Cole's bill. The switchboard operator referred her to our friend, who kept her on hold while he checked his files for a signed release-of-information form. He then proceeded to confirm the dates of Sonnet's stay and answer all her questions." *So far, so good,* Jenny thought. She pulled in a calming breath. "Eve asked me to keep her informed."

"Then you won't have to invent excuses for calling her," said Peter. "That's great, honey! Really terrific. She's playing right into our hands."

For the rest of that week, Jenny passed along information to the Vandivers. On Tuesday she told Eve that Sonnet remembered leaving the shopping center with "an older woman." On Wednesday she reported that Sonnet recalled being forced into a car by a man. "It seems she may have been abducted, after all," Jenny said.

After a conspicuous silence, Eve inquired, "Does she remember what this man looked like?"

"No, but she has the feeling he was someone she'd met."

"Does she remember where he took her?"

"She says to a house somewhere in Santa Rosa. She can't describe the exact location, but wherever it was, the place was full of cats."

This set the stage for the tapes of Sonnet's voice Hal Joyce had spliced together. On Thursday, Jenny phoned the Vandivers at a time she had reason to believe they would not be home and ran the tape for their answering machine. The message was brief, an accusation and a warning.

"You won't get away with what you've done."

On Friday morning, Jenny paid a visit to the main branch of Citizens Bank. She was waiting in line to cash a check when Reed walked through the main entrance, into the lobby. He looked drawn, haggard, pale as death; his steps were unsteady as he approached.

"Good grief! You look awful," Jenny exclaimed without thinking.

Reed summed her up with a disparaging glance. "Thank you for those kind words, Jennifer. I might say the same about you."

"Sorry," she said. "The long hours I've been working don't seem to have helped my social graces any more than they've helped my appearance."

Reed's mouth twitched into a parody of a smile. "Forget it," he said. "All is forgiven." She smelled alcohol on his breath when he bent down to kiss her cheek. His lips were cold, his hands clammy. It was all she could do not to recoil from his touch.

"I've been working long hours, too," he said, "putting the finishing touches on the house for Hal Joyce's crew. Did Eve happen to mention they're due in town on Monday?"

"No, she didn't. Mostly we've talked about Sonnet."

"Ah, yes. Eve's told me about her miraculous recovery. Both of us are looking forward to seeing her again."

There was a sarcasm in Reed's tone, malice on his face, a mote of hostility in his eyes.

He's on to us, Jenny thought. *He knows what we're up to.*

Aware of the hazards in this game of cat-and-mouse, wondering who was the cat and who the mouse, she edged away from him. "I—I see a teller's available. I won't keep you any longer."

She wanted to escape, simply turn tail and run as fast as she could, as far as she could, but she sensed that Reed was watching her. To lull his suspicions, she concluded her business before she left the bank.

That evening she recorded another message from Sonnet on the Vandivers' answering machine. "Big shot," this one jeered. "You think you're clever. You probably think you can get away with murder, but you won't."

Later that night, when Peter phoned, Jenny said, "I'm frightened for Carla. Even though I know she isn't Sonnet, with that wig and the makeup and the way she's performing, she almost has me convinced she is."

"That's the general idea, isn't it? To convince Reed Vandiver that Sonnet survived his attempt to kill her? To play on his conscience, plant seeds of doubt in his mind? Isn't that what we planned?"

"Yes, but—"

"Nobody twisted Carla's arm, honey. She was Sonnet's friend. She's got a stake in this, just like the rest of us. She *wanted* to play this part. But believe me, it'll be all right. Everything's going like clockwork. We've been careful in choosing the details to string Reed along. I think we came up with specifics he believes only Sonnet could know. After the line you've been feeding him, and hearing those tapes, I think one look at Carla will send him over the edge."

"But what if he goes after her?"

"He won't get far. He's under surveillance, and Joyce has beefed up security. Carla has bodyguards with her constantly."

Jenny twisted the telephone cord between her fingers, envying Peter's confidence. "I wish it were over."

"I wish it were, too, for your sake. I know how rough this has been for you, but hang in there, Jenny, one more night. Gus and I will be with you first thing tomorrow. By this time Monday, Vandiver will be so damned scared, he'll make a break for it, and when he does, we'll be ready for him."

Will we? Jenny wondered. *How can we be sure?*

If the ruse succeeded, if they convinced Reed there was a remote possibility that Sonnet could have survived, he would be desperate. And the more desperate he became, the more dangerous he would be—and the more unpredictable.

How could they hope to foresee his reaction? He might do anything, go to any lengths to avoid a murder charge.

ON SATURDAY, IT BECAME apparent that the situation was as volatile as Jenny feared. At 7:10 that evening, the operative who was keeping track of the Vandivers' comings and goings notified Peter that the subjects had left their house. This was Peter's cue to leave the third message from Sonnet on the Vandivers' answering machine.

"I saw what you did to the old lady," this one taunted. "Why don't you confess and get it over with?"

At 9:43, the Vandivers returned home; an hour later, Gus McAvoy called. "Something's up," he told Peter. "Looks to me like this bird's had all he can take. He just left the house again, and he's headed north on Highway 12, drivin' the blue Mercedes."

"You on his tail?"

"Yeah, me and Joey and one of the local cops. But he's just a rookie, so we sure could use some help. We can't get too close or Vandiver'll spot us, and he's goin' like a bat outta hell. If he turns off on a secondary road, we're gonna lose him."

"I'm on my way."

Peter rang off and bolted for the door, with Jenny close behind. "This is it!" he shouted, slamming out of the house.

She broke into a trot, taking two steps for every one of his as he dashed for his car. "I'm coming with you," she declared.

Peter didn't argue. He didn't have time. He climbed behind the wheel and she piled in on the passenger's side.

"See if you can raise Gus," Peter said, "and if you do, keep the line open."

Jenny gripped the cellular phone with one hand and clung to the door handle with the other as Peter gunned the engine and the car shot out of the driveway. Seconds later, they were speeding toward the freeway.

"We'll take 101 to the Highway 12 exit," Peter said.

"That way's the quickest," she replied.

The convertible top had been removed, and the wind roared past her ears; strands of hair flew over her eyes. She shoved it back, anchoring it in place with spread fingers, while she dialed Gus's number. The investigator came on the line just as they swung onto the on ramp.

"That you, boss?"

"It's me," Jenny said. "What's happening?"

"Nothing's changed. We're playin' leapfrog with each other, keepin' Vandiver's taillights in sight, but there's no traffic to speak of. I'm afraid he'll spot us."

The Highway 12 exit sign whizzed by, a green-and-white blur overhead. The Maserati gained speed as Peter guided it through the steep, banking curve of the interchange. They ran the stop sign at the bottom of the slope, sailed over a bump, and careened through a left turn in what seemed like midair. When the wheels touched down, Jenny's head whipped forward. Her chin struck the telephone and her teeth clicked together.

"What was that?" Gus asked.

"N-nothing," she answered. "We're headed your way on 12." And closing the gap more swiftly than she could believe. She glanced at the speedometer and watched the indicator climbing toward one hundred miles per hour.

"Keep your eyes peeled," said Gus. "This guy's really flying."

"So are we."

She braced herself, scanning the roadway ahead while the lights of the city gave way to the less-populated outskirts and finally to the dark countryside. In the next five miles, they passed three vehicles: a station wagon, a Nissan Sentra and a pickup towing a horse trailer.

"No sign of the Mercedes at this end," she reported.

Gus muttered an oath, cursing the deserted highway. "Where do you estimate we'll intercept?"

"Just a minute. Let me check the map."

"Glove box," said Peter.

Jenny handed over the telephone and found the road map and a penlight. She had to fight the wind to fold the map open to the relevant section.

Peter wedged the handset between his ear and his shoulder. "Gus? It's Peter. What's your position...? Are you sure...? My God! We're practically on top of you."

Jenny glanced up, looking for landmarks. "Where is he?"

"Two or three miles this side of Kenwood." Peter frowned and leaned over the steering wheel as headlights appeared in the oncoming lane, dimmed, then brightened, then dimmed once again.

"Is *that* him?" she asked.

"Yeah," Peter growled, returning the signal. He stamped on the brake and the Maserati skidded to a stop on the graveled shoulder.

Jenny peered through the windshield, dismayed, watching two more sets of headlights take shape in the distance. She clamped her lips together, smothering a protest, as McAvoy's sedan drew abreast of them.

Gus lowered his window and offered a halfhearted wave. "Looks like we lost 'im."

"Looks like it," Peter agreed. "Any idea where?"

"Best I can figure is back there in Kenwood. If Vandiver spotted us on the south side of town, all he had to do was switch off his lights and pull into the trees." Gus scratched the back of his neck and added disgustedly, "I hate like hell to admit this, boss, but by now that SOB could be most anywhere."

Peter remained silent, gripping the wheel so hard his knuckles blanched, until the other two cars in the caravan pulled in behind McAvoy's and stopped. He spoke without looking at the investigator.

"I don't know about you, but I'm not ready to throw in the towel."

"Me neither, Pete."

"You said one of these guys is a local cop. Maybe he has a suggestion."

Gus opened his door and stepped out. "I'll ask," he replied, ambling along the roadside.

"'For want of a nail,'" Peter muttered, when McAvoy had moved out of earshot.

Jenny looked up from the map, startled. "Pardon me?"

"We needed more backup, dammit! On Monday we would've had it." Peter vented his irritation by punching the steering wheel. "Vandiver held out this long. Why didn't he wait a couple more days?"

Looking at the map, Jenny traced the beam of the penlight along the yellow line that represented Highway 12, absorbed in thought, dredging up memories of her telephone conversation with Eve on the morning after Edwina's death. What was it Eve had said? Something about Dolf Kagan—

"Reed saw the lights!"

"What?" Now it was Peter who was startled.

"Reed saw the lights at Kagan's place. He'd been out that way the night before."

Peter stared at her, transfixed.

"The winery," Jenny said. "The old Thiebault Winery on Soledad Road."

Peter needed no further reminders. She hadn't finished speaking when he started the engine and spun the wheel, pulling along the blacktop until he was parallel with the unmarked cruiser.

"Follow us," he said.

In the next instant, the Maserati roared off down the highway.

THERE WERE NO LIGHTS on at the Kagan house tonight. Shortly after they passed the driveway, Peter turned off the headlights and eased back on the accelerator so that the car glided quietly down the hill to the Thiebault property.

A blue Mercedes was parked in front of the main building.

Peter held the telephone handset to his ear; the connection with Gus was noisy with static but open. "Vandiver's here," he announced.

"Wait for us. We're right behind you," Gus replied.

Peter pulled onto the headland just beyond the entrance to the drive. After a three-minute wait, the others arrived. Peter and Jenny got out of the car to meet them. She stood to one side while the men went into a huddle, speaking in whispers, plotting strategy.

Gus said, "Vandiver might be armed. He's got a permit to carry."

Peter said, "Armed or not, he's dangerous."

The rookie from the unmarked cruiser said, "I'm out of my jurisdiction here, but I put out a call to the sheriff for reinforcements. Maybe we should wait till they get here."

"We can't afford to wait," Peter said. "He's already had twenty minutes to do whatever he came here to do. We have to catch him with the evidence."

The others agreed that this made sense.

Gus took charge of deployment. "I'll cover the front." He pointed to his operative and the rookie cop. "You two work your way around to the back. If there's any windows on the south side of the building, keep an eye on them." He glanced at Peter. "I assume you're not packing."

Peter unbuttoned his sports coat and held it open to show that he was unarmed.

"Scout the north side of the building," Gus directed. "If there're no windows or doors, go around to the back. Once we're in position, we'll try to sneak inside and grab him, but if he makes a break for it, the three of you can flush him out the front."

Jenny stepped into the huddle. "What about me?"

"You can stay here and watch for the reinforcements. When they get here, show 'em where we are." Gus glanced around the circle. "Got it?"

"Got it," said Peter. "Let's go."

The men started toward the winery, keeping low, using the shadows of the cypresses that lined the drive for concealment. Near the end of the drive, they fanned out and sprinted across the open area that surrounded the building, two to the south, one straight ahead, toward the huge main doors, and one to the north.

En route to his assignment, Peter stopped at the Mercedes. He reached through the window on the driver's side, removed the ignition keys and made a soundless sprint for the corner of the building.

When he was out of sight, Jenny shifted her attention to Soledad Road. There was no sign of the reinforcements.

Hurry. Please hurry.

She turned to look at the winery again. An expectant hush lay over the building. She strained her eyes, but saw no movement. She held her breath, but heard no sound aside from a rustling of leaves nearby.

The breeze, she told herself.

But there *was* no breeze.

She whispered, "Who's there?" and received no answer. The night remained utterly still.

She took a few tentative steps along the drive toward the clearing, then stopped to listen.

The rustling of leaves was repeated. Closer now. To the right and slightly behind her.

She whirled in the direction of the sound. "Is someone there?"

No answer.

"Peter, is that you?"

Again there was no answer.

An animal, she decided. A raccoon. Or in this remote, sparsely populated area, maybe even a deer. But on the heels of this thought came the unmistakable *crack* of a twig breaking underfoot.

She opened her mouth to call out just as she was captured in a stranglehold and a hand was clamped with suffocating strength over her mouth and nose.

"Don't scream," Reed commanded in a harsh whisper. "If you scream, I'll kill you right now." To prove his intent, he exerted more pressure on her windpipe.

She couldn't breathe! Instinctively, she clawed at his forearm, and he caught hold of her wrist and twisted her arm behind her at an angle so acute, she thought the bones would snap. She reached up and back with her other hand and tried to scratch him. She tried to gouge at his eyes, but he slapped her hand away.

"Bitch!" he snarled, adjusting his hold so that both her arms were anchored behind her, imprisoned against his chest.

Dear God, she thought, *this can't be happening.*

She bucked and fought with all her strength, struggling to break free, and he grabbed a handful of her hair and tugged it, viciously twisting this way and that, dragging her head from side to side. But in his concentration on that torment, his hold on her arms slackened enough that she was able to jab an elbow into his rib cage.

He grunted and doubled over, but recovered quickly. His grip on her hair tightened. "If you want to play rough, I'm willing to oblige." Tears spurted from her eyes as he pulled her head back and delivered a clublike blow to her temple.

Her knees buckled. She saw stars. Klaxons sounded in her ears. Her lungs were on fire with the need for oxygen. A layer of darkness engulfed her and she went limp. She was numb with despair, aware that she was fast losing consciousness, when Peter's voice rang out.

"Let her go, Vandiver, or you're a dead man. We've got you surrounded. You haven't got a chance."

Reed froze for a moment, then turned in a circle, staring coldly at each of his four captors. "If I'm dead, she dies with me." He released his hold on Jenny's neck, and she drew in a gasping breath. He roughly shoved her away so that Peter could see the revolver that had appeared in his other hand, and with lightning speed, Reed pressed the barrel of the gun to the base of Jenny's skull. The metallic *click* as he thumbed the hammer sounded as loud as rifle fire.

"As you can see, we have a stalemate. If you shoot me, I shoot Jenny."

"Careful, Pete. The bastard means it," Gus warned.

"You bet your life I do. So, Darien, if you want to keep her alive, you'll give me the keys to your car and get out of my way. You won't try to stop me from leaving, and you won't try to follow me. If you do, I'll kill her."

Peter advanced a step closer, spreading his hands to show they were empty. "What's the point, Vandiver? We found Sonnet's body back there in the winery. We know you killed her. We know you killed Edwina Farber. We know about the money you embezzled. By tomorrow morning, all of Santa Rosa will know what you've done. By afternoon, the news will be all over the state."

The wail of sirens pierced the night; Peter used the distraction to move in closer. "I know how it is for a man like you. You value your reputation above everything else. It's more important to you than your family, your friends, your business. Your social standing means more to you than your life.''

The sirens grew louder. Headlights raced toward them. Bands of red-and-blue light pulsed in the darkness. Jenny counted one...two...three vehicles. Reed must have counted them, too. Although he kept the revolver aimed at her, she sensed that his resolve was weakening.

Now that she could breathe, her head was clearer. She had recovered some strength, but she didn't struggle. She stood docile and passive, her gaze fixed on Peter, waiting for an opportune moment.

"What'll you do? Where can you hide? Soon everyone will know what you are."

Every word Peter spoke took its toll upon Reed. The hand holding the revolver was trembling. Jenny saw his throat work. She heard his labored breathing, and with the arrival of the patrol cars, she realized that he was weeping.

"Give me the gun," said Peter. "Let Jenny go and I promise I'll see to it that you get the best possible defense."

Reed had stopped listening to Peter's arguments. He seemed mesmerized by the vehicles that had converged at the end of the drive. When the officers began leaving the cars, he brandished the weapon.

"Back off!" he ordered. "Keep the hell away!"

Jenny's throat felt raw, but she managed to whisper, "Please, Reed, don't do this. Think of Eve. She loves you so much. Please, for her sake, won't you give me the gun? Peter will help you. You can trust him. And you can trust me. We were friends once—"

Reed threw back his head and shouted with laughter.

"Friends!" he howled, pushing Jenny away.

His decision made, Reed raised the gun to his temple and slowly, almost lovingly, squeezed the trigger.

Epilogue

At 1:05 that Sunday morning, Reed Vandiver was pronounced dead. Fifteen minutes later, Sonnet's body was disinterred from the huge oaken wine cask in which Reed had hidden it. A deputy sheriff took Jenny's statement. Other officers questioned Peter and Gus and Joey. The coroner arrived, as did men from the crime lab. Officers swarmed over the winery, gathering evidence. Photographs were taken and measurements made. The hearse departed with its grisly cargo, and shortly after its departure, the officer in charge informed Jenny and Peter he was satisfied with their statements.

"We'll notify you if your testimony's required at the inquest," he told Peter, "but for now, you and your friends are free to leave."

And with that, the ordeal was over.

At 3:10 a.m., Jenny and Peter got into the Maserati and drove away from the winery along Soledad Road.

Jenny didn't look back. Peter put a Brahms symphony on the tapedeck, and she listened to the music and tried not to think.

The moon had risen. It bathed the hilltops with silver and tinted the valleys shades of gray. The moonglow leached out colors and distorted proportions. Elongated shadows made the gnarled old grapevines that dotted the hillsides seem as tall as trees.

The landscape had the look of a painting by Dali. Surreal, Jenny thought. *Un*real.

But the landscape was real, and so were the events of the past few hours.

She concentrated on the music and tried not to think, but it didn't work.

They were nearing the end of Adobe Canyon Road, approaching Kenwood and Highway 12, when she said, "Peter, I've been thinking..."

"What about?"

"Sharon and how horrible it will be if she hears about her sister's death on the radio. It occurred to me that if you leave for Sacramento after you drop me off, you could tell her personally, and...comfort her."

Peter glanced at Jenny, bemused, surprised. "The same idea occurred to me, but I wasn't sure how you'd feel if I took off like that."

"Well, I'd rather have you stay, of course, but Sharon needs you."

"And you don't?"

"I need you, too," Jenny confessed, and Peter rewarded her with a smile.

They had reached the junction with Highway 12, and he braked for the stop sign and turned to her.

"There's an alternative," he said. "You could come to Sacramento with me."

"Right this minute?"

"Yes, right now."

"How can I come with you? I don't have any clothes with me. I don't even have my toothbrush."

Peter shrugged. "There are stores in Sacramento. We can buy whatever you need."

"What about my book?"

"I've got pencils and paper. I've got a computer. You can work on your book at my place."

"B-but my manuscript! My notes!"

"Betty could courier them over to you, and we can come back later this week and pick up the rest of your things."

Lights swept over them as another car approached the junction, and Peter downshifted and pulled out of the way. He switched off the ignition and confronted Jenny.

"Some time ago, I asked you to consider moving to Sacramento. I haven't pressed you for an answer because I know it's asking a lot. But tonight I almost lost you...." His arms went about her and hauled her close. His voice was hoarse with emotion as he continued. "It made me realize it's not enough seeing you every other weekend and talking on the phone between visits. I need more than visits. I want to see you every day. I want your face to be the first thing I see in the morning and the last thing I see at night. I want to be able to touch you, kiss you, hold you, make love to you, sleep with you.... I want to be with you always. So the question is, do you want to be with me?"

Jenny's throat felt thick. She swallowed to clear it. "Is this an ultimatum?"

"Yes, I suppose it is." Peter straightened and moved away from her. "Relationships are like people, honey. You can't stand still indefinitely. Not if you want to stay healthy. You reach a point where you have to progress beyond physical intimacy to emotional intimacy, because if you don't, some part of you dies."

"And you think we've reached this point?"

"I have," said Peter. "I don't know about you."

Jenny stared at the stretch of highway, literally at a crossroad.

In one direction lay Santa Rosa. The familiar. The known. The security of the life she had made for herself over the past three years. The certainty of her work. The challenge of occasional loneliness. The possibility of pleasure.

In the other direction was Sacramento. The unfamiliar. The unknown. If she chose that direction, the only thing certain was uncertainty.

But she would have Peter and the possibility of love.

She wanted him. Oh, how she wanted him! She wanted to be with him every day. She wanted to love him and be loved by him. Always.

She could have all this. It was hers for the taking. All it required was a leap of faith.

Peter started the engine, shifted into first and eased the car toward the stop sign. There was no traffic on Highway 12. For as far as Jenny could see in either direction, the road was clear.

She met Peter's gaze. He cocked an eyebrow at her. "Well?" he said. "Where to?" And suddenly, both of them were smiling.

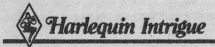

Two exciting new stories each month.

Each title mixes a contemporary, sophisticated romance with the surprising twists and turns of a puzzler... romance with "something more."

Because romance can be quite an adventure.

Romance, Suspense and Adventure

Six exciting series for you every month... from Harlequin

HARLEQUIN
American Romance®
Harlequin celebrates the American woman...

...by offering you romance stories written about American women, by American women for American women. This series offers you contemporary romances uniquely North American in flavor and appeal.

◆

HARLEQUIN
Temptation®

Passionate stories for today's woman

An exciting series of sensual, mature stories of love...dilemmas, choices, resolutions... all contemporary issues dealt with in a true-to-life fashion by some of your favorite authors.

◆

Harlequin Intrigue®
Because romance can be quite an adventure

Harlequin Intrigue, an innovative series that blends the romance you expect... with the unexpected. Each story has an added element of intrigue that provides a new twist to the Harlequin tradition of romance excellence.

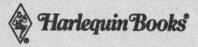 *Harlequin Books*®

PROD-A-2R